I0825534

Advance Praise for *Trump's Superpower*

"A bold and inspiring novel that brings the Founding Fathers back to remind us what America stands for. With wit and historical insight, *Trump's Superpower* asks the question every patriot should ponder: What would our Founders say about America today?"

—Julio Gonzalez, CEO,
Engineered Tax Services

"*Trump's Superpower* is a charming and patriotic novel that reveals important lessons about our founders."

—Larry P. Arnn

TRUMP'S SUPERPOWER

A Historical Novel About the Founding Fathers & One Founding Mother

JOHANNA NEUMAN

A POST HILL PRESS BOOK
ISBN: 979-8-89565-548-1
ISBN (eBook): 979-8-89565-549-8

Trump's Superpower:
A Historical Novel About the Founding Fathers & One Founding Mother

Cover design by Jim Villaflores

Post Hill Press
New York • Nashville
posthillpress.com

Published in the United States of America
1 2 3 4 5 6 7 8 9 10

To my father, Seymour Neuman, who loved
American history and the Fourth of July

&

To my brother-in-law, Bill Lyddan, my
partner in all things MAGA

TABLE OF CONTENTS

Part I
The Rebellion

Part II
The Revolutionary War

Part III
The Constitution

PART I

The Rebellion

"There, I guess King George will be able to read that without his spectacles!"

—Businessman John Hancock

SCENE 1

The Arrival

Benjamin Franklin was the first to arrive.

This annoyed Priscilla Babcock, who was assistant director at the National Archives in Washington, DC. Anyway, that's what her business card called her. At thirty-two, with joint degrees in public history and museum administration from Georgetown U., she saw herself more as the custodian of American cultural history. As she once explained to a friend, "My unofficial job is to edit any historic narratives that offend modern sensibilities. Think of me as the Mark Zuckerberg of American history." In this, she often clashed with the Director, an eminent scholar who was ninety-five years old, and who had never been in lockstep with the intelligentsia anyway. But he was African American and widely admired—you could say world-famous—so she tried to make sure these matters never crossed his desk.

Of all the Founding Fathers, Ben was the most popular with the public. Or at least, he outsold all of them at the museum gift shop. Armed only with the good name and admirable values of his father, Josiah, a candlemaker who prized work over laziness, Ben had become a printer, postmaster general, lawmaker, diplomat, and inventor whose kite experiment established that lightning was a form of electricity. As Philadelphia's most famous citizen, he was best known for civic causes, lending his name and reputation to a public library, a discussion club, and a university. Plus, he was witty and charming. In his early life, he had owned house slaves, but later he led efforts to abolish slavery. No doubt Americans saw in his biography their own aspirations, an everyman for the centuries. Maybe, like Elon Musk, he had been on the spectrum.

Normally, she would have enjoyed talking to this actor, who certainly looked the part—if only to test her Franklin knowledge against his. But she was much too busy preparing for what the White House kept calling "One Big Beautiful Reenactment." The OBBR script needed work, the loudspeakers were on the fritz, and the Director kept interrupting to find out when he could meet his star players. As she sat on a wooden chair on the National Archives stage, clipboard in hand, looking out at the 290 seats she hoped would be full for the performance, she realized she would have to skip lunch—again—to get everything done.

"Dr. Franklin, you are prompt, as always," she said, standing to greet him after he hobbled on a cane from the back of the auditorium as it sloped toward the stage, a smile masking her impatience. She was surprised that he was already outfitted in the appropriate costume—knee-length breeches, a fitted waistcoat, and a long coat. She had arranged a circle of wooden chairs on stage for the arriving characters, and he gladly took one.

"Early to bed, early to rise, my dear," he said congenially. "It will be a big occasion for all of us. I delight that you stuck with the July Fourth date."

"I know some historians believe we should celebrate on August 2 because that's when a third of the fifty-six delegates finally showed up in Philadelphia to sign the Declaration of Independence. But at the Archives, we believe in honoring the date of popular memory."

"Actually I was thinking you might have chosen July 2. That is the day we in Congress approved a motion from Richard Henry Lee of Virginia. I will not soon forget it. *'These United Colonies are, and of right ought to be, free and independent States, that they are absolved from all allegiance to the British Crown, and that all political connection between them and the State of Great Britain is, and ought to be, totally dissolved.'* John Adams always argued the Lee motion marked the real beginning of our drive for independence."

"I certainly did," said the actor playing John Adams as he too arrived onstage, standing to speak to Ben. "I still think July 2 would have been more accurate. I told Abigail there would be exploding fireworks and boat parades on that date across the land, far into the future."

"You could make a case that it was King George the Third who announced our independence," said Ben. "Wasn't that the year before when he refused to accept our Olive Branch Petition?"

"Good point," said John. "He issued the Royal Proclamation where he said we were in a state of rebellion. In a way, he was right. The General was already leading the Continental Army. Men were already dying. But no matter—the nation we founded is now two hundred fifty years old, and we are here, though who could have imagined the size of this city. A muddy swamp when last I saw it!"

"My dear Mr. Adams, if you only knew. I arrived yesterday and acclimated myself by taking a tour on the Boomerang Yacht. As the boat cruises down the Potomac River, a guide explains the memorials one after another—Jefferson, Washington, Lincoln—as they appear on the horizon. You would not believe the size of the monument they built to the General!"

"Ah, Ben, you seem to have forgotten our history. The General was the country's father, who led us to victory in war and then in governance. Of course, his monument is the largest!"

"Can we return to the General? His monument soars five hundred fifty-five feet into the sky, and by law, it is the highest building in the city. Our tour guide said it took eleven years to build—the Civil War kept interrupting. As a result, the monument has three different kinds of marble, with three different shades of white. I suggested vinegar might help erase their differences. When I asked why the nation went to war against itself, my fellow tourists looked at me oddly."

"For your information, Ben, they have a whole course on the Civil War in the Earthly Library."

"I rarely bother with the Earthly Library. After all, we all experienced earthly adventures enough to last a lifetime when we were here. By the way, how did you arrive?"

"I came by something called a train. I stopped in Boston, to see how my old city was doing. It, too, is a major metropolis but still maintains some of its colonial charms. The train runs on wheels, guided by tracks. I calculated travel time was about the same as a horse and rider could gallop in one day, but not nearly as comfortable as one of those finely upholstered seats in General

Washington's carriages. Arriving, I was stunned at how big the District of Columbia is."

"A major world capital," said Ben. "I seem to recall a debate on its size in your legislature."

"Yes, that one delegate was quite excited about it. I forget his name, but he read the draft of the Constitution and fumed that the new federal city was to be ten miles square."

John stood and began waving his arms around, imitating the delegate. "'Ten square miles!' he railed. 'Too large a space to give to the uncontrolled discretion of the central government. It will only lead to a reign of tyranny over the states. I will never vote more than one square mile.'"

"If that delegate could but see this district now. This city is still constrained by those ten square miles and by the height of the General's memorial, but the reach of the US government extends to every state where a federal agency houses federal employees. The federal government is by far the largest employer in the country—eight million workers. We bequeathed a monster!"

"That was before President Trump started cutting waste and fraud," said John. "I understand he stood up a new agency, the Department of Government Efficiency. They call it DOGE."

"But it is not alone the size of the government; it is the size of the country," said Ben.

"Fifty states, reaching across the whole continent and beyond," said the actor playing Thomas Jefferson as he, too, arrived on the stage. "The spirit of 1776 lives on."

"You should know," said John. "You who doubled the size of the country with that ridiculous purchase from France of Louisiana and all the territory west of the Mississippi River."

"How could I not?" said Tom. "Napoleon was making noises in Saint-Dominique, putting down a slave rebellion off our coast.

It was your party, John, that worried he would next invade our country. I was protecting the port of New Orleans as a matter of strategic national security."

"I just heard about this yesterday on my tour," said Ben. "I understand we also got two Canadian provinces in that deal—Alberta and Saskatchewan. I also heard yesterday President Trump is thinking of reacquiring them. Plus Greenland."

"It surprised me Napoleon was willing to sell all that land for only $15 million," said Tom. "Ben, do you remember Robert Livingston?"

"America's Cicero," said Ben, brushing away a puff of sawdust from the set builders. "I always admired his eloquence, intellect, and political acumen."

"I sent him and James Monroe to Paris to sign the deal, and he called it 'the noblest work of our lives' because it made our country one of the world's major powers."

Priscilla interrupted their chatter. It was driving her nuts that they were staying in character—though she was pleasantly surprised at how tall, regal, and handsome this Jefferson actor was.

"I'm afraid the stage hands have much to do to prepare for the performance," she said. "Might I suggest you three adjourn to the Old Ebbitt's Grill? The Archives would be happy to pay for your lunch, and I'll have the Director's chauffeur drive you there."

"How old is this Old Ebbitt's Grill?" asked Tom.

"It opened sometime before the Civil War. I read that President Lincoln sometimes convened his Cabinet there. And I believe your portrait is on the wall, Mr. Jefferson."

She caught herself and smiled. Now she was treating them like the real Founding Fathers who couldn't be expected to know these things. But in fact, she reminded herself, they had likely all been to DC before. Reenactments on this side of town were as common as pizza.

"Of course your portrait is on the wall," said John, smirking. "Everyone always swooned for the Man of the People. Few know that his soul was poisoned with ambition."

"Aren't we all guilty of that?" said Ben. "No bickering. We are here to celebrate our nation."

"Take this, Dr. Franklin," said Priscilla, handing him a pager. "I'll beep you when it's time to come back for rehearsals."

"I beg your pardon, dear?"

"This little instrument will beep at you when I program it to do so."

"Does it run on electricity?"

Priscilla sighed. Should she keep up the pretense?

"As you know, Dr. Franklin, we use batteries, but the pagers have long-lasting ones. That's why they're still in use in hospitals."

"If I agree to carry this little item with me," said Ben, "I wonder if you could do me a favor."

Priscilla sucked in her breath. If anyone added more request to her to-do list, she would scream.

"What would that be, Dr. Franklin?" she asked sweetly.

"Could you arrange a private tour of the White House for us?"

Oh God, she thought, *what a sight that would be.*

"The Capitol too," said Tom.

"I'll see what I can do."

They began to leave the stage. Just then, a familiar figure burst on the scene.

"You do not dare go without me," Mercy Otis Warren said from the top of the auditorium. "You would not get far, anyway. As you may have noticed," she added, smiling at Priscilla, "women are now in valued positions of much glory."

John whispered something to Ben, but Mercy overheard him.

"I did call you a monarchist," said Mercy, "because you acted like one. You wanted us to call the General 'Your Excellency' instead of 'Mr. President.'"

"I wanted the position to be honored," said John. "If you come to lunch, I will not sit with you."

"That suits me. You ruined my writing career."

"I made your writing career!" raged John.

"At first, yes, and I am grateful. But when my *History of the Revolution* cast doubts on your character, you summoned all your friends to condemn me. I never published again."

"I always meant to tell you I rather enjoyed your account," said Tom. "I ordered it for my entire Cabinet to read. Beautifully written."

"Coming from you, that is quite a compliment," said Mercy, linking her arm through Tom's. "Perhaps you can accompany me to lunch."

"Charmed."

John looked like he was going to say something nasty to both of them, but just then Alexander Hamilton walked down the aisle, bowing slightly to his fellow founders.

"A reunion at last," he said.

"You have not lost your strut, I see," said John.

It was true. Alex believed he was the most brilliant of them all, the handsomest, too, and it showed. His climb from an immigrant of no standing to first secretary of the Treasury of the new nation had defied all expectations. His predictions—about the banking system, tariffs, the Constitution, even US libel laws—had all withstood the test of time, in history's judgment. And his attempts to recruit slaves to fight in the Continental Army had proved his political instincts were sharp. Sometimes he thought he understood American values before the nation did.

For her part, Priscilla thought the Hamilton actor was very much his likeness—the piercing violet eyes that some histories mentioned, the slight but athletic build. And like the others, he arrived in a costume of the period—tailored suit, knee-length coat with a high collar, with a waistcoat, trousers, and a white linen shirt with ruffled cuffs. At this rate she was going to save a lot of money on costumes.

"There he is, the Founding Father who became a Broadway star," smirked John.

"That was quite the surprise, was it not?" said Alex. "I had never heard of rap music."

"I never knew you were Puerto Rican," said Mercy.

"Hardly," said Alex. "My parents were Scots, who happened to be living in the British island of Nevis when I was born. Later my mother moved with me and my brother to St. Croix. So a mixed heritage of Scottish and British, with a little Caribbean."

"I read in the Earthly Library that in today's America, people take pride in being a country of immigrants and second chances," said Mercy. "Maybe that is why rappers embraced you."

"I was hoping to see the play while we were here," said Alex.

"What a marvelous idea," said Ben. "We should all go see it together."

"Alas, Mr. Miranda canceled the performance at Kennedy Center here after Trump shook up the board of directors," said John.

"Why did he do that?" asked Tom.

"Trump likes classical art. He thought the performances had grown too promiscuous. Now they are performing mainstream plays, and they are usually sold out."

"This city sizzles with life," said Alex. "When I traded the capital away from Philadelphia to the banks of the Potomac, I imagined it would become a small outpost in a swampy nest of mosquitos where no one would choose to stay for long. And now, this metropolis!"

"I hardly think that was your gravest mistake, Alex," said John. "Why on earth did you agree to that duel with Aaron Burr?"

"You have no idea how often I have asked myself that question," said Alex, staring off into the distance, watching as a stage hand adjusted the lights. "As I have always said, when the sword is once drawn, the passions of men observe no bounds of moderation."

Tom had been silent until then.

"What are you doing here anyway?" asked Tom. Since Hamilton's arrival, he had stayed close to the edge of the stage, as though the air in the room had become suddenly unbreathable. "I do not remember seeing you at the signing on either July 4 or August 2."

"I was fighting the war as General Washington's top aide-de-camp," Alex shot back. "As for you, I do not recall you being in Philadelphia for the Constitutional Convention either."

"I was serving my country abroad, sir, as a diplomat in France."

Priscilla interrupted. "It's true, I wasn't expecting Alexander Hamilton until rehearsals for the play's second act, when we switch from the rebellion to the war. Aren't you early?"

"Yes, I saw the script, and I know my main role comes later in the reenactment. But I was so excited at the chance to see what had become of the nation that I requested an early departure to Earth. I stopped first on Wall Street, where everyone was buzzing about AI and cryptocurrency. You could say my own time here was cut short. I couldn't wait to get back."

"When is the General arriving?" asked Mercy, looking toward Priscilla. "I would think he would be instrumental in the story of our founding."

"Certainly. The actors playing the General and his manservant are due here next week."

"Billy Lee is coming too?" said Alex. "Wonderful news. Few know this, but when that valiant slave was not handing General Washington a spy glass or arranging maps for our war council meetings, Billy Lee gave me excellent advice. He had a keen intuition about people."

"Example?" asked Ben, perking up.

"He told me he distrusted Benedict Arnold from the beginning. After Arnold dishonored the cause, Billy Lee told me he was not surprised. He said you could tell the nature of a man by his eyes. And, he added, Arnold never looked anyone in the eye, except to glare."

"Alex, why are you really here early?" asked John. "Surely not to see the rest of us."

"Frankly, I am fascinated by President Trump and his whole Make America Great Again movement. Plus, I have a crush on Melania, so I long to meet them both."

"He was the best president after I left the White House," said Tom.

"Who was?" asked Alex.

"Trump."

"Not Lincoln?"

"They both rescued the nation from its worst instincts. In 1860, the North and the South both revered America, so once he finally found the right generals, Lincoln could remind each side that they were brothers who shared revolutionary history. In 2024, Trump had to liberate the country from a cabal of tyrants who had no love of country, or God, or history. He had to remind Americans that they were created as a constitutional republic, not a communist dictatorship."

"A rare spot of agreement between me and the gentleman from Monticello," said Alex, pacing on the stage as if already in performance. "But you can't understand Trump unless you understand FDR. Both of them upended the DC establishment—Franklin Delano Roosevelt, in the wake of the Depression, to impose government solutions to all economic issues; Trump to undo the federal bureaucracy the FDR Democrats installed."

"You were always about business," said Tom. "I regret agreeing to your scheme for the central government to swallow all the state war debts after the Revolution. Virginia had already paid off its losses. All we got out of the bargain was this swampy, overgrown capital."

"It takes a businessman to understand bureaucracy," said Alex. "I learned when I stopped at my old firm on Wall Street that President Trump hired a businessman, Elon Musk, and tasked his team of computer geniuses to use technology to find waste and fraud in the government."

"Yes, John mentioned it earlier. I tried something like that, but there was so much resistance I abandoned the idea. It makes me wonder if President Trump ever tilled the land as a farmer. He seems to understand innately the need of pruning costs to make profit."

"Only if you consider concrete a farm commodity," said John. "He is a builder, a creator of massive projects."

"I like this idea of cutting the size of the federal government," said Tom. "The people should be free to pursue happiness, not report to bureaucrats."

"Another area of accord," said Alex. "Proves what I have long said. Business drives politics."

Priscilla put her hand to her head. She could feel a migraine coming on.

"Are we upsetting your composure?" asked Mercy. "Would you like us to leave?"

"Thank you for your concern. I do have much to do. Perhaps I can show you the way."

Priscilla escorted them to the elevators, pushed the button for the basement-level garage entrance, and sent them on their way. As the elevator door closed, she drew a long breath. Funny, they didn't teach you how to handle actors in museum admin school.

Waiting downstairs was their driver, who introduced himself as Claude Debussy. Dressed in a suit, he was a gentleman with a French accent and a great smile. He opened the doors for them.

"You were born elsewhere?" asked Ben.

"Yes, I was born in Haiti, and came here with my parents at the age of seven," said Monsieur Debussy, bowing slightly. "The Director has asked me to be available during your stay whenever you like. I can drive you anywhere you want, and I know quite a lot about the city and its history. Immigrants are great students of their new countries, isn't that right, Mr. Hamilton?"

"Ah yes, Mr. Debussy. We immigrants press our noses to the windows of the successful, seeking to learn all their secrets and emulate their habits."

"This Old Ebbitt's Grill—does it have good vegetarian food?" said Ben.

"I thought you gave that up when you noticed fish eating other fish," said John.

"I did not discover that until the Constitutional Convention."

John rolled his eyes.

"I believe you will be pleased, Dr. Franklin," said Mr. Debussy. "Lots of vegetables."

"Ah, how I miss the research and growing of seeds and plants," said Tom. "One of the greatest lessons I learned from the General was not about military strategy or governance but about crop rotation. His system was genius."

"I know nothing about crops except I miss them when they are brewed," said Alex.

"I hope this grill is not too far," said Mercy. "Travel has made me hungry!"

In this precarious way, with reputations and history interrupting their memories, the party of five piled into the limousine and left the theater behind.

"Quite a conveyance," said Ben.

"How fast does it travel?" asked Alex.

"I keep to the speed limit," said Mr. Debussy. "But if I floor the gas pedal we could easily hit one hundred miles per hour."

"Imagine if we had one during the war," said Alex.

"It might have spared Paul Revere's horse," said John.

"Mr. Debussy, might I ask you to make a slight detour?" said Ben. "I would like to show my colleagues the exterior of the President's House."

"You will not believe its size," he said to the others.

*****

After they had left, Priscilla Babcock returned to the stage, and her clipboard.

Summoning the Founding Fathers from Heaven had been the Director's idea. Thomas Sowell was a man of faith—perhaps, she thought, the last person at the Archives who believed in God.

She assumed they had not come down from Heaven, but were actors hired by Director Sowell because they were passionate about their characters. Though it dawned on her after the morning's conversation that they seemed to know an awful lot of details she didn't. And she had two college degrees!

SCENE 2

Old Ebbitt's Grill

"Like an old British pub," said John, pulling a seat out from under the round table. "Stools made of wood and wood on the walls and on the floor, a tribute to the trees."

"If they have fifty states now, they must have taken all the Indian lands on the other side of the Mississippi," mused Alex. "Imagine how many trees they must have chopped down for that."

"I guess Tom's Louisiana Purchase, unconstitutional though it might have been, started the whole land boom, and now the nation is enormous," said John.

"It would be amazing if the Trump administration buys Panama," said Alex. "I doubt even Andrew Jackson would have thought of that."

"Despicable man," said Mercy. "Imagine killing all those Indians, just for Oklahoma."

A waitress approached their table.

"My name is Evelyn, and I'll be your server. What can I get you folks to drink?"

"What is your most popular drink?" asked Alex.

"Diet Coke."

"Let us have a round of that."

"What kind of ale do you have?" asked Ben.

"Sam Adams is very popular," said Evelyn.

They all burst out laughing as Ben ordered a round of that too. She departed to get their drinks.

"Do you think Sam would be amused to be remembered as a beer?" asked Ben.

"Beer was his father's business, but his calling was revolution," said Alex. "I remember he warned against complacency. 'If ever vain and aspiring men possess the highest seats in government, we will need our patriots to prevent the country's ruin.' Seems like the nation's history has proved him right."

"Once I heard him say, 'It does not take a majority to prevail, only an irate, tireless minority, keen on setting brushfires of freedom in the minds of men,'" said Mercy. "I suppose that is what they did, he and Tom Paine and Patrick Henry—they set brushfires of freedom in the minds of our countrymen."

"I too wonder why Sam's not with us," said John. "It seems his presence is essential to telling the story of the Revolution."

"Maybe he's not yet in Heaven," said Ben. "To tell you the truth, I was surprised to find myself there, not having been a churchgoer."

"Surely creating a moral country of God-fearing citizens is enough for admission, otherwise I would not be there either," said Tom."

"Some believe it is not your good works but your faith that guides admissions," said Mercy.

Evelyn brought the drinks, and they raised their glasses in salute to Sam Adams.

"This beer is good," said John. "Better than his father's, as I recall."

Alex spit out his Diet Coke. "I believe this is some sort of hallucinogen."

The menu held many surprises. Alex was delighted by the idea of beef between bread.

"Who do you suppose Mr. Hamburger was?"

"In advance of this trip, I only read the books deemed essential," said Ben. "That was enough reading for one eternity. And there was no mention of your hamburger anywhere in those books."

"They did not mention Diet Coke either," said Alex.

"In answer to your question, I think Mr. Hamburger was German," said Tom.

"A Hessian?"

"Of more recent vintage I believe."

"There is enough food on this menu to feed a family of seven for a year," exclaimed Mercy. "Coconut curry lentil soup, whatever can that be?"

"I believe beans with spices from Bombay, which became part of the British empire," said Tom. "Did you see Buffalo chicken wings? Maybe chickens and buffaloes together?"

"That sounds dreadful," said Mercy.

"What appeals to me," said Ben, "is a salad of roasted beets and Honeycrisp apples. At least I understand the words. And maybe a cheese board, if some of you might join me in its partaking."

"I probably should have the oysters Rockefeller because Mr. Rockefeller was a famous New Yorker," said Alex. "But I must say this beef-and-bread meal we inherited from the Germans sounds enticing."

"Did you notice it comes with something these Americans call 'french fries'?" said Tom. "In Paris, they called them *pommes frites*, and they were a great indulgence. I may join you in this hamburger, Alex. Are you having yours with cheese?"

"Sounds barbaric," said Alex. "But I was intrigued by the option of adding bacon."

"For me, the familiar," said John. "New England clam chowder."

"And for me," said Mercy, "the coconut curry soup. Because life is short."

Evelyn returned for their order, taking down her notes on a pad too flat and shiny to be paper.

"My dear lady, what is that machine?" asked Ben. "Does it run on electricity?"

Evelyn looked at him dubiously.

"Say, you guys look familiar. Are you visiting from out of town?"

"Yes, we are," said Ben. "We are performing at the reenactment of the nation's founding."

"Ah, for our birthday! Of course! You seem to have rehearsed your roles very well. And you all look very convincing, except for the lady. Who are you supposed to be—Martha Washington?"

"My name is Mercy Otis Warren," said Mercy. "I am the reason we have a Bill of Rights."

"A bit of an exaggeration," said John, his eyebrows lifted.

"Not in the least," said Mercy. "You called us dissidents and deplorables, but we were right. The Constitution without the Bill of Rights—I doubt this country would have lasted two hundred fifty years."

Evelyn left to place their orders. John turned to Tom.

"This is all your fault, you know. That lofty language you put in the Declaration of Independence about how we all were created equal unleashed what I called, then and now, an excess of democracy. Once it was written down, once it was trumpeted as the promise of democracy, everyone wanted in—slaves, children, Indians, women! Abigail never stopped talking about it."

"John, human rights can never be excessive. It is our greatest legacy from the Enlightenment."

"Not sure about that," said Alex. "I agree it was our great legacy from thinkers like John Locke. You could even say it was the linchpin that held together Western civilization. But pure democracy is pure anarchy. I have made no secret of my admiration for the British form of government. And surely history is replete with examples of too much democracy."

"For instance?" asked Tom.

"The Chartists in England, the Jacobins during the French Revolution."

"You could make the case that those industrial workers in England who wanted the right to vote and those rebels in France who wanted the king beheaded won the reforms they were seeking," said Tom, "as we did ours."

"An excellent point," said Ben. "Sam Adams and his allies in the Sons of Liberty were castigated as revolutionaries, but they prevailed. I heard someone say once that 'radicals start movements but legislators finish them.' What do you think, Alex?"

"I think there may be something in that, about radicals and legislators. But what destroys such movements is corruption. That's another thing that makes Trump such a unique character. He does not want for money and can crack the whip on government spending."

"It is odd Sam did not last longer in politics," said Mercy. "Perhaps some men are made for revolution but not governance."

"He was already fifty-four in 1776," said John. "Older than any of us, except Ben of course."

"I was a lad then, a mere seventy-one! I lived for another thirteen years, a record in my family."

"Sam was quite famous in Europe," said John. "When I arrived in France on a diplomatic mission, people always assumed I was the famous Adams, that revolutionary Samuel Adams."

"Did you know Sam was so proud of serving in the Revolutionary War he wore his cocked hat and military coat as long as he lived, even as governor of Massachusetts?" said Mercy. "But I always thought mingling with politicians brought him no joy. His passion was for rebellion."

Just then, their food arrived, and they all dug in with great appetite. Mercy thought everything spicy, Ben thought his bland, but Alex proclaimed his hamburger the best meat he'd ever tasted.

As they were delighting in these new culinary sensations, a young boy walked up to Ben, with a man trailing behind who might have been his father.

"Are you Ben Franklin?" the kid said excitedly. "My dad showed me your picture on the one-hundred-dollar bill. Can I have your autograph?"

Ben smiled weakly and adjusted his bifocals.

"Do you have a document for me to sign?"

The boy took his Make America Great Again hat from his head and a pen from his pocket.

"Where would one acquire such a hat?"

"All the shops have them." The boy watched eagerly as Ben signed the hat. "Thanks!"

"Alex, why am I on the hundred-dollar bill?" Ben asked. "True, I made money as a printer, and some of my books did well. *Poor Richard's Almanac* sold ten thousand copies a year for nearly twenty-five years. But I wanted notice for my achievements, not for my money."

"Be grateful!" said Alex. "I am worth ten dollars, and I was almost kicked off by a woman!"

"You're lucky you were not on the penny," said Mercy. "I read that Trump has eliminated them, so now poor Abraham Lincoln has no monetary home."

"Ah, but he does, on the five-dollar bill," said Alex. "Odd that they put him on the penny to begin with. He was the one who started issuing paper currency to pay for the Civil War. Maybe they'll put him on the new digital currency everyone was talking about in New York."

Evelyn returned with their check. For some reason she gave it to Alex.

"Are you playing Alexander Hamilton?" she asked.

"Yes," he said, taking the bill.

"I thought you were Puerto Rican."

"So I heard."

When she walked away, John, in full smirk mode, teased Alex about being a Puerto Rican.

"If you had been raised properly, perhaps you would not have tried so hard to impose your will, first on the troops and then on the treasury."

"Mr. Adams, you need to apologize to me, back across the centuries, for branding me born out of wedlock. I think your expression was 'the bastard brat of a Scotch peddler.' Besides, if I had not been born to disadvantage, I might not have been driven to excel as I did."

"You called me mentally deranged and unfit for the presidency!" growled John.

"Well?"

Alex smiled, happily signing the check to the Archives' account.

"Alex, I know you and I were on opposite sides of the federalist debate," said Mercy. "But I have always admired your intellect. I think you would have made a great president but for your pride."

"I like to think I would have been like Trump, standing on the shoulders of those who came before. Trump is always quoting us, as if we are his superpower. In any evident, thanks to the Constitution, as an immigrant I was not eligible."

"Mercy, what are you talking about? Mr. Hamilton here always carried himself as an American Napoleon," said John. "That stupid proposal to stand up a permanent army and march all the way down to Peru, liberating people to join our country—what were you thinking, Alex?"

"At least I did not aspire to be the monarchist-in-chief, John."

Turning to Tom, Alex added, "I never understood why you abandoned the Federalists. And I also never understood why you took up with a slave woman."

Tom grew sullen.

"Sally Hemings was my father-in-law's child. I never got over the shock of Martha's death at the age of thirty-four. It comforted me to see my Martha's face in Sally's. We had six children together, and four survived to adulthood. I liberated them when they came of age. And frankly, Alex, she may not have been a slave, but your Maria Reynolds was not your wife either."

"The Reynolds were bankrupt. Her husband sent her to my door to lure me into blackmail payments," Alex said defiantly.

"You were always such a snob, Tom. You might have been a more pragmatic leader if you had been disadvantaged as I was."

"I am grateful for my upbringing," said Tom. "Besides, the larger part of being a leader is to inspire hope, to offer a dream of a better tomorrow."

"I agree," said Alex. "In fact, I wish I'd figured it out sooner."

Eager to change the topic, Ben interrupted. "I was fascinated to learn on my tour yesterday that some scholars believe the Civil War was not fought over slavery, but over national sovereignty."

"Yes," said John. "President Lincoln freed the slaves, changing the war's purpose. I wonder if he and his Cabinet dined here when they made that decision."

"Do you mean the Confederacy believed it was lawful to secede from the union?" asked Mercy.

"The Constitution we ratified gave the South every right to secede from the union on objecting to laws it viewed as unconstitutional," said Tom. "I am not as avid a reader in the Earthly Library as John, but I have read that after the war, Jefferson Davis, the president of the Confederacy, was never tried for treason. Technically, he had done nothing illegal."

"We were supposed to be forming a new country of thirteen free and independent states, with each retaining the ultimate authority over internal matters," said Mercy.

"We had to create a central government or the colonies would have collapsed," said Alex. "The whole would not hold without some entity directing the sum of the parts, with a real leader. Tom, perhaps that is why Lincoln was greater than all but the General."

"Some actor said Trump was," said John. "Someone who played a tough guy in the movies. I thought the Earthly Library said his name was something like Sylvester Stallone."

"A movie?" asked Ben.

"Moving illustrations," said John.

"Was that in our reading? How I wish I had been born later," said Ben, sounding a bit rueful. "What an invention!"

"I think you were right, Ben. It would have been better to have been born now. There are so many more opportunities to make money!" said Alex.

"Indeed, but then we would not be Founding Fathers," said Tom.

"And this country would not be what it has become," said John.

"But I wonder what exactly this nation *has* become," said Mercy. "Is it still a constitutional federal republic? Was it ever?"

"I never assumed the government as we created it would ever last this long," said Tom. "I remember arguing that the earth belongs to the living, that the dead have no power over it. Maybe each generation needs to fight anew for its breath, for its liberty."

"I disagree completely," said Alex. "It was our destiny to expand the frontier. The venture West—so dangerous and so violent and so long anticipated by those of us who led at the beginning—turned the Americans into rugged individuals with a belief in hard work and tremendous faith in self-reliance. It is in our bones. Anyway, I hope it still is."

"If so, perhaps the United States owes a great deal to Britain's progenitor customs," said Tom. "Those second and third sons born to nobles, with no future and no prospect of inheritance, came here and seeded our democracy. To explore is endemic to the American soul."

"Having inherited nothing from my father, I wholeheartedly agree with that," said Alex. "But I wonder if Mercy is right. I wonder if America is now what we intended—a representative republic. Or whether the country descended into a rivalry among competing fiefdoms."

"Not sure those are different," said Mercy. "After lunch, let us go to one of those souvenir shops and see how they are portraying us. It could tell us a lot."

"Or not portraying us," said John.

"And I want to get a Make America Great Again hat," said Ben.

"But why?" asked John.

"It would cover my bald spot, for one," said Ben. "But also, I enjoy being on trend."

As if weary of their political observations, they turned their conversation to memories, revolving around family, money and beloved farm animals. Ever the Renaissance man, Tom even recited a poem he had written as a young man, pretending to be an old one:

> I have seen the sea all in a blaze of fire.
>
> I have seen a house high as the moon and higher
>
> I have seen the sun at twelve o'clock at night
>
> I have seen the man who saw this wonderous sight.

Then they went out on the town.

SCENE 3

The Arrest

At Mercy's suggestion, they first queued up to take a tour of nearby Ford's Theatre, where President Lincoln was assassinated. The line was filled with foreigners and Americans—Mercy thought she heard French, Spanish, Arabic, Hebrew, and even Hindi.

"So many from other countries, here to honor an American president," she said.

"Assassination is a dastardly deed," said Ben. "But nothing is certain except death and taxes."

"Quite a few of our presidents have met violent ends," said John. "I am grateful I was spared, although voters did send me packing before I was ready to leave." He looked pointedly at Tom.

"John, that was two hundred twenty-six years ago! My goodness, I thought you might have gotten over it by now. We all have regrets."

"And yours?" asked John.

"You may recall that one of my early drafts of the Declaration included criticism of King George for creating and perpetuating the transatlantic slave trade. I wish I'd kept that in."

"Now that would have bankrupted us," said Alex. "Without slave labor, it is hard to see how the whole experiment would have worked."

"I think that sad but true," said Mercy. "Listen."

Behind them, a young man was saying to his friend, "You know, this whole effing country was built on slave labor. They probably built this theater."

"Yeah," said his friend, "the sign says built in 1863, so makes sense."

"Remind me," said Mercy, "why was that passage removed?"

"The Continental Congress took it out," said John. "Delegates reasoned that if they were about to declare war on the British Empire, they needed all colonies—North and South—on board."

"The truth is more complicated," said Alex. "All the colonies needed the slaves. In the South, they needed free labor to produce tobacco, rice, and cotton for export. In the North, they depended on the transatlantic trade of rum, sugar, and enslaved humans."

Tom looked introspective.

"I always thought that passage in the original Declaration contained some of my best writing." He recited, "'He has waged cruel war against human nature itself, violating its most sacred rights of life and liberty in the persons of a distant people who never offended him, captivating and carrying them into slavery in another hemisphere or to incur miserable death in their transportation.'"

"Stop mumbling, Tom. People are starting to stare at you," said John.

"I was enjoying the recitation," said Mercy.

After touring the theater, the box where Lincoln was assassinated, and backstage where his cloak and gloves were on display, they followed the crowd across the street to the boarding house where the sixteenth president was carried after the shooting.

"A sober sight," said Tom, "such a tall and important figure, squeezed into such a small bed. That is why I built my own sleeping quarters at Monticello, so I could get a good night's sleep."

"I cannot imagine that any of us had a swifter path to Heaven than this man," said Ben. "A hero."

Somber, they walked out into the sunshine and followed the crowds to the gift shop. They spent several minutes there and took photos with various shoppers. Mercy was horrified.

"Christmas ornaments, T-shirts, hats, and little golf balls with dimples on them, all with Lincoln's likeness," she said. "Busts of Lincoln. Portraits of Lincoln with his son. Signs that proclaim Lincoln was the GOAT, whatever that is. Have we been reduced to a nation of souvenir collectors? There is even a replica of the Gettysburg Address written on parchment!"

"Must be printed," said Ben, examining it. "These lines are too precise to be handwritten."

"A masterful speech, that," said Tom. "'Four score and seven years ago, our fathers brought forth, on this continent, a new nation, conceived in liberty, and dedicated to the proposition that all men are created equal.'"

"An excellent writer," agreed Mercy. "Which does not explain why his image appears on this jar of...something called barbecue sauce."

"So brilliant of him to use the occasion of death, a battlefield in Pennsylvania where so many Confederates and Yankees had died, to remind the nation of their debt to us," Tom continued, oblivious to Mercy's remark. "'We here highly resolve that these dead shall not have died in vain, that this nation, under God, shall have a new birth of freedom, and that government of the people, by the people, for the people, shall not perish from the earth.' Just brilliant."

"From what I have read, the Civil War changed this country," said Ben. "Even the English language changed. In our day we used to say, 'The United States are.' After the Civil War, the formulation changed to 'The United States is.' A correction of grammar, and history."

"I am not sure that is a good thing," said Tom. "In reuniting the country, it seems Lincoln took us further from our foundational principle that government derives its consent from the people."

"Are you suggesting that the central government as a behemoth started then?" asked Ben.

"Perhaps. I read that Noah Webster, a wordsmith who wrote a dictionary, said, 'Liberty and Union, now and forever, one and inseparable.' Perhaps, if the Civil War settled the conflict between the states, it also tilted the power equation in the federal government's favor."

"I actually think that shift was more pronounced under a man named Woodrow Wilson and his urban progressives," said John. "We designed a government bound by the Constitution, with the states as our great experiment in self-governance. Progressives believed in an unelected shadow government of bureaucrats to run the country no matter who was in office."

"If the Civil War was a contest over sovereignty, then perhaps the Confederacy was an unwilling ambassador of states' rights," said Mercy. "And its defeat set them back. For my part, I just wonder why they could not have just abolished slavery."

"Because the South needed it," said Alex. "That whole region was a House of Cotton and Rice. And all of it needed to be harvested. Anyway, that is what the courts ruled."

"Ah, the courts. A bane in my presidency," said Tom. "Thanks to John's 'midnight appointments.'"

"Those were lawful measures as I was leaving office."

"Lawful, perhaps, but sneaky nonetheless."

There was a silence then, as they left the souvenir shop.

"Look." Mercy pointed across the street. "Something called a wax museum."

Ben smiled.

"I knew a Madame Tussauds in Paris once."

"What is a wax museum?" asked Mercy.

"We will find out," said Tom, taking her arm.

It was dark and cool inside, and at first, they had trouble making out what the building housed.

"Why is it so cold in here?" Ben asked the burly young man behind the counter.

"Sir, this is summer in DC. We couldn't stay in business without air-conditioning."

"Air cooling?" asked Ben. "Does that run on electricity?"

"I guess. How many tickets to you want?"

"Tickets for what? What is this place?"

The man named Christina looked at the group of five as if seeing them for the first time.

"Say, some of you are in here."

"As what?" asked Alex.

"Maybe, statues of famous people like you," said Mercy.

Tom looked at her in wonder.

"Is that true, young man?" asked Ben.

"Christina," said the young man angrily. "My name is Christina. My pronouns are she and her."

This silenced them, and they withdrew to consult.

"Do we have money for tickets?" Mercy whispered.

"Why on earth would that young man pretend to be a girl?" John wondered.

"Weak character," said Ben. "As I wrote in *Poor Richard's Almanac*..."

"We've all read it, Ben," said Mercy.

"No one thought to give us any money," said Alex. "At Old Ebbitt's Grill, we put the bill on the Archives account. At Ford's Theater, they waved us in, as if they were accustomed to seeing us walking around town. So glad we resisted the temptation to buy anything at the souvenir shop."

Just then, they heard a beeping sound. It seemed to be emanating from Ben's pocket.

"Crickets," said Ben. "I believe there are crickets in my pocket!"

"Sir," the man named Christina yelled, "could you please silence your pager?"

"My what, young man? Oh yes, this must be the gadget Priscilla Babcock gave me."

"I wonder how you turn it off," said Alex.

By this time, Christina had left the desk to hover over them.

"If you don't silence that pager," Christina said, "I'll have to ask you to leave."

Ben looked at the still-beeping instrument, puzzled.

"Can you show me how, young man?"

"I am not a young man!" said Christina. "I am a proud transgender woman."

"How can you be a woman when you have an Adam's apple?" asked Ben.

At that, Christina roared back and punched Ben in the nose, knocking his bifocals to the ground and pushing him into Alex, who was luckily strong enough to hold him upright.

"See here—Ben is the oldest of us, and you should show him respect," said Mercy.

"It's bad enough that evil racist Trump made me give up my pronouns," yelled Christina. "If you people are still here when I get back from the crying room, I'm calling the police."

"The constable?" asked John as he looked for Ben's glasses on the floor.

Christina screamed and ran to the back of the building.

"Found them!" John exclaimed.

"Look," said Alex, "he left the gate open."

On that news, Ben seemed to recover, and they walked through the opening. Once inside they were amazed to see a collection of statues of many famous people made of wax.

"Look, I think that's Shakespeare," said Mercy. "I saw an illustration of him once."

Ben looked up to see a rendering of himself. They stood next to his statue, the others gathering around him. A tourist wandered by and snapped a device, making a clicking noise.

"A good likeness," said Mercy.

"Marvelous idea for a building," said Tom.

"Seems a waste of space to me," said Alex, "unless of course it makes a lot of money."

"My goodness, Alex, you are right across from me," said Ben.

"That looks nothing like me," said Alex.

"It really does not resemble you," agreed Mercy. "I would have thought, you being a famous person on Broadway, that they could have created a better likeness."

John looked petulant.

"Be grateful you're in the museum, Alex," he said. "I am quite sure I have been relegated to the dustbin of history, toppled by that magnanimous Man from Monticello."

"Let us look," said Mercy, walking further into the vast space. "Oh, dear Father, there's Tom!"

The Jefferson statue was even a better likeness than Ben's, and they all gathered round like soldiers saluting their leader. As they oohed and ahhed, they heard the sound of sirens.

"Such a noisy city," said Alex. "I should have kept the capital in Philadelphia."

"I hardly think that would have been any quieter," said Ben.

Just then the doors of the museum burst open, and a squad of uniformed men marched up to the group and announced they were all under arrest.

"Whatever for?" asked John.

"We have a video that shows you jumped the turnstile and entered without paying," said one officer whose nametag said Sergeant Bilk. "Also, that guy in the bifocals misgendered someone, and in the District of Columbia we still call that a hate crime."

"Ben? My dear man," said Mercy, "Ben Franklin is the kindest man I know. He hates no one."

Sergeant Bilk looked at them for the first time, recognizing Ben and Tom.

"Hey, is this some sort of prank?" Sergeant Bilk asked. "You are actors?"

Alex looked at Tom, who winked at him. Before departing Heaven, they had been instructed to tell curious Americans that they were actors.

"Yes, we are here for the birthday affair in a few weeks. We just came to look at our likenesses."

"All good," said Sergeant Bilk, "but you can't look at anything without paying. I can let that one slide for now. But you," he added, pointing at Ben, "should not insult transgender people by misgendering them, even if President Trump tried to disappear them. A lot has changed around here lately, but that hate crime law is still on the books, and I intend to prosecute you to the hilt."

There was much silence at that.

"Is this a language you know?" Tom whispered to Ben.

Ben shook his head.

"You are the wordsmith among us, Tom, so if you are unaware, I am as well."

"Do you think transgender means those men who liked to dress as women?" asked John. "Why do you suppose they traveled their gender? Or how?"

"Remember during the war, there was a woman who dressed as a boy so she could serve in Washington's army," said Mercy. "Perhaps it is something like that."

"Surely the Archives will not allow Ben to be arrested," said Alex.

"OK, that's enough of this conversation. We're taking this man in for a hate crime. What's your real name, sir?"

"My name is Benjamin Franklin, and my pronouns are he and him."

"Take him down to the DC jail," Sergeant Bilk told one of his officers. "See if you can get his real name out of him."

"Why is it that the man behind the counter is allowed to choose his own name, but Ben is not?" asked Mercy.

"I was on the Earth for eighty-four years," Ben mumbled. "I come back once, and I find myself arrested!"

"Not to worry," said Mercy. "I had five sons. I know something about getting boys out of trouble."

As the police car whisked Ben away, sirens blazing, Alex crossed the street and told Mr. Debussy what had happened and that they would like to walk back to the Archives on foot. Alex prided himself on having a good sense of direction, and the others said they would enjoy the fresh air.

"Good thing Ben's not here," said Tom, whose daily regimen on Earth had included a cold foot bath every morning and a long horse ride. "I am not sure he could have made the march."

"Perhaps, but he would have figured out a way to hire a conveyance," said John. "Trust me, I saw the man operate in France. A born dealmaker."

"What an extraordinary encounter that was," said Mercy. "To think Americans no longer know whether they are men or women."

"It is worse than that I fear," said Alex. "I wonder if they even know they are Americans."

"Why do you say that?" asked Tom.

"Did you hear their questions on the tour? They seem like empty vessels, unlearned in anything concerning this country or the world it grew out of. From their questions, I thought the foreigners were better informed about America than the Americans were."

"That seems true," said Mercy. "I heard one man ask why Lincoln was born in a log cabin. They do not talk about history. They talk about shopping and what to buy and where to eat."

"Maybe options for both are greater now," said Alex. "Besides, are we not guilty of that too? We just arrived for a reenactment, and yet we rushed to lunch and then went touring and shopping."

"Are you saying we have become a nation of acquisition?" asked Mercy.

"We always were," said Alex. "One reason the debt got so large. All those luxuries that Americans wanted to import from Britain."

"It was the women," said John. "My Abigail schemed to get imported lace from Flanders or England. She liked to wear it on her collars and cuffs. It made her feel special."

"Oh, the irony there," said Mercy, "to blame the women for the interest in fashion. I seem to recall many a colonial gentleman dressed in fancy gear, outfitted with gloves and top hat."

"Point taken," said John. "As Alex says, maybe we are all guilty of being consumers."

"At least we also consumed history and literature," said Tom. "I wrote that if a nation expects to be ignorant and free, it expects what never was and never will be."

On their return to the Archives, they took the elevator back up to the auditorium.

"Where have you been?" Priscilla said, barely controlled fury in her voice. "And where's Ben?"

"He was arrested," said Mercy. "Something these Americans call a hate crime."

Priscilla saw her plans collapsing. There would be notoriety—the media would blow things up into a firestorm. Rehearsals would be disrupted. The reputation of the Archives would be tainted. The Director would be furious. Suddenly she felt herself swaying and reached her arms to her chest. Then the world started spinning and she toppled to the floor.

"I think she has fainted," said Tom. "Did any of us bring smelling salts?"

SCENE 4

The Airbnb

By the time Priscilla recovered, the Director had arrived. He sent her home. Then he approached the author of the words that animated his museum's very core.

"An honor to have you with us, sir," Thomas Sowell said with a smile, reaching for Tom's hand. "An honor to have all of you."

"Can you get Ben out of prison?" asked Mercy. "He was really so insulted. My apologies to all of you, but I believe Ben is the quintessential American. I know that Tom's Declaration was a gorgeous piece of writing, underlined by principles of democracy that inspired nations around the world to model their governments on ours. And that John was a stalwart for constitutional writing and legal foundations. And that Alex literally won the war, sold the peace, and then saved our country's finances. And I like to think that my poetry and history played a small role in righting the ship to protect individual rights. But without Benjamin Franklin, well…"

She paused for breath, visibly agitated.

"Go on," prodded Tom.

"Without Ben, this nation as a concept would not exist. He taught us all the importance of a work ethic, of lifting ourselves to achievement. His inventions were revolutionary, from the lightning rod to the Franklin stove, from his famous bifocals to glass musical instruments. And then this exemplary American used his celebrity as an inventor to convince doubters in France and England that we were serious people. He came home to craft our Constitution. No, I do not see how the United States could have happened without him."

The Director smiled at her. He took her hand and kissed it lightly.

"I assure you I have a good relationship with the warden at the Correctional Treatment Facility. I hope to have Dr. Franklin released quickly. In fact, if you forgive me, I will go make my first call now. In the meantime, as it's been a long day, I suggest you retire to the house we've rented for you in Georgetown. Mr. Debussy will take you. There are provisions for your comfort."

"What about the rehearsals?" asked Alex. "I assumed that was why Miss Babcock paged Ben."

"We will postpone those until tomorrow," said the Director. "Hopefully with Dr. Franklin."

"Is Georgetown named for the General?" asked Mercy.

"Indeed."

He gave them all a nod and left the room.

"I like him," Tom said to John as they went downstairs to the waiting car. "A tall, well-built, obviously intelligent man of African descent, older than we imagined people could live, serving at the highest levels of the United States government. Remarkable, do not you think?"

"I told you earlier today what I think—an excess of democracy. Look at this place—Blacks and women in charge, men who think they're women, what Sergeant Bilk called hate crimes for speech. Think of how many of us would have gone to jail if we had been punished for speaking our minds. Why, Patrick Henry would have been arrested on the floor of the Virginia General Assembly! You could make a case that this country was founded on hate speech! And Mrs. Warren, with her inflammatory pamphlets urging the states to reject the Constitution unless we added a Bill of Rights—they would have jailed her too!"

"I do not think my writings were inflammatory," Mercy chimed in.

"For goodness' sake, Mrs. Warren," said John, "you called me an English loyalist!"

"Mr. Adams, you were very autocratic sometimes, as you are being now. Besides, you know better than most that I studied Greek history and European literature with my brother James and his tutor. I like to think my writings reflected the literary pinnacle of Western civilization."

"I concede that," said John, looking thoughtful. "That is the reason you and I and Abigail were such fast friends. And we were very fond of your husband."

"What do you say, just for the birthday, a truce?" asked Mercy.

John smiled at Mercy, hesitatingly, for the first time in 230 years, since her book's publication.

"Thank you, Mr. Adams," she said, smiling back. "However, I have to disagree with you about one thing. I am not sure today's incident was about free speech. Think about it. Ben did not so much speak his mind or even pontificate on a heady subject. All he did was call that person named Christina 'a young man.'"

"An excellent point," said Alex. "You know when I was here last I handled a libel case, defending a New York journalist accused of libel by one Thomas Jefferson. You remember the Croswell case, I assume, Tom? Anyway, I convinced the New York Supreme Court that a man could only be convicted of libel if his intent was malicious or if the accusation was untrue."

"Do you think that could apply in Ben's case?" said Mercy. "A matter of free speech?"

"Perhaps," said Alex.

"It is difficult to understand how calling Christina a 'young man,' would be a crime," said Tom.

"Great irony there," said Alex. "Ben, who thrives on inventions rather than politics, who lives in the tactile world of objects and creations, accused of a crime of what, culture?"

"I am more bothered by what the incident says about today's Americans," said Mercy. "If a child lashes out at playmates with naughty words, he is not arrested—he is schooled. Are Americans so soft, so lacking in spine, that they can no longer handle what amounts to a child's tantrum?"

"I suppose we will find out if Ben is ever put on trial," said John.

The Airbnb in Georgetown had big picture windows overlooking the Potomac. The house had bedrooms for everyone, and each person had a separate room for the taking of baths. Priscilla had stocked their kitchen with cheeses and Madeira wine—the Director had suggested such a menu would be familiar to them. Privately, she had rolled her eyes. There were lots of restaurants in Georgetown if they decided to go out.

"Quite the view," said John. "How I wish Abigail could see this."

Alex ran to a bedroom and bounced on the mattress. "Divine!" he said.

Mercy took the wine from a cabinet she decided to call the Closet That Kept Everything Cold and gave it to Tom to pour. He looked at it with a frown.

"Madeira? Anything French?"

Mercy suggested he look in the cabinet and select whatever bottle pleased him. She put out the cheeses and some loaves she found in a box.

"Comforting food," said John. "But I have to admit, I did like my chowder at Old Ebbitt's Grill."

"I loved my hamburger," Alex chimed in as he emerged from the bedroom.

"Before we go to bed, we should discuss what happened today," said Mercy.

"Besides what we ate for lunch?" asked John.

"I suspect Mercy means what happened to our country," said Alex. "At times today I wondered if this country is what I was defending in *The Federalist Papers*. Or if the foundation has fractured into a million interests, like stakeholders in a business."

"We were all so united during the war," agreed Mercy. "I remember the spinning parties where we women weaved our own clothes so we as not to import British goods. I remember how the women hungered for every scrap of news from the front. I blush thinking about our gossip."

"Women, gossiping?" said Alex with feigned incredulity.

"It seems like everything that came afterward—the war, the Constitution, the fight over ratification—it divided us in factions, fighting with each other instead of the king," Mercy continued. "Then this country went to war so often—our Civil War, those two world wars, the Cold War, those things they call the forever wars. I expected our greatest bequest to future generations was the pursuit of happiness. Our descendants seem eager to fight new wars."

"That was what the General warned about in his Farewell Address," said Alex. "And I should know, I wrote it for him, and I have the drafts to prove it."

"You wrote it well," said Tom, reciting: "'Against the insidious wiles of foreign influence—I conjure you to believe me, fellow-citizens—the jealousy of a free people ought to be constantly awake, since history and experience prove that foreign influence is one of the most baneful foes of republican government.'"

There was silence for a few minutes as they pondered George Washington's words. Something about the birthday seemed to be softening the enmities between them.

"James Madison also worried that direct democracy would inspire great turbulence and die an early death," said Alex. "In Federalist 10, he called it 'spectacles of turbulence and contention' and warned that anarchy could trample the rights of the citizens."

"Yes, yes," said John. "That is the point I was trying to make earlier. Too much direct democracy is dangerous. Aristotle was sure it would lead to mob rule."

"That is why we included an Electoral College in the Constitution," said Alex. "And that's why I was surprised to see a tyrannical takeover of the US government by that senile old Joe Biden. The US government teetered on the edge of authoritarianism."

"From what I gather it was not this President Biden, but a gang of schemers behind him—sent by that man Obama—who were more interested in government power than public will," said John.

"Trump keeps calling him the 'autopen president,'" said Alex. "If he never really signed anything himself, it might put all his achievements in legal doubt."

"He or even the cabal could not have been as bad as those presidents before the Civil War," said Mercy. "From what I hear, they just kept delaying the slavery question, leaving the landscape so scarred with unworkable compromises that a war was perhaps inevitable."

"To be fair," said Tom, "corruption in government has a long history."

"The Continental Congress was lobbied by merchants to end the molasses tax," said John. "And I understand that by the 1850s, Samuel Colt gave away free pistols to congressmen."

"My question," said Mercy, "is how did we get from a celebration of the individual and his inalienable rights to this overgrown city where citizens of the republic can be arrested for calling a man by a man's name? How did we go from enumerating the rights of the states and the citizens to a gigantic federal government with its claws choking the life out of the living? And how did we acquire a military so large it itched to fight wars in every decade?"

"I have long believed," said Tom, "bad government grows out of too much government."

"Must be true," said Mercy. "Think about all those buildings we saw today."

Tom nodded.

Suddenly there was a rattle at the front door, and in walked Ben.

There was shouting and back clapping and a shy hug from Mercy. "Wine?" she asked.

Ben laughed.

"You know I am a beer man, Mercy."

She showed Ben the Closet That Kept Everything Cold. He was ecstatic to discover another cooling invention. He pulled out a Sam Adams. Then he eyed another contraption on the counter called Two-Slice Toaster, and he was lost in wonder, pressing the buttons for bagels, defrost, and cancel, imagining the machine's uses. Mercy called out from the living room to see if he was all right.

"Born too early," he said ruefully as he joined the others. "If only I had lived now instead of then."

"I, for one, am glad you were born when you were," said Mercy. She seated him in their circle, put before him a plate of cheeses and bread, and sat back to listen.

"What ever happened?" asked John.

"It was frightening," said Ben. "There was a cage between me and the driver, as if I might attack him. They had my hands constrained in some metal contraption. It hurt badly, but I must say the design was creative. That gadget Miss Babcock gave me kept beeping, until finally a policeman grabbed it and smashed it. Which told me he had no idea know how to turn it off either!"

"And then?" said Mercy.

"Once at the jail, they released my hands from bondage and took my image—with a marvelous invention called a camera—and made me sign some papers. They wanted me to sign as John Doe One-Five-Five-Seven, but I said I'd never heard of the fellow and refused. They took me into a cell and slammed the door shut. The room had bars on the front door, two beds and one person."

"Who was that?" asked John.

"John Doe Three."

"Why was he there?"

"That is rather an interesting story. Apparently, he was down on his luck and had accepted a bribe from something called the FBI," said Ben, sipping his beer. "You are an avid reader in the Earthly Library, John. Have you any idea what those letters stand for?"

"I believe it is the Federal Building of Interrogation," said John, "though I am not sure."

"The United States government has a whole building dedicated to interrogation?" asked Tom.

"And then what happened?" asked Mercy.

"He showed up, as directed by the FBI, to protest the 2020 election that Biden won. There was chaos at the Capitol. In the melee, this very same FBI arrested him for insurrection."

"Insurrection!" said Mercy. "I have not heard that word since Shays's Rebellion, when all those farmers protested having to pay high taxes after spilling blood for the Revolution. I always thought it cruel of our governor in Massachusetts to punish them so severely."

"Without the backlash against Shays's Rebellion, I doubt we would have had the votes to even call a constitutional convention," said John.

"I was in Paris then, but I was surprised to hear that the convention created to amend the Articles of Confederation decided instead to invent an entirely new constitution," said Tom.

"There was no choice," said Alex. "The states were fleecing one another, especially those with port cities. We were headed for a civil war over trade and taxes!"

"Please," said Ben. "Can I return you to our present country? This poor gentleman has been in jail since 2021. Five years!"

"So you enjoyed his company," said Mercy.

"Very much. He was very intelligent—we even discussed the Sixteenth Amendment, which in 1913 first imposed an income tax on Americans to fund the central government. He is not a fan."

"I so wish they had not done that," Alex said. "When the Constitution took effect in 1789, I worked hard to straighten out the nation's disastrous financial situation. That is why your State Department, Tom, had five employees while mine at Treasury had forty. The central government assumed all the states' war debts, and I stood up a new National Bank. I had it all set up to get revenue from tariffs on imports. You could say I was the Donald Trump of my day."

"I wish there we could free John Doe Three. He was the only person all day—apart from you present now, of course—who treated me as if I really were Benjamin Franklin."

"Wait until you meet Director Sowell," said Tom.

"John Doe Three even asked for my signature, and you know how he expressed himself? He said, 'Can I have your John Hancock?' I laughed out loud."

"My reputation in history might be more robust if only I had written my name larger," said John.

"John, it is long since time for you to drop your resentments," said Mercy. "We were privileged to be there for the creation of this great nation, and now God has favored us to be here for its two hundred fiftieth birthday. We have much to celebrate."

"To sleep for me," said Ben. "It has been an unexpectedly exhausting day."

"Wait until you see the beds," said Alex. "Like Heaven."

The next morning, opening the front door of their Airbnb, Mercy found a copy of *The Washington Post* on the doorstep. The headline summed up the events of the previous day nicely:

"Man Claiming To Be Ben Franklin
Arrested For Hate Crime."

"Ben," she called out as she closed the front door, "you are famous."

"I rather thought I had been earlier."

"Yes, I suppose it would be more accurate to say you are newly famous."

She showed him the newspaper.

"Oh, my heavens. Your Mr. Sowell will not be happy with me."

"Wait until he hears you want to free one of DC's most notorious prisoners," said Alex, his hair tousled by deep sleep. "I could get used to the fluffy comforters down here."

"I am sure you could arrange one," said Mercy. "Ben, come look at this coffee machine!"

Ben followed Mercy into the kitchen and proclaimed the Moccamaster a great invention.

"That smells rich," said Tom as he joined them.

"Have you been sleeping this whole time?" asked John as he joined them.

"Of course not. I took my ice bath and then went for a long walk along the Potomac."

Just then there was a knock on the door. Mercy went to open it.

"Director Sowell, do come in. And thank you for rescuing Ben."

"It was my deep honor. I thought we should all talk about legal matters."

"John's your man for that," said Mercy.

"And a great lawyer too," Ben said.

"At your service," said John.

"Would you like some coffee?" Mercy asked their guest.

"Yes, please, black."

Once they had arranged themselves around the large table in front of the picture window, Director Sowell addressed them all.

"We were able to effect the release of our friend Ben Franklin temporarily, so that he can participate in the OBBR," he began. "But he may have to stay on Earth afterward."

"Could not he just die again?" asked Alex.

"I suppose he could," said Mr. Sowell, "although that is a bit beyond my rank."

"What about the rest of us?" asked Mercy. "Could we stay with him?"

At this Mr. Sowell stared into his coffee cup.

"The matter is complex," he said. "You see, I only prayed to God for the five of you, plus the General and Billy Lee, to come down for the reenactment."

"And you have forgotten how to pray?" chuckled Ben. "I will never forget, at the Constitutional Convention I suggested we ask a clergyman to pray over our deliberations. I was voted down! Someone argued that if word got out that we were in need of prayer, the public would panic."

"Why does Ben need to stay behind?" asked Tom.

"To stand trial." Silence greeted this statement. "For a hate crime."

"Director Sowell," said Mercy, "as I told you last night, Dr. Franklin is not capable of hate."

"Yes, I asked about the prospect of a plea bargain, but local officials are eager to prosecute."

"A plea bargain?" asked Alex.

"An agreement where the defendant pleads guilty, and in return, prosecutors spare him the harshest sentence."

"Even if he is innocent?" asked Alex. "My goodness, these Americans seem to have forgotten the concept of defending their honor!"

"You could certainly teach a class in that," said Tom.

The conversation lapsed, the five of them contemplating this news.

Finally, Ben spoke.

"If possible, I would like to, as Alex says, defend my honor. There is nothing hateful in calling a person 'a young man.' I would be happy if my fellow patriots would like to stay with me. But if they have more pressing issues to attend to upstairs, I understand. I rather miss my daughter."

"I'm afraid we will have to get you a new name," said the Director.

"But he is known around the world as Benjamin Franklin!" protested Mercy.

"And a great name it is. But that is precisely why I can't get him a driver license under that name. We would be laughed out of the Department of Motor Vehicles."

"With respect, I do not think it a good idea to let Ben drive," said John. "I remember once in Paris we took a carriage to see the sights. I can report he has a dreadful driver!"

"What name would you like, Dr. Franklin?" asked the Director.

Ben looked down, his face a combination of shame and confusion.

"A name is a privilege, and if you have worn it well, if you have earned with it a reputation, it is difficult to abandon. If I must have a new name—this would be temporary, Director Sowell?"

"Yes, Dr. Franklin, just for the duration of this court case."

"In that case, only for this court appearance, I would select Josiah Folger."

"Your father's first name?" asked the Director.

Ben nodded.

"And my mother's family name. I managed eight decades here without being arrested. The first thing my father said on seeing me in Heaven was, 'Well done, son.' I'd like my parents to be with me on this unexpected journey."

"Are you all agreed to stay?"

"I wonder if I might return after the reenactment," said John. "How I miss Abigail."

"You cannot leave, John."

"And why is that?"

"Because I need an attorney, and you're the smartest one I know. I was astonished you won freedom for Mum Bett, a slave, on the strength of the idea that all men are created equal!"

"I cannot claim that, Ben. The case was won by another lawyer, much younger than I, named Theodore Sedgwick. After he won that lady's freedom, she changed her name to Elizabeth Freeman and, as a paid employee, worked for the Sedgwick family the rest of her life."

"But you wrote the Massachusetts Constitution!"

"Yes, I penned the phrase, 'All men are born free and equal, and have certain natural, essential, and unalienable rights.' And I told Sedgwick I had an inkling those words could make a successful case. But I suspected that for Mum Bett's case to be successful, it would also require men of conscience, judges open to judicial activism. Sedgwick appealed to their better angels."

"We are agreed, then, on John Adams for the defendant?" asked the Director, smiling. "I rather like the sound of that."

Both John and Ben nodded.

"Very well, then I will pray accordingly."

SCENE 5

Rehearsal

As in Robert Trumbull's famous portrait of the Declaration of Independence, Thomas Jefferson stood at the front of a desk, handing the document to John Hancock, seated in a chair. Finished in 1817, the painting depicted the moment that launched America's war against British rule.

"Quiet on the set," said Priscilla. "Let's take it from the top."

"Mr. President," Tom said, addressing the actor hired to play Hancock, who sat upright in the chair. "We, the Committee of Five, are honored to share with you this Declaration of Independence. This outline of our grievances, and attendant insistence on our rights, is addressed to the king. We ask that it be delivered to England."

With that, John placed on the desk a king's crown, sitting it atop the Bible that belonged to the Congress. "We have divided this crown into thirteen parts to represent our unity."

Priscilla cued Ben to leave, toward stage left. A young actress approached and said, "Doctor, what have we got—a monarchy or a republic?"

To which he replied, "A republic, if you can keep it."

With that, Priscilla signaled the sound man to play the recording of church bells.

"My dear, I did not utter that line for another eleven years!" interrupted Ben. "That was after we had written the Constitution, not after we declared our independence from the king."

"My goodness, you're right," said Priscilla. "My apologies. That line has to move to act three. Was anything memorable said at the signing?"

"As a historian and a playwright, I think not," said Mercy, seated with Alex in the front row. "I understand that when the Declaration was voted on, Philadelphia Hall was utterly silent."

"I agree with Mrs. Warren," said John. "If you have read Dr. Benjamin Rush's account, you know there was a 'pensive and awful silence.' As we were called to sign, I imagine all of us thought we were signing our death warrant. I certainly did. We were traitors to the king, likely to be hanged as such. The event was deeply solemn, do you see?"

"But once the document was signed, didn't church bells ring out?"

"Yes, they did," said John. "All day and almost all night."

"The church bells should wait until all have approached the desk and recorded our signatures," said Ben. "We should convey the utter, fearful silence in that place. The decision we had just made, to take on the Crown, weighed heavy on all of us."

Priscilla nodded.

"I am surprised to hear you are in accord with this, John. I thought you said the Declaration was too passionate for your liking, too much like scolding the king," said Tom.

"Who told you that?" asked John.

"You did," said Tom. "It was in that letter you wrote to that man Pickering, years later."

"Ah, one of the drawbacks of us both dying on the same day," said John. "You know everything."

"You died five hours after me," said Tom, "so you could have penned some final barb."

"Did you know, Miss Babcock, that Tom and I both died on July 4, 1826, on the fiftieth anniversary of the Declaration of Independence?"

"I did know that," she said. "Historians have made much of it, wondering if you planned it that way. I wonder if there's some way to presage that in our reenactment."

What was happening to her, Priscilla wondered. She had bungled the timing of the famous Ben Franklin line, and now she was talking to these actors as if they were the real characters.

"To answer your question, Tom, yes, I did think the Declaration was rather emotional," said John. "But I knew it had to be written by someone from Virginia, the fulcrum of our nation, bridging North and South, free and slave, mercantile and farm. In the end, you were the solution to the most difficult problem we faced—how to make thirteen clocks strike at once."

"By the time I wrote the Declaration, scores of local communities had already declared themselves for independence," said Tom. "Slaves were clamoring for their freedom, and freed slaves were volunteering to fight with us. There was a high fever in the air, a kind of anticipation of a pivot, a passionate assertion of Tom Paine's *Rights of Man*. By definition, emotion was the connection that fueled politics across the nation, and maybe even now, across the generations."

"Quite so," said Mercy. "And it should also be noted that the first official call to leave the king's rule came a month earlier on

June 7, when Richard Henry Lee of Virginia rose in Congress to report that the Virginia Assembly had instructed its delegates to 'declare for independence.' Delegates from New York, New Jersey, Pennsylvania, Delaware, and Maryland were still dubious. Congress did what it usually does in such consequential situations—it deferred the vote on Lee's motion until July 1. But it did hire General Washington to defend Boston."

"I left Congress shortly after the General did," said Tom, "he to wage war, me to study, surrounded by books of philosophy, Locke, Aristotle, architects of all the great civilizations."

"I believe you took the Bible as well, did you not?" asked Mercy.

"Of course, I had the Jefferson family Bible. And I might have stayed in that study forever—how I loved to read and think—but when word came of Mr. Lee's resolution, I knew I had to begin the work of composing. I put down my books, ended my study, and began to write."

"I do not know if you are aware, John, but Abigail got a sneak peak of the document sitting on your desk and sent me some excerpts. I was overwhelmed."

She and Tom began reciting the opening in unison.

> When, in the Course of human Events, it becomes necessary for one People to dissolve the Political Bands which have connected them with another, and to assume, among the Powers of the Earth, the separate and equal Station to which the Laws of Nature and of Nature's God entitle them, a decent Respect to the Opinions of Mankind requires that they should declare the Causes which impel them to the Separation. We hold these truths to be self-evident, that all

> men are created equal, that they are endowed by their Creator with certain unalienable Rights, that among these are Life, Liberty and the pursuit of Happiness.—That to secure these rights, Governments are instituted among Men, deriving their just powers from the consent of the governed.—That whenever any Form of Government becomes destructive of these ends, it is the Right of the People to alter or to abolish it, and to institute new Government.

"So magical," said Mercy.

"It surprises me, looking back, that the draft was completed within weeks," said Alex.

"No one could have written it as well," said Ben. "Even loyalists appreciated the majesty of it. Tom, do you remember John Dickinson?"

"I remember him as a great thinker about governments and public opinion. His *Letters from a Farmer in Pennsylvania* set out the colonial argument for opposing British taxation more persuasively than any previous work. And if I am not mistaken, he also wrote the first draft of our first Articles of Confederation, did he not?"

"He did," said Ben. "And he called for a convention in Philadelphia to write a new constitution."

"I remember once he wrote that a good constitution promotes a good administration only if it respects the supreme sovereignty of the people."

"Miss Babcock, this man, so able and learned, opposed the Lee resolution," said Ben. "It was a measure of how complex the decisions were. It seems to me this nuance should be reflected in the play. He seemed to know it would erase him in history's eyes. Listen to what he said:"

> My conduct this day I expect will give the finishing blow to my once too great—and my now too diminished—popularity. Yet I had rather forfeit popularity forever, than vote away the blood and happiness of my countrymen.

"I like that," said Priscilla. "I'll have the scene expanded to include the prequel of Congress delaying the vote, and then assigning Mr. Jefferson to write it, then Mr. Dickinson's intellectual dilemma, and finally the processional to the desk. Maybe as you walk, you can talk among yourselves about who wrote the document and why the Committee of Five amended it."

"Excellent idea," said Ben. "Also, I see nothing in the script about the Continental Army learning that the Declaration of Independence had been signed. I believe they were at Ticonderoga in western Pennsylvania by then, in August."

"I remember it well," said Alex. "The troops were all whooping and hollering, and we lined up, voluntarily, to take a loyalty oath to the new nation. No one asked us to. That was our instinct."

"May I add my perspective?" said Tom. "I believe it a mistake to begin with the Declaration of Independence. So many events led up to that moment. You could go back to 1763, when the British signed a treaty ending the very expensive French and Indian War. If not for an effort to recoup those costs, Parliament would never have imposed the Stamp Act on us two years later."

"And that, in turn, would never have resulted in the Boston Massacre in 1768," said John. "We lost five Americans there to

British bullets. Or the Destruction of the Tea in 1773, or even the debate in Congress, where the vote was almost lost. Our first tally was nine states to four—New York sent no instructions, Pennsylvania and South Carolina were opposed, and Delaware was divided. Only because we adjourned until the next day was the union cause spared."

"Miss Babcock, forgive me if this sounds forward, but may I have a try at the script?" asked Mercy. "I used to be quite good at that sort of thing."

"I have a rather extensive record of writing myself," said John.

"An excellent idea," said Ben. "Miss Babcock, the five of us were discussing the script, and think it would be improved by the skilled pen of Mrs. Warren, with an assist from Mr. Adams. She is the Revolution's first memoirist, if you will, and he, the Constitution's first lawyer."

"I'd like to add another idea," said Alex. "I think Mrs. Warren should also narrate the play. She understands both the Federalists and the Anti-Federalists and has an excellent memory for detail. This would not only introduce her to Americans of 2026—and so few of them seem to know who she is—but knit the three acts of rebellion, war, and governance together in one voice."

"I agree," said Tom. "Mrs. Warren is the solution to the problems plaguing the script."

Priscilla bristled, unaccustomed to actors criticizing the script. But perhaps they were right. Clearly, she was losing her touch when she predated Franklin's famous line. She sighed, wondering if she had lost her mind altogether. And would she now lose her credibility, handing the script to two actors? Still, she was exhausted, and she sensed that Director Sowell had somehow approved this conspiracy to wrest the script from her hands.

Looking from John to Mercy, she said, "I thought you two were mortal enemies."

"Reunions are marvelous occasions for repairing history," said Mercy, smiling at John.

"I'll have lunch brought in so you two can get to work on the new script," said Priscilla said to John and Mercy. Turning to the other three, she said, "Please don't go too far." Looking at Ben, she added, "Or get arrested for anything."

Ben bowed slightly.

"We have an errand," said Ben. "We will be in Mr. Debussy's capable hands."

Priscilla detected a note of triumph in this actor's voice. Or was she getting paranoid? How did these people know so much about the nation's history? Who were the two actors now writing the play? She gathered from what the Ben Franklin character had said that they were in touch with Director Sowell. Should she worry?

Ben, Tom, and Alex exited stage right.

"This is our moment to rescue John Doe Three," Ben whispered. "Anyone have ideas?"

"We should visit him first," said Alex.

"If only to eye the prison's vulnerabilities," agreed Tom.

They found Mr. Debussy and explained their mission. He smiled.

"I will be happy to drive you to what they call the DC Gulag, named after the infamous labor camps during the Bolshevik regime in the Soviet Union. I'll be waiting for you when you exit. And if for some reason you are, well, detained, use these numbers to contact me."

"Numbers?" said Ben.

"Just ask anyone at the jail. They will know what to do. If you are arrested, you are entitled to reach out to one person via their numbers. I am your contact."

On arrival, they were searched with a baton, and had to walk through a machine.

"How barbaric," Ben whispered to Alex.

Once cleared, they stopped at the front desk. Ben spoke first.

"Madame, excuse me, I was here the other day—time goes so quickly in this place—and wondered if I could visit the man with whom I shared a room."

Samantha looked up from her paperwork.

"Ah, Mr. Franklin," she said, smiling. "Yes, I heard of your visit. Everyone has. Did this roommate of yours steal something from you?"

"Oh, no, my dear," said Ben. "I just wanted to…that is…"

"What Dr. Franklin meant to say," offered Tom, "is that John Doe Three gave him something to safekeep for him."

"Yes," said Alex, "and he means to return it."

Samantha picked up her phone.

"Captain, you're gonna want to see this," she said. "Ben Franklin has some friends. Also John Doe Three may have given him a package."

The captain was an African American but looked nothing like Director Sowell. He was light-skinned and very thin and lanky, with his pants kept aloft by suspenders.

"Ingenious," Ben whispered to Tom.

"Nothing you would ever have need of," Tom whispered back with a smile.

"Gentlemen," the captain said. "What can I do for you?"

"Sir, you see, the man I was placed with in my jail room the other day gave me a keepsake to hold for him. I just wanted to return it."

"And these are your friends?"

"Yes, this is Thomas Jefferson. And next to him is Alexander Hamilton."

"I see," said the captain. "Samantha, can you get me the file on room number seventeen?"

The young lady turned to her desk, and soon her fingers were clicking on a board of numbers and letters, her eyes riveted to a screen. Ben strained his neck to see what she was doing.

"My dear, what do you call that device?" he asked.

"A computer," Samantha answered. "We use it for keeping records."

She thought they were pushing the act a bit too far, but she'd heard about method actors. Maybe that's what they were. She would play along.

"Could it keep one's words in a safe place?" ask Tom.

"Oh yes, we have millions and millions of words stored in here, possibly billions."

"What about money?" asked Alex. "Could you store that in the computer too?"

"Sure," said Samantha. "Most people do their banking online."

"With currency?"

"No, with instructions to a computer to withdraw or move the money elsewhere."

"Instructions controlled by what?"

"Other computers."

Alex looked at her uncomprehendingly. Her screen started blinking.

"Here it is," she said to the captain. "It appears room seventeen is no longer occupied."

"No longer occupied!" cried Ben. "When did that happen? How will I find John Doe Three?"

The captain stood looking over Samantha's shoulder at the screen.

"Looks like he was released yesterday to the feds," he said.

"The feds, as in the Federal Reserve?" said Alex.

"No," said the captain, "as in the FBI."

"Thank you for your time, sir and lady," said Tom.

They returned to the car where Mr. Debussy was waiting.

"How did it go?"

"Not well," said Ben. "Apparently John Doe Three is in the hands of the FBI. I fear my notoriety may have gotten him into trouble."

"The FBI is nearly impenetrable," said Mr. Debussy. "Even in their new location, you can't access the building without a photo ID. And you can't visit without passing a security clearance review months in advance. I think it's time we bring Director Sowell in on this little project."

"A good plan," said Alex. "In the meantime, perhaps you can drive us to some of the famous monuments in town. I understand there's a statue of me at the Treasury Department."

When they arrived, Ben asked, "Why is Alex on the south side?"

"Good question," said Mr. Debussy. "When your statue was dedicated, Mr. Hamilton, the north side, which sits on Pennsylvania Avenue, featured a huge fountain. Only later did Congress decide to remove the fountain and commission a statue of Albert Gallatin, chairman of the House Ways and Means Committee, who was treasury secretary after you."

"A great bane in my side, always fighting me from Capitol Hill, complaining about war debts and expenditures," said Alex. "He was an immigrant, too, but from an aristocratic Swiss family. His first language was French. I always suspected he looked down on my less august roots. He insisted everything be done in the Swiss way. I kept arguing that we were our own country."

As they approached the statue, Tom said, "Look at how young you were. I suppose we all were."

"Not all of us," said Ben, as he ambled to join them. "Look at all that gold. If you'd had all that wealth back in the day, you could have retired the war debt and opened another National Bank."

"It says it was built in the Roaring Twenties," said Alex. "They were wealthy in those days."

"Do you want to go round the front to see your nemesis, Mr. Gallatin?" asked Tom. "I suppose you hated him because he liked me. We agreed on policy. I liked his sense of laissez-faire."

"Modesty does not become you, Tom. When your election was pushed into the House of Representatives, I hear he was instrumental in your winning."

"On the thirty-sixth ballot," said Tom.

"I am willing to look," said Alex. "He cannot touch me now."

As they approached Gallatin, Alex started laughing.

"At least I look young and virile," he said. "Albert looks short, old, and angry."

"Quite an epitaph, that," said Tom.

"Indeed," said Ben, as he caught up with them. "What do you think, gentlemen, better to be esteemed in death or revered in life?"

"Only one way to find out," said Tom as they piled back into the car. "Mr. Debussy, may we next see Ben's monument?"

"I believe mine are mostly in Philadelphia," said Ben.

"Dr. Franklin, you have one here too. It depicts you not as a founder but as a printer. Maybe because it's in front of the first post office building, near where the Trump Hotel once stood. And if Eric Trump is successful, the family may repurchase the hotel from the Hilton Company."

"With proximity to power like that," said Ben, "by all means, let's go have a look."

SCENE 6

Slapped

Ben's statue was right in the middle of Pennsylvania Avenue, at the corner of Twelfth Street Northwest.

"The statue was a gift from Stilson Hutchins, founder of *The Washington Post*, erected in 1889," said Mr. Debussy. "He wanted to honor your history as a newspaperman, Dr. Franklin, and this statue's original location, on Tenth Street, was right in front of the *Post*. It was moved in the 1960s to Twelfth Street, perhaps because that is the site of our first post office."

"But it depicts me neither as a postmaster general nor as a newspaper printer."

"True," said Mr. Debussy. "This statue depicts you as a diplomat in the court of Louis the Sixteenth, when the US signed its first treaty with a foreign power. You are tall and imposing—eight feet tall I believe—and you are surrounded by books, while holding documents."

"I have not looked that good in a very long time," said Ben.

"The 1890s—that was the Gilded Age I believe," said Alex. "Maybe we were popular then."

"An odd concept that we would swing up and down in popularity," said Ben.

Ben insisted they next visit Tom's monument.

It was the architecture at the Jefferson Memorial that most thrilled the man it honored.

"Like an illustration I once saw of the Pantheon in Rome," he said as Mr. Debussy drove up.

"Yes, the designers set out to mirror your tastes in architecture. They visited the buildings you had designed at Monticello and the University of Virginia," said Mr. Debussy as he led them to the monument's centerpiece. "Did they do a good job?"

"In great style," Tom said, "in great style."

"In the middle of the Rotunda, as if greeting visitors, is a bronze statue of your likeness in black granite, holding the Declaration of Independence in your left hand."

"Towering!" said Alex.

"It stands nineteen feet tall and weighs ten thousand pounds," said Mr. Debussy. "It was dedicated in the spring of 1943 on the two hundredth anniversary of your birth, Mr. Jefferson. President Franklin Delano Roosevelt officiated—he was a big fan of yours. But this was during World War II, when metals were in high demand by the military. Organizers had to use a plaster version. The granite one you see now was not finished until after the war."

"Humbling," said Tom. "Perhaps later generations liked us better than our contemporaries did."

"Perhaps because we knew you better," said Alex.

"Gentlemen, gentlemen, no need to be testy," said Ben. "We are here to celebrate something I never dreamed possible—the republic held!"

"And celebrating we are," said Tom. "I feel reinvigorated. Rest assured, Ben. Alex and I have been quarreling for most of our careers. No reason it should stop now."

"Many people believe this memorial is the most beautiful in the city, sitting on the banks of the Tidal Basin, surrounded by nature," said Mr. Debussy. "On the walls are your famous sayings."

"Let us test Tom to see if he remembers them," said Alex, reciting: "'I have sworn upon the altar of God eternal hostility against every form of tyranny over the mind of man.'"

"I remember it well," said Tom. "From a letter I wrote to Dr. Rush before my election in 1800."

"What about this one?" said Ben, quoting: "'No man shall be compelled to frequent or support any religious worship or ministry or shall otherwise suffer on account of his religious belief.'"

"That was certainly my conviction, but I do not remember putting it quite that way."

"And this one," said Ben: "'I tremble for my country when I reflect that God is just, that his justice cannot sleep forever. Commerce between master and slave is despotism. Nothing is more certainly written in the book of fate than that these people are to be free.'"

"I remember writing that several times, including in my *Autobiography*."

"Yes," said Mr. Debussy, "it was a mash-up of several of your famous utterings."

"What a dramatic word," said Ben. "I like these newly invented phrases."

"Is not the Declaration of Independence here?" asked Alex.

"Yes, on the Southwest Wall, the most quoted words in our history: "'We hold these truths to be self-evident, that all men are created equal, that they are endowed by their Creator with...'"

Just then, a young boy ran up to Tom and slapped him hard across the face.

"Are we acquainted?" Tom asked his assailant, rubbing his cheek.

"You kept slaves!" yelled the young boy, of black skin and deep charcoal eyes. "How could you write these nice words and not understand how you were hurting human beings?"

Tom knelt down to the boy's level and asked his name.

"Tommy," the lad said. He hesitated for a moment. "My name is Thomas Jefferson Blackett."

"And you are so upset with me, because your namesake disappointed you?"

The boy nodded.

"Your mother?" he asked, standing up to greet a handsome woman standing behind the boy.

"Kendra Blackett," she said, reaching out to shake his hand. "I apologize for my son."

"No need," said Tom. Then he turned to Tommy.

"I am an actor, but I imagine if Thomas Jefferson were here, he would say that he freed many of his slaves when they turned twenty-one, and few of his contemporaries did. He might also say he is sorry slavery was not abolished when he wrote these words in 1776. It was in his original draft, but the idea was defeated by the Congress."

T. J. Blackett looked up at his mother.

"I'm sorry if my son hit you, but please understand he is also a great fan of Mr. Jefferson's," she said. "Tommy was overwhelmed by the power of Jefferson's words about how we are all created equal. I know you're an actor, but he saw you as the real thing." She smiled.

"I appreciate your son's passion for history."

"May I take a photo of the two of you together?" she asked.

Tom nodded his assent. Tommy looked a bit sullen, which made Tom wonder what punishments lay ahead for him at home. The woman retrieved a small device from her bag.

"A moment please," said Ben. "Can you tell me what that device is? What does it do?"

"It's a phone," she said.

"What is a phone? Does it work on principles of electricity?"

"I suppose so," she said. "I mean, I have to charge it every night."

"But what is its purpose?"

"If you need to reach someone," she said, wondering who these guys really were but figuring she'd just go along with the ruse. "Every person has a number, so you type it in and hit the send button. You can talk to people all over the country. And if you don't have time to talk, you can also send them quick texts. It also works as a camera and a computer to research things."

Ben looked thoughtful, thinking about the numbers Mr. Debussy had given him earlier and about the computer the clerk was using at the DC Gulag.

"So we are no longer a nation of humans but of numbers?" he asked. "Does every American have one of these devices?"

"Actually, I think just about everyone in the world has one."

"All over the world?" Ben said, his eyes wide with wonder. "I must sit down."

Mr. Debussy rushed to retrieve a wheelchair and some water for Ben from the staff office.

Before it was over, all the Founding Fathers had posed with little Tommy—who was smiling at the attention—and Mr. Debussy asked Mrs. Blackett if she could send him a copy of the photos.

"Of course," she said. "Here's my business card if you need to reach me."

"A business card?" asked Alex as he looked over Mr. Debussy's shoulder and tried to memorize the numbers on the card. "Kendra Blackett, owner and instructor, Bikram Yoga Ivy City."

"You own a business," Ben said. "And raise a family. And presumably care for a husband?"

Mrs. Blackett smiled.

"We call it multitasking," she said. "It's like living on all tracks at the same time."

"How industrious," said Ben. Reaching for her hand, he kissed it, bowing slightly.

"I gather you are the actor playing Benjamin Franklin," she smiled. "Charmed to meet you."

Just then Alex reached to shake Mrs. Blackett's hand.

"I play Alexander Hamilton," he said, offering his hand. "You are quite a beauty."

Mrs. Blackett smiled and escorted Tommy to the exit.

"Mr. Jefferson, I'm not sure I should tell you this, but I'm afraid little Tommy's outburst may be part of a larger battle being waged over your memorial and your memory," said Mr. Debussy.

"Whatever for?" asked Ben. "Tom was a great blessing to our nation."

"Come with me," said Mr. Debussy, escorting them downstairs to a basement museum. A sign read "Closed for Renovation." Below it was a note from the renovation team.

> This memorial is run by the National Park Service, home to scholars who are working to convert this monument from an overly patriotic presentation of Mr. Jefferson's words into a more

> comprehensive portrayal of his slave ownership and radical ideas. Thanks to the generosity of philanthropist Marcus Rosen, we are working to revise this exhibit to correct the historic record. As Senator Tim Kaine of Virginia recently said, "The notion that rights don't come from laws and don't come from the government, they come from the Creator is extremely troubling." We hope the exhibit will re-open soon.

"Correct the historic record?" said Ben. "Eliminate God from our foundation? Goodness."

"I'm afraid these scholars are left-wing activists who see everything through the prism of race and gender," said Mr. Debussy. "They won't be happy until the little Tommys of the world are all brainwashed into believing that their heroes had feet of clay."

"But the General also owned slaves," said Tom. "Is there an effort afoot to tear him down too?"

"Not that I know of, certainly not while Trump is in office," said Mr. Debussy. "The president has ordered the Park Service to restore this space so visitors can see a Jefferson Memorial that celebrates rather that condemns the man who wrote those glorious words."

"The whims of the madding crowd are always difficult to navigate," said Alex. "I suppose these critics think they can wait out the Trump administration and do their evil later."

"I am beginning to think," said Ben, "that they're not trying to discredit us as people so much as to dishonor us for what we achieved. In a way, they are denouncing not only the founders but the nation we founded and the Constitution we left behind."

"I agree," said Alex. "Whatever did we fight for if not for the future generations? And if they no longer value our legacy, perhaps we should return to our heavenly fold quickly."

"First, it might be good for Mr. Franklin to eat something," said Mr. Debussy. "You never know what inventions he might next encounter. Mr. Jefferson had a rough morning too. As for you Mr. Hamilton, you encountered an old foe at Treasury. Perhaps we could all benefit from a cool space and some healthy nutrition."

They marched down the steps, more solemnly than when they arrived. Mr. Debussy tried to tell them about the grounds with their famous cherry blossoms. But by then, Tom and Ben were lost in thought, contemplating the toll of their decisions even on later generations.

"Are we going to Old Ebbitt's Grill again?" asked Alex. "I rather liked that German sandwich."

"With your permission, I'd like to take you to a new place, rather exotic. Plenty of vegetables for Mr. Franklin and Mr. Jefferson, and for you Mr. Hamilton, a German sandwich made not from meat but from beans. It's called a Vegan Burger."

"Sounds like something Washington's army was forced to eat," said Alex.

Mr. Debussy pulled up to a quaint place called Teaism and parked the car.

"This is a popular place with the young, and it's a great deal less formal than Old Ebbitt's Grill."

"Why do the young like it so much?" asked Ben.

"Because the cuisine is from Asia."

"How did the Orient get its cuisine to America?" asked Alex.

"Ever since the Wright Brothers invented the airplane, all kinds of cultures have exchanged their foods. The airplane travels through the skies, so it's far quicker than a ship."

"When was the airplane invented?" asked Ben.

"About a hundred years ago," said Mr. Debussy.

"Like a bird, flying through the air?"

"I suppose so," said Mr. Debussy. "But in this case, the wings and tails are made not of nature but of metal and aluminum and other man-made composites."

"Do you think we could see one of those?" asked Ben.

"I believe our trip to the Air and Space Museum is scheduled for next week."

"These young people are wearing so few pieces of clothing!" observed Alex.

"That young girl's bosom, barely covered like that—shocking and thrilling," said Ben.

"And look at that young man's short pants," said Tom. "Is that a color from nature?"

"It's called teal, a manufactured color," said Mr. Debussy. "It's popular in the southern states, and in summer, there are probably more visiting Americans than residents in DC. You'll excuse me, I'll go place our order."

"That air cooling feels wonderful after that encounter at your memorial, Tom."

"I am not sure if I was surprised more by the child's knowledge of our history or by his personal connection to it. For me it was a revelation of the power we still hold in the imagination of these Americans. In fact, I left me thinking that perhaps they have lionized us too much. And then, to learn there are those in government who wish to erase us, or anyway me—it was shocking."

"Watching you interact with that boy, I kept wondering what it would be like to encounter someone who knew that I once had two slaves," said Ben. "I won one of them as payment for a printing debt from a customer, and I freed him as soon as I could. But the other lived with me until his death. Later, of course, I founded Pennsylvania's first abolition society and petitioned Congress to outlaw slavery. But I guess the Anglicans were right. We were all sinners once."

"Mercy thinks slavery was our original sin," said Alex. "If so perhaps the Civil War was our penance. This generation judges Tom harshly, perhaps the General too, because they kept slaves. We all agreed to compromises that compromised human lives. If original sin is a reference to the Garden of Eden, Adam and Eve were not erased. Why should we be?"

"Perhaps these are the socialists Director Sowell warned about in his research," said Ben. "How did he put it, Alex?"

"He said, 'Socialism's record of failure is so blatant only an intellectual could ignore it.'"

"And then we come to the essential question," said Tom. "How did our Constitution—rooted in principle, armed with checks and balances, grounded in the consent of the governed—how did such a foundation allow for the confiscation of our history by activists who privilege government programs over free will?"

"Perhaps that is why God sent us down here," said Ben. "Perhaps we are meant to remind Americans of their heritage."

Tom looked out the windows, as Alex and Ben studied his face.

"Perhaps it is the manner of the war," said Tom. "We cannot dictate to contemporary Americans how to think or what to do. But perhaps we can remind them of the legacy we left them."

"And why it matters," said Ben.

"I doubt I would be a good messenger," said Tom. "I lived a life of contradictions—I wrote of the rights of man but denied those rights to my slaves. I ran for president as a small government candidate, and then I doubled the size of the country. Perhaps these are unforgivable."

"That makes you the perfect candidate," said Ben. "Who among us is lacking in contradictions?"

"I plead guilty to that as well," said Alex. "Perhaps it is a function of being human."

Just then, Mr. Debussy arrived with a huge tray of food, followed by an Asian man carrying yet more food.

"If Mercy were here, she would declare this another meal that could feed Washington's army!" said Ben.

"For Dr. Franklin, lentil soup with cilantro, with a side order of sweet potatoes with miso sauce," Mr. Debussy said. "I believe these are those purple sweet potatoes from Japan, very nutritious."

"How fondly I remember my first smell of cilantro," said Tom.

"For Mr. Hamilton, the vegan burger. And for Mr. Jefferson, the grilled salmon bento box."

"And what are you having?" asked Alex.

"I love their Thai chicken curry," said Mr. Debussy. "And for dessert, I've brought us all a plate of salty oat cookies. It is their signature dish. Divine."

They ate quietly for a time, raving about their food—"Not a hamburger, but delicious in its own way," proclaimed Alex—silently pondering the day's events.

"When I told Mrs. Powel outside Independence Hall that we had created a republic, if Americans could keep it, I never dreamt it would hold this long. But after that encounter at Tom's memorial, and the news that wealthy activists are trying to erase Tom's contribution to his nation, and to the world, I wonder if maybe the foundation is wobbly."

"Maybe it was always wobbly," said Tom. "After all, to free the slaves took a Civil War."

"Our times called for creativity," said Alex. "Maybe they are called for again. But I suggest we talk to Director Sowell before we reach any conclusions on the nation's fate. If President Trump has launched a war against these activists, perhaps we can join forces with him instead of embarking on our own."

"An excellent idea," said Ben.

"I'm afraid we must delay the rest of the tour for another day," said Mr. Debussy. "Miss Babcock says Mrs. Warren and Mr. Adams have rewritten the first act. She'd like you back for a reading."

"Can we have these cookies with us?" asked Ben. "They remind me of the sweet oatmeal made at one of the boarding houses in Boston I used to stay in."

Mr. Debussy brought him a small box with flaps that folded into themselves.

"Ingenious," said Ben. "You know, Alex, maybe we were wrong about these Americans. All these inventions—do not they suggest a sense of innovation, or drive?"

"I agree," said Alex. "Perhaps there is more to these Americans than, well..."

"Then their clothing might suggest?" said Tom, finishing the sentence.

"Or less," said Ben, "perhaps less."

SCENE 7

Whose History?

Mercy was a great woman of letters. She had livened the script enormously, adding a few memories of her own from the female perspective.

"I remember James told me that when they presented the Declaration, it was noon," she explained. "So I have the clocks striking twelve notes."

"I love how you added some background," said Ben. "Like why the General was not there, and why so many others were absent, too, deferring their signatures until August."

"I like that you quoted so much of the document," said Tom. "Gives it more depth."

"At the risk of piling on praise, I do appreciate that you reminded the audience of the what they call the Boston Tea Party and its complaints of 'no taxation without representation,'" observed Alex. "It affords the play an economic founding."

"Of course," said Mercy. "My brother James coined that phrase. His nickname was Jemmy, and he would have been a brilliant revolutionary if his health had held."

"The bar fight with Tories," said Alex. "I read that his mind was never the same after that."

Mercy teared up, only nodding her head.

John had said little, smarting as his colleagues all congratulated Mercy. Angrily, he grabbed the script, eager to highlight the passages where he had inserted his own language. As he read, the features on his face softened. He handed it back to Mercy with a smile.

"It seems you and I, Mrs. Warren, make a good writing team after all," he said. "Perhaps we should collaborate on the second act."

Mercy smiled so widely her eyes crinkled.

"I would like that, Mr. Adams. I would like that very much."

Priscilla nodded her assent, though she looked like she might faint again. This constant staying in character by a group of actors she did not hire was bringing out the snark in her.

"Perhaps we should put your names in the program notes."

"Not necessary," said Mercy. "All of us are accustomed to writing under pen names."

"Besides, it might confuse the audience about our real identities," said Alex.

Ben turned to John.

"John, you would not believe what happened to us this morning. Tom was assaulted."

John sprang from his seat. "Are you well?"

"I am fine. It was a slap on the face by a ten-year-old boy."

"The impudence of these young Americans. Whatever for?"

"The young boy was upset that Tom had written 'all men are created equal' but did not end slavery," said Ben. "It has given us all a lot to think about."

"Not to mention that my memorial is being redesigned to minimize my contributions and emphasize my ownership of slaves."

"Oh dear," said Mercy. "Who is doing that?"

"Scholars in the government who seem to think they know better than we do what happened," said Alex. "Ben thinks they're not so much erasing the founders as deleting the founding. Not fans of the Constitution or the Bill of Rights, apparently."

Just then, Director Sowell walked in, taking a chair in their circle.

"I heard about the encounter from Mr. Debussy. Are you all right, Mr. Jefferson?"

"My soul is bruised, but I am fine. I keep replaying the debate over slavery in Congress. I suppose we had no choice."

"Without question," said Alex. "We would have not survived without slave labor."

"But at what cost?" said Mercy. "The Civil War was the bloodiest of our history—and we have fought a lot of other wars, despite the General's warning us against them."

"Economically, it took the South a century to recover."

"And so we are all guilty," said Tom, "we who were there at the beginning."

"I beg to differ, Tom," said John. "We made the compromises needed to form a union. Then the nation we birthed fought a mighty war to correct them. That seems the essence of our legacy. We gave them the tools to overcome our weaknesses."

"I suppose God has already forgiven us," said Ben, "or we would not reside at his right hand."

Priscilla sighed. Then she briefed Director Sowell on the need for them to hire another.

"I believe there's a British actor named Ben Barnes," said Priscilla. "He played Samuel Adams in that TV miniseries called *Sons of Liberty.*"

"A bit of irony there," said Tom, "though I suppose we were in one way or another all British."

"I could coach him," said Mercy. "Those early meetings of Sons of Liberty were held in our home in Plymouth, and it was there that we laid the founding for asking each colony to form a Committee of Correspondence, so we could bind the new nation together."

"No need," said the Director. "My prayers have been answered. Sam Adams is on his way."

Another hire she was not consulted on, thought Priscilla. Another actor claiming to be Heaven sent. Sometimes she wondered if the Director was losing his mind. Among the actors playing the founders, there was much cheering at this news.

"I cannot wait to see him again," said a smiling Mercy.

"Nor I. But I wonder, can we arrange to view this—what did you call it, Miss Babcock, a TV miniseries?" said Ben. "I would love to see how this generation portrayed the founding."

"A marvelous idea," said Director Sowell. "I will arrange for you to watch it in our media room, or maybe at one of the larger theaters around town, complete with popcorn and Dr. Pepper."

"Popcorn?" asked Ben.

"And who is this Dr. Pepper?" asked Alex. "Another German perhaps?"

"All will be revealed later," said Director Sowell, a smile spreading on his face. "But in the meantime, I have a delicate issue to discuss with you, my heavenly cast."

"Would you like me to leave the stage?" asked Priscilla. She had long given up trying to police the ninety-something head of her agency, though she did sometimes worry about him.

"I suspect it would spare you another fainting spell."

"Very well," Priscilla agreed, curious but privately relieved.

After she left, the founders looked at Director Sowell.

"I understand some of you were at the DC jail this morning, looking for Ben's John Doe Three."

Ben looked down. Tom locked eyes with Alex. John looked at them, astonished.

"Dr. Franklin, we are all in a bit of a dilemma over your brief stint in jail and the cause of it. And now I understand you seek to broaden the problem to include your prison cellmate."

"Director, John Doe Three has been in jail for five years. Do you not think that excessive?"

"Yes, of course I do, especially for the crime of what the government euphemistically called 'trespassing,' and especially because President Trump has already pardoned the other January 6 defendants," said the Director. "But if he is to be pardoned, it must come from the president's pen, nor ours."

"Might we petition the White House to pardon him?" asked John.

"I'm afraid you have no legal standing, as you are merely, well, visiting. I suppose the Archives could petition for his release, although it would be highly controversial."

The Director paused and looked at Ben.

"On a pardon for John Doe Three, I will consult the board of directors, on one condition."

Ben looked up.

"And what would that be, Mr. Director?"

"No more freelancing."

Ben looked quizzical.

"No more attempts to free John Doe Three on your own."

Ben nodded but did not look happy.

"Perhaps Sunday we should go to church to atone," said Mercy.

"I believe we have already done that," said Ben. "Sunday might be a good day to walk the streets of Georgetown."

"I prefer that option myself," said Tom, and Alex quickly nodded his assent.

"Maybe John and I can find a church in Georgetown and meet you for lunch later," said Mercy.

"If I may have your attention," said Director Sowell. "Then it's settled, no more meddling with the Department of Justice?"

They all nodded.

"Good. Now, there is one more thing I need to discuss with you. It has been brought to my attention by some historians that the Archives has an obligation to broaden our contemporary understanding of the Revolution."

"Director Sowell, I have never heard you sound so tentative," said Mercy.

"As these contemporary Americans like to say, spit it out, man!" agreed Alex.

"This is a delicate subject for me. For the last seventy years, maybe longer, academics have worked hard to excavate the stories of people of color, the slaves, the Indians, people long ignored in our national narrative. This is a good thing, important contributions to the historic record. But sometimes they are added not to flesh out the full picture but to ignore or minimize the contributions of, if you will, the original cast."

"Are these the same people who are trying to tear down Tom's legacy at the Jefferson Memorial?" asked Ben.

"Trust me, I am working intensely with the White House to keep these woke scholars from demolishing the achievements of the founding generation. They have already dimmed Mr. Jefferson's star at Monticello. Now they are working to minimize the Fourth of July by promoting Juneteenth as the national birthday of independence."

"What is Juneteenth?" asked John.

"It is said to be the date, in 1865, on which the last slaves still in captivity, I believe in Texas, found out they had been freed. The National Park Service has taken to referring to June 19 as 'National Independence Day.' Many believe it a deliberate slap at July 4."

"No reason not to celebrate both," said Tom. "But Ben thinks these radicals want to minimize the founding altogether."

"That is the concern," said the Director.

"And these are the same radical historians who want us to change the story of the founding by including in the script—what did you call them—marginalized people?" asked John.

"I prefer to believe these historians want to broaden our understanding of what happened."

"Example?" asked Ben.

"There were quite a few men of color, free and slave, who fought for the Continental Army. True, many more fought for the British, who promised them their freedom in return. But in the 1790 census, forty percent of the Blacks in Connecticut reported they had fought in the war."

"Not in the Continental Army," said Alex. "I often suggested it. But the General would not hear of it. He thought it would perturb the army's esprit de corps."

"Perhaps they served in the state militias," said Mercy.

"If I understand you, Director Sowell, you are asking us to present these newly discovered characters in the play we are performing," said Tom. "And this makes me wonder, whose history we are portraying—is it the one we remember or the one we never saw?"

"I don't blame you for wondering, given that abominable rewrite at your memorial. In contemporary circles we say the woke mob has come for you. Trust me, we are fighting very hard to defeat it. But in this case, I do think it would be prudent to include some faces you may not have noticed, yes. Also, historically accurate."

"Do you have anyone in mind?" asked John.

"We could use Atticus Crispus, of black and Native American ancestry, killed at your cousin Sam's side, the first person to die in the Boston Massacre."

"What is a Native American?" asked Mercy.

"That's what we call the Indians."

"You mean the Savages?" asked Tom. "My dear Director Sowell, every one of us has family ancestors who were brutally assaulted, some of them scalped, by those heathens."

The Director turned his laptop screen in their direction.

"May I introduce you to Hendrick Aupaumut, born in 1757. His parents converted to Christianity and moved with ninety other Indians to Stockbridge, where he grew up in an environment that combined Indian and European ways. At eighteen, he enlisted in the first company of the Continental Army in that area of Massachusetts. During a battle at White Plains, New York, Indians from Stockbridge fought bravely. After that battle, the General promoted Aupaurmut to captain of his company, citing 'the good opinion I have of your bravery and attachment to the US of A.'"

An uncomfortable silence settled on the group as they pondered this story.

"I served as the General's aide-de-camp for six years, and I never heard of this," said Alex. "I suppose it would do no harm to include him."

"By my count we have now added two of the Savages to our play," said John. "And what does this esteemed board of historians suggest we do about a person of color for the play?"

"Of course, we have Atticus," said Director Sowell, "but I would like to add another, the slave Peter Salem. Named for the city of his owner's birth, he served as a minuteman at Lexington and Concord. Then he was freed by his owner so he could remain in the Continental Army. After that he gained fame at the Battle of Bunker Hill, where he is said to have been responsible for killing Major John Pitcairn, an influential officer in the Royal British Navy."

"I feel this all very personally," said Tom, shifting uncomfortably in his chair. "It seems the modern profession of historians is keen on exposing slave owners as wicked people, and they have certainly tarred my reputation with the Blackett family and no doubt others. I never treated my slaves with cruelty. And yet now we are being asked to portray them as Revolutionary heroes. Next, we will be elevating them to the presidency."

"I believe that has already happened," said John. "Did you miss the lecture on Barack Obama?"

"My goodness," mused Mercy, "the stage will be quite crowded with people we never met."

"And there's one more perspective I need to request, that of a woman. You might have heard of her—Deborah Sampson, who disguised herself as a man and served in the Continental Army. The contemporary audience might be delighted to learn of her exploits, everything from how she hid her anatomy to how she kept private her monthlies."

"Mr. Director!" said Mercy, her cheeks blushing. "Surely we must not discuss such things in public!"

Director Sowell sighed and sat back.

"I'm afraid that is the way of the world now, my dear. The more scandalous, the better."

"I am not at all sure I want to continue authoring this play," she said. "I was raised in a Puritan family—one of my ancestors survived the *Mayflower*—and I value humility as well as honor."

"Maybe it was not a good idea to come back to Earth," said John, looking at Mercy. "I myself was raised as a Congregationalist. I believe the Christian faith is the best that was or has been ever since. If Mercy wants to return to Heaven, I will join her."

"John, if you leave," said Mercy, "who will represent Ben in court?"

"I am beginning to think I should skip the trial," said Ben. "After all, if I am nowhere to be found on Planet Earth, what could a judge possibly do to me? The only reason to stay is to explore the world of new inventions. Perhaps I can just manage to take some home with me."

"Are you suggesting our lives could be improved by technology?" asked Mercy. "May I remind you we live in Heaven?"

"I, for one, am not ready to leave," said Alex. "It seems so vibrant down here. I now appreciate why Lin-Manuel Miranda portrayed me as a man of color. It may be inaccurate, but it makes me proud. I like this trend of uncovering new history."

"Even if your role is exaggerated?" asked Tom.

"I suppose you think only those of us who survived the Revolution should comment on our motives," said Alex. "But for the rest, I do think succeeding generations are welcome to make of us what they will. As you said yourself, Tom, every generation is entitled to rebel."

The fire in Director Sowell's office cracked—he was one of those rare characters, like Richard Nixon, who liked a roaring fire in the middle of Washington's humid summers even as the air-conditioning blasted—and they all sat silently. Finally, he spoke.

"Mrs. Warren, I want to apologize if I shocked you. But if you and Mr. Adams rewrite the rest of the play as you did the first section, with you serving as narrator, you can control how or how much we say about these new characters if you decide to include them at all."

Mercy looked pale.

"There will be Hessians during the war scenes, those awful Germans who came to fight for the British. So perhaps it would not be so bad to have some Savages on our side."

"It seems I have introduced a flurry of doubt into your hearts, and I am sorry about that," said the Director. "Why don't we all muse on the topic for a bit and reconvene for another session later?"

With that, almost as if he had been listening, Mr. Debussy knocked on the door and escorted them to their limousine, driving them in silence back to their Airbnb in Georgetown.

Once inside, their conversation resumed.

"Perhaps we are all getting caught up in too much pride," said Mercy. "If Americans in 2026 want to believe the Continental Army included all color of mankind, what is the harm in that?"

"Quite a bit if it was not true," said Tom. "Though an interesting question. Does American history belong to us or to them?"

"There's the rub," said Ben. "Does it belong to we who created it or those who are living it?"

"I have been thinking about that too," said Mercy. "Perhaps we should welcome these new characters to the OBBR. First, because the Director is a scholar, who would not steer us wrong. And second, because widening our circle connects our generation to this one."

Tom walked to the Closet That Kept Everything Cold and withdrew a bottle of wine, a Bordeaux, exhaling as he uncorked it and smelled the soothing aroma of relaxation.

"Here's to the play," said John, raising his glass. "Or maybe to its demise. After all, they can always hire actors to play our parts, and then they can write it any way they want."

"Nonsense, they will always need us," said Alex. "If only for verisimilitude."

"Well," said Ben, "at least we get to go to the movies."

SCENE 8

Movie Night

For their movie night, Director Sowell had managed to borrow a viewing theater at the Air and Space Museum. What he had neglected to anticipate is that they would be captivated by the planes and space ships that were sprinkled throughout the lobby, people-movers that that defined the nation's history of space conquest. As he tried to lead them through the museum to the theater, he marveled at how like children they became, derailing any schedule he had in mind.

"Look at the wings on this one," said Ben. "And is that the seat for the driver up there?"

"Yes, they call it a cockpit."

"How do women climb up in the seats?" asked Mercy. "I wonder if I would get seasick."

"Pales next to the space ship," called Alex from just ahead. "Come look at this. They call it a capsule. Difficult to believe human beings could even squeeze themselves into this thing."

"How vast a mission is this, to collapse time and space," said Tom.

John had walked ahead, following Director Sowell. He waved to the others to hurry up.

"We'll miss the movie!" he called.

"Can we return?" asked Ben.

"Yes, of course," said Director Sowell. "I believe we have it on your schedule for next week, a private tour by an amazing American, one of the few willing to suspend belief and embrace the idea that you five might actually be visiting from a different realm."

"And who would that be, Director?" asked John.

"His name is Chesley Burnett Sullenberger the Third, but everyone calls him Captain Sully. On January 15, 2009, flying an airplane into New York, he discovered that both engines had been disabled by birds. He managed to land the plane right on the Hudson River. All one hundred fifty-five passengers aboard survived. That brush with death seems to have made him a believer."

"I have a better idea," said Alex. "Could we ask Captain Sully to fly us somewhere?"

Ben cheered, and Tom applauded.

The Director smiled.

"I'll see what we can arrange."

With that, he led them to a darkened room with huge leather chairs.

"Talk about a deluxe saddle," said Alex.

"The seats recline," said Mr. Debussy, who had joined them for the outing. He sat down and demonstrated the chair's features.

"Goodness," said Ben, "You mean you can get a massage while watching a movie?"

"What are these holes in the chairs for?" asked Mercy.

Mr. Debussy placed a Dr. Pepper in her drink holder.

"Many Americans put these chairs in their homes during the pandemic," said the Director. "For my part, I prefer watching in a theater. The movie looks and sounds more majestic to me."

"Yellow fever?" asked John.

"No it was a disease called COVID that leaked out of a lab in China."

"Is that why many Americans wear napkins on their faces?"

"We call them masks. They were required during the pandemic, but their efficacy has since been questioned by science. It seems to me the only ones still wearing them now have severely compromised health or are living in fear."

"Do you mean all Americans have a big screen like that in their homes?" asked Ben.

"Something like that, yes."

"And yet they go to work?"

"I suppose you could say that they now prefer luxury within their work. It's complicated."

They each took a chair and began playing with the controls.

"Too many options," said John. "Can my chair be returned to sitting straight up?"

"Yes, of course," said Mr. Debussy, readjusting the controls to default.

Their chauffeur also showed them all the bar where they could replenish their food and drink. Alex delighted in the pizza, and Ben jumped on tasting his first Dr. Pepper.

"These Americans must like food that awakens their tastebuds," he said, "as if their senses have been dulled by too much luxury, requiring more and more impulses to rouse them."

"Sometimes I think movies have gotten like that too," said Director Sowell, "gratuitous scenes put in to wake you in case you have been napping."

"Easy to see how that could happen in these contraptions," said John.

"This TV series is a little more high-end than that. *Sons of Liberty* was produced twenty years ago, before the world grew quite so crass and calculating. There's a warning of violence on its label. But of course, you witnessed these scenes firsthand, so we have no need to warn you."

"I look forward to seeing it all from a secondhand perspective," said Mercy.

"First I have a surprise for you," said the Director. He nodded at Mr. Debussy, who walked out of the room, only to return with a special guest joining them for the evening.

"Sam!" screamed Mercy.

"Cousin!" yelled John. "What a delight to see you here."

Tom rose to shake Sam Adams's hand. "Mercy is a delightful writer, but we could not have re-created this story without you, Mr. Adams."

"Heartily agree," said Ben.

"Make it unanimous," said Alex. "It was to my great fortune that you nominated George Washington to command the Continental Army. He became something of a father figure."

"So I heard," said Sam. "So, what have I missed?"

"It's not beer," said Mr. Debussy, "but try a Dr. Pepper."

With that, the lights dimmed, and images filled one wall with an intensity that unnerved Ben.

"I might not need my bifocals for this," he said.

"How handsome you look, Sam," said Mercy.

"I rather fancy that all the Adams men are handsome," said John.

Sam looked from one to the other, perhaps overwhelmed by the newness of it all.

"Let's watch the movie, shall we?" Director Sowell said diplomatically.

Unfolding on their screen was the very Revolution they had all helped birth—John Hancock bankrolling Sam's efforts to arm and train a ragtag army, Sam organizing and schooling them in how to outmaneuver the British despite their meager numbers, Paul Revere who rode for days without stopping to find their hiding place and warn them that the British were coming for them, and Dr. Joseph Warren, a valiant doctor who volunteered to participate in the Bunker Hill battle not as a major general but as a private, killed in the third British attempt to take the hill. It was said that his valor inspired many to volunteer for the war, to fight for their country.

They were entranced.

"I wonder if Joseph Warren was a relative of my husband," said Mercy, "although my James was older by a generation, I believe."

"Specialists can dig through the history for you," said Director Sowell. "They are called genealogists, and they can learn a lot about your heritage just by taking your blood."

"I always thought it was sad that the General's doctors bled him out," said John. "Now it turns out that could have learned more from studying his blood than emptying it."

"But what did you all think of the depiction of the Revolution?" asked the Director.

"It made me marvel all the more that we managed to win," said Tom. "To beat a mighty world power like the British. How young we were, how arrogant!"

"I suppose arrogance is the purview of the young and the need of every revolution," said Ben.

"If any of us had succumbed to fear, this whole noble revolution might not have been," said Ben. "And because of Tom's beautiful pen, because of the power of his words and the nobility of their sentiment, the world will never forget the truth of our cause. You elevated all of us, Tom."

Tom bowed his head and smiled.

"May I say something?" asked Sam. "The movie was entertaining but hardly revealing. I do not think it captured why so many everyday folks put down their tools and picked up their guns."

"The motives," said Mercy. "What would you tell today's Americans if you could?"

"I would introduce them to the ordinary people who showed unbelievable courage, the night we destroyed the tea."

"Go ahead," said John.

Sam stood and pulled out a cap from his back pocket. He threw his voice into a low register.

"My name is Thomas Melville. You might wonder, and, yes, I am the grandfather of Herman, of *Moby Dick* fame. The boy was thirteen when I died, and I must say I had no idea he had it in him. I'm told the book was a meditation between man and nature. What always drove me was politics. I entered Princeton at fifteen years old and graduated with a degree in theology. I was twenty-three when the destruction of the tea occurred. It seemed a chance to change the arc of history. I had watched my friend Dr. Warren die in battle at Bunker Hill, one of our greatest citizens, felled by evil. And it filled me with rage. What nobody knows is that I found some of the tea in my shoes afterward and years later gave it to General Lafayette."

"You never told me that," said John, "about the tea."

"Of course not," said Sam. "I could have been arrested! Wait until you hear this one." He pulled his hair down and adopted a voice in high register.

"Hello, my name is Sarah Bradlee Fulton."

Mercy started laughing, and they all joined in.

"When two of my brothers—Nathaniel and Thomas—told me about plans for a tea protest, I suggested disguising the men as Mohawk Indians to conceal their identities. On the night, I smeared their faces with red paint and dressed them in borrowed Indian costumes. It took four hours to dump all that tea, and as they snuck back into town, still under darkness of night, they stopped in to our home so I could remove their makeup and return the costumes to the Loyal Nine, a revolutionary group formed to protest the Stamp Act eight years earlier."

"I had no idea there were any women involved," said Mercy. "How delightful."

Next Sam took off his hat entirely.

"Hey there, I am John Crane. At twelve years old I substituted for my father in the French and Indian Wars. After working as a carpenter, I joined the militia in Boston. My vision was so good I could see a bullet passing through the air. I was made brigadier general in one of the militias. As far as I know, I was the only patriot injured in the tea protest. I was in the hold of the one of the three ships involved, the *Beaver.* We were tossing lots of East India Company tea overboard, so we could not be taxed for it. As men dropped tea into the harbor, I was knocked unconscious by a falling crate. I guess my friends thought I was dead, and they dragged me to a carpenter's shop near the harbor, covering me with a pile of wood shavings. The next day, I woke up. You could say God woke me. And I lived to see America win her independence."

"Imagine having vision that good," marveled Ben.

"He must have been a good man for God to spare him like that," said Mercy.

"You're going to have to really use your imaginations for this one," said Sam, who ruffled his hair again and asked Ben to borrow his cane.

"My name is George Robert Twelves Hewes. I lived to ninety-seven. On the night of the destruction of the tea, I stood on the *Dartmouth*, tossing the East India Company's product into Boston Harbor. It thrilled me that I, a lowly shoemaker, stood shoulder to shoulder with John Hancock, the wealthiest man in Boston. Do you see? The Tea Party represented the end of deference in the colonies. Once, those of us who worked with our hands would bow or remove ourselves from the walkway whenever someone prominent came by. The destruction of the tea ended that. Because shoemakers felt themselves equal to the prominent, and the wealthy, for their own economic reasons, had decided on rebellion. On that ship, and in the Revolution, we were all brothers."

"That one is prescient," said Tom. "I had not thought of it until now, but maybe that is the moment America became a less formal society. And I had never heard of the man."

"This one I imagine will be familiar to all of you, because of the poem," said Sam.

"My name is Paul Revere. I was a silversmith in Boston. You may have heard, I am sure, of my midnight ride to warn that the British were coming to kill them."

There was much laughter at this.

"What you may not know is that I also led the patriots' first wartime intelligence network. My riding compatriot, Samuel Prescott, and I organized sixty horseback riders carrying messages back and forth between the Continental Army and the militias. At Lexington and Concord, we learned the British were planning to capture and destroy our supplies, so we got word to the troops, who had time to hide them. We only had seventy-seven militiamen in that battle, to their seven hundred Red Coats. But they retreated, and we had the chance to fight another day."

"That defined so much of the war," said Alex, "the chance to fight another day."

"Oh, I wonder if that does not also define life," said Mercy. "God keeps giving us new mornings, full of promise. But what about you, Sam, when do you enter the picture?"

"May I present to you my final vignette. My name is Sam Adams, founder of the Sons of Liberty, and on the night of the destruction of the tea, I discovered British soldiers in the audience at Old South Meeting House, dressed in citizen clothes, spying on us. I kicked them out. I went up to the balcony to give our signal—'Boston Harbor, a teapot tonight!' Then I helped the rebels board all three boats. 'You are patriots,' I said. 'You are ready. My Sons of Liberty, time to let the tyrants know what we think of their tea. Use those tomahawks to open the hatches. With three hundred forty-two chests below, and more than ninety thousand pounds of tea to dump, make sure they get really wet.'"

"I love this telling," said Mercy.

"So do I!" said Director Sowell. "Mrs. Warren, can we put this in the script?"

"I will not finish the script without it!"

"I appreciate that personalized rendition of history," said Tom. "I have always thought emotion played an enormous role in politics, especially in revolutions. Look to France for proof of that."

"In France, emotions descended into violence," said Ben. "They substituted the guillotine for our Constitution. But the destruction of the tea killed no one. It was an act of political protest against injustice, a wakeup call for Parliament, and perhaps for the colonies too."

"Everyone felt that," said Alex. "If the Crown can destroy Boston, will New York be next?"

"Do you think today's Americans have revolutionary spirit?" asked Sam.

Alex nodded.

"In the early 2010s, a group of Americans banded together to call themselves the Tea Party. They were protesting President Obama's efforts to force them to buy health insurance. Some believe their energy was later transferred to the Make America Great Again movement that propelled President Trump to power, not once but three times—in 2016, 2020, and 2024."

"I thought Mr. Biden won in 2020," said Tom.

"Many believe that election was stolen," said Alex.

"You mean like in 1800?" asked John.

"The election of 1800 was not stolen," said Tom. "You lost, not only to me but also to Aaron Burr. Still, during this visit I have begun to wonder if perhaps everything after us was imitation."

"I disagree," said Alex. "As Ben has noted several times, these Americans are inventing new products constantly. And it seems President Trump and his powerful Cabinet have righted the ship. Government spending has been trimmed, and ambition to create is on the rise."

"I am not sure that is decided," said John. "The big cities are a mess. And it may take generations to recover what President Reagan kept calling the spirit of American exceptionalism."

"Was it ever exceptional, this country?" asked Sam. "Were we really so unique in history?"

"I believe so," said Ben, "We risked our reputations, everything we had become."

"Suddenly I am glad we journeyed here," said Tom. "I was perfectly content in Heaven, but now I see that it was important to ponder the questions we left behind. The trip has convinced me that despite our lapses—especially the decision on slavery—this land was better because we had lived here. And maybe it is time we reminded our fellow Americans of it."

"This movie ended with the Boston Massacre," noted Mercy. "That was before we even declared our independence or commissioned the General to lead the fight."

"I agree," said Sam. "It seems as if this is mere prequel."

"You are both correct," said Director Sowell. "The movie ends with the Boston Massacre because it is the first of a three-part series. If you like, we can schedule another movie night for the remaining episodes."

"Oh, yes, please," said Mercy. "After all, otherwise we will not know how the story ends."

There was much laughter at that.

"It makes the performance we are rehearsing that much richer," said Alex. "Altogether pleasing. And that Dr. Pepper, my goodness, it should be called Dr. Burp!"

Director Sowell ushered them to their car.

"One more thing, Director Sowell," said Ben. "I wonder if you could arrange to equip our living quarters with computers, like those we first saw at the DC jail?"

"And those portable phones that everyone has," said Alex. "Then we can take photos of ourselves next to our statues."

Director Sowell smiled.

"We will happily arrange iPhones and laptops for all of you. I'm actually surprised you didn't run into Steve Jobs in the heavenly realm."

"And who might that be?" asked Ben.

"A visionary in technology. He invented the iPhone and the iPad, and he brought beauty to computer design."

"I imagine in these fraught times you might convince me otherwise, but I'd like to visit Monticello, if only to hear what the docents say about me."

"Our calendar is bulging with activity, but I'll see what I can do."

"Sam, any special requests?" asked the Director.

"Director Sowell, I appreciate the invitation, and it was an unexpected treat to see all of you. But this is not my place. And if I do anything on this planet before returning to the other realm, I would like to see Boston again—to walk Griffin Wharf, to visit Concord, and to go home."

"If you are sure that's what you want, I will arrange the trip to Boston," said the Director. "As for going home, well, I leave that to you."

"It saddens me you are leaving, but I respect your decision," said Mercy. "We are much enriched by your having come. Those stories will personalize the play, making it more poignant."

Sam smiled.

"You always were a great storyteller."

"Gosh," said Director Sowell, "what a godsend to have all of you here."

PART II

The Revolutionary War

"They had the splendor, we the advantage."

—General Nathanael Greene

SCENE 9

The General

They met the General at his home, which had been cleared of visitors for the occasion, though the docents kept finding excuses to enter the drawing room, if only to pinch themselves at the sight of the acting company assembled, all in their colonial garb.

"It is wonderful to see you again," said Alex, with a hug. "I have missed your company."

"And I yours," George smiled, grimacing at how his teeth hurt again upon leaving Heaven.

"What great work we did together."

Director Sowell beamed at the sight before him and reached to shake the General's hand. Then he shifted direction to shake the hand of Billy Lee, the loyal valet slave who had accompanied the General everywhere, assisting him with myriad tasks, from delivering messages to laying out his clothes and later centralizing his voluminous papers. As if to illuminate the great devotion between them, Washington had freed Lee in his will, with a lifetime allowance.

"I wonder, Director, if I might be called Will now? It is the name I took on the General's death."

"Of course. It is a great honor to have both of you with us, a great honor."

"I must say I was surprised at the assignment," said the General. "I always believed that our independence would not have been won without Divine Intervention. As a result, once in Heaven, I bothered myself little with current affairs, avoiding the Earthly Library and other temporal matters. I had no idea, until the reading assignments for this trip, that the nation had lasted so long. I suppose that in itself is worth a toast."

He raised his glass, filled with his favorite Madeira, and said, "To these United States of America!" Everyone echoed the sentiment.

"Our longevity was entirely due to your restraint, General," said Director Sowell. "It is widely believed among historians that if you had not resigned your command after the British surrender, if you had not detached the soldier from the ruler, we might have become a monarchy."

"The king marveled that you walked away from power," said Tom.

"He was a king," said George. "I never aspired to hereditary rule. In fact, as my friend Dr. Franklin can tell you, I never aspired to the presidency."

"You were, then and now, the obvious choice," said Ben.

"And no one else could lift us above our differences, knitting these thirteen colonies together, North and South, free and slave, Federalist and Republican," said Mercy. "You were our unifier."

"Mrs. Warren, I see you are as lyrical as always," said George.

"America has become very informal now, General. Everyone calls me Mercy."

"Then call me George."

"I doubt I could ever call you by your Christian name, General," she said, smiling.

At that, they all started speaking at once. Alex leaned in to tell the General about the computers that could simulate a battlefield in seconds and this new artificial intelligence that could advise commanders on the best strategy. Tom asked John if he would be a Republican now that Trump had wrested the party from the authoritarians. Director Sowell conversed with Will about his journey from slavery to freedom. And Mercy asked Ben why he became a vegetarian.

"What a marvelous segue to the lunch menu," interjected Director Sowell. "We are having vegetables grown here at Mount Vernon with wild rice, pistachio nuts, and raisins, served with plum port, along with homemade French bread. Shall we adjourn to the gardens?"

A long wood table had been set up in the air-conditioned greenhouse for lunch, but it took some time for them to arrive there. The General insisted in giving them a tour of all the plants and species he had brought from his travels, and the joy in his face at being reunited with them was evident to all. Stopping at one boxwood garden, he cheered that the fleur-de-lis was still carved in its bushes, a nod to the Franco-American alliance that proved so decisive in winning the war.

"We would not have won without the French," said Ben. "Or that is what I kept telling them."

There was laughter at that.

"Congress was dysfunctional," said Alex. "We rarely had enough money for uniforms or even food. Every request required all thirteen colonies to agree."

"There must have been moments that tried your soul, General," said Tom.

"A few, but I kept God close. After I arrived in Boston in June of 1775, my biggest challenge was to integrate the efforts of the state militias with the new Continental Army."

"You should have seen him," said Alex. "He rode in on his beautiful gray horse, Blueskin, his posture upright and his eyes intent on the target. You could feel the air fill with hope."

"We in Boston had taken the brunt of the abuse for years," said John. "People were tired of being taxed and punished, sick of British troops ordering them around at the prod of a musket."

"Before I took command, a militia group captured the British garrison in Fort Ticonderoga, New York. We were still outnumbered, but the Green Mountain Boys—so-named because some were from Vermont—surprised the guards."

"The fort was not important militarily but the catch was impressive," said Alex, "seventy-eight cannons, six mortars, and three howitzers."

"How did you transport them back to Boston?" asked Mercy.

The General smiled.

"Colonel Henry Knox was a big man—six feet, two hundred fifty pounds—and he volunteered to take a team to New York and bring those arms down from Ticonderoga, no matter how much snow they faced."

"And he did?"

"It was impressive," said the General. "Took months, traversing over three hundred miles of snowy trails, frozen streams, and steep hills, pulled on sleds pulled by horses and oxen."

"And what did you do with them?"

"Something I had wanted to do for a long time. We went on offense. I told Colonel Nathanael Greene to fire on Boston from the north, to divert the attention of the Red Coats. We hit them for three days. On the third night, Colonel Knox and I took the troops, with all those cannons, to Dorchester Heights, an elevated hilltop overlooking Boston from the south."

"We had to climb the hills, at night, in silence, dragging all that armament," said Alex. "In the morning, at first light, British General Howe looked up at Dorchester Heights and said, 'These fellows have done more work in one night than I could make my army do in three months.'"

"A gift from Providence," said the General. "Especially when they abandoned Boston."

"I've always wondered why you let them escape," asked Mercy.

"They sent word if they were not allowed safe passage, they would burn Boston and all its residents to the ground."

"I remember you worried about what General Howe would do next," said Will.

"I was pretty sure he would head to New York," said the General. "But New York is an island surrounded by eight hundred miles of water. Would he land in Long Island, Manhattan, Brooklyn, Staten Island? I had to know. I did not have enough troops to cover every port."

"Remind me," said Will, "is that when you hired Nathan Hale?"

"Yes, I told Alex to find a soldier willing to take an assignment as a spy. I needed someone to frequent New York's taverns and pubs and churches and overhear something important."

"Only one soldier volunteered," said Alex. "His name was Nathan Hale, and he was from Connecticut. The British captured him, and two months later he was hanged."

"Awful," said Mercy.

"An honorable death," said the General. One British officer wrote that as he was marched to the gallows, Hale said, 'I only regret that I have but one life to lose for my country.'"

"The tragedy is that he never had the chance to convey any information to us," said Alex "and the British routed us at New York, with the largest expeditionary force that ever landed on American shores, almost decimating the army."

"It galls me still that Britain held that valuable port until the end of the war," said the General. "They had nine thousand of our men in Brooklyn Heights trapped, surrounded on all sides with the East River to our back and no feasible route to victory. I evacuated and retreated to Manhattan."

"It saved the Continental Army," said Alex.

"And the patriot cause," said Mercy.

"During World War II, British Prime Minister Winston Churchill had to evacuate hundreds of all Allied soldiers in little boats from Dunkirk," said the Director. "Something like that?"

"Very much like that. But we still had to figure out our next move. The General was adamant that we pocket a victory before the end of the year."

"The British were not the only ones coming for me," said the General. "After Brooklyn Heights, there were those who wanted me fired."

"Names?" asked the Director.

The General shook his head, even now unwilling to condemn his foes.

"There was a cabal of them," said Alex, "led by Major General Horatio Gates."

"We were in a precarious position," said the General. "We were nearing the end of 1776, when many of our enlistments were up, our recruits leaving. Desertions had already thinned our ranks. And conditions were deplorable—some of our soldiers were dying of starvation."

"Was that when we read to the troops from Tom Paine's book?" asked Alex.

The general nodded.

"We read to them around campfires," said Alex. "I kept this from you, General, but we also offered them liquor."

The general smiled.

"I knew."

"Was this Paine's *Common Sense*?" asked Will.

"No, that book was published in January of 1776," said the general, "and I believe it helped push Congress toward adopting the Declaration of Independence in July."

"Quite right," said John.

"But by December, the tide had turned against us in New York," said the general. "And Tom Paine had a new pamphlet out, called *The American Crisis*."

"What was that one about?" asked Will.

"Gloomy, reflecting our fortunes. 'These are the times that try men's souls.' And, 'Tyranny, like hell, is not easily conquered. Yet the harder the conflict, the more glorious the triumph.' I planned a new attack, and told my war council we would leave on December 24."

"Ah, the Delaware," said the Director.

"How better to catch the enemy sleeping? I told my team we would leave on boats, at midnight, crossing the Delaware River at McConkey's Ferry. Once on the other side, we would march ten miles to Trenton and surprise the fifteen hundred Hessians occupying the town for the British."

"Did you really get down on one knee in the boat and pray?" asked the Director.

"Who better to appeal to in our troubles than the Lord?"

"And that portrait, of you crossing the Delaware with the American flag flying behind?"

"An exaggeration. This was Christmas of 1776. It was not until the next June that Congress approved the flag—thirteen stripes, alternating red and white, and thirteen white stars on a blue field."

"So what flag did you use?"

"The Pine Tree Flag, with the green tree and the words, 'An Appeal to Heaven.' It worked."

"We took more prisoners of war in Trenton than we did almost anywhere else," said Alex. "They were mercenaries, fighting not for God or country, only because the British paid them."

"Their collapse in battle told me two things," said the general.

"Let me guess," said Mercy. "First, British were having trouble recruiting."

"Exactly."

"And the second?"

"We were gaining in public opinion abroad. Dr. Franklin did a remarkable job on the Continent, spreading the word about our courage, swaying other nations to join our fight."

"The other thing Ben did for us was procure the services of a Prussian military leader," said Alex.

"I will not soon forget the first time I set eyes Baron Van Steuben, a Prussian military officer Ben recommended as a drill master," said the general. "Through a translator, he told me, 'I can whip your troops into formation. I can make of them the greatest soldiers in the world. I can organize them to defeat the British Army and Navy. I can swear in three languages.'"

"Impressive résumé," said the Director. "I wonder if he's still available."

"Van Steuben was loud, flamboyant, and crude," said Alex. "The troops said he knew only two words in English. 'Halt' and 'damn!' But no one disobeyed. He ordered the men to build latrines and new housing structures to improve sanitation, this in a camp where many died of disease. He taught them how to shoot their rifles quicker, and better use their muskets. He made them march in circles, he wrote a book of regulations called *Order and Discipline*. By the time the Continental Army left Valley Forge, we looked and acted more like a professional tribe."

"And that made all the difference?" asked Mercy.

"Eventually," said the general, looking at John.

"It always angered me that Congress did not provide for the troops," said Alex. "Every decision had to be approved unanimously by all thirteen states. Not all were eager for war, nor on any hurry."

"Not true," said John. "It is only that we had no authority to act."

"Congress has been saying that for two hundred fifty years," said Alex.

"Then Dr. Franklin delivered again, a robust navy from the French," said the general. "And I gained a new staffer, who became something like a son to me, the Marquis de Lafayette. He told me, 'Yorktown will be their Marathon.' He meant in 490 BC, when outnumbered Greek forces toppled the mighty Persians. And he added, 'If we win there, we win the war.'"

"Yorktown was our glory," said Alex. "We finally outnumbered them—twenty thousand soldiers, to their nine thousand. We suffered four hundred casualties, to their eighty-five hundred. Cornwallis had no choice but to surrender."

"A British band played '*The World's Turned Upside Down*.' That is how it felt to us too."

"General, when did you come home here to Mount Vernon?" asked the Director.

"There were a few more battles, and it took the British almost a year to evacuate our land. But by late 1783, I bid farewell to my officers in New York and traveled to Congress, meeting in Annapolis, to resign as commander in chief. Then I rode here, to become a planter again."

"Is that line about King George true?" Will asked Ben.

Ben nodded.

"Most in Europe thought the General would cling to command or become the leader of this new nation, or even a king. To just walk away from power, voluntarily, that was unheard of. The king was sitting for a portrait by American artist Benjamin West, who told him he'd heard General Washington was planning to resign his command. It was widely reported that King George the Third said, 'If he does that, he will be the greatest man in the world.'"

"Did you think you would be called back to duty as president?" asked Mercy.

"Honestly, as I rode home to Mount Vernon, I did not know for sure. We did not yet have a constitution, and without a code of conduct, we still did not have a country."

"You served so long, and so admirably," said Mercy. "No one would have blamed you if you had turned down the presidency."

"My dear Mrs. Warren, to my knowledge, in the two-hundred-fifty-year history of our country, no one has ever turned down the presidency."

There was silence in the greenhouse then.

"I want to return to the question of Providence," said John. "After the Constitution was drafted, I said that the document would work 'only for a moral and religious people. It is wholly inadequate to the government of any other.' Director, is the US of A still a moral country?"

"More so every day," said the Director. "Something of a religious revival is afoot, with young people, especially young men, returning to religion and tradition. President Trump underwent his own rebirth after Butler."

"What is Butler?" asked Ben.

"A small town in Pennsylvania where a big thing happened. Donald Trump was on the campaign trail—these days candidates for the presidency actually ask for the vote rather than delegate that job to surrogates. He was before a huge crowd, tens of thousands. A shot rang out, aimed at his head, but at the last moment he turned to look at something else, and the bullet grazed his ear."

"Providence," said the General. "Something like that happened to me during the French and Indian Wars. The king had asked me to carry a message to the French, telling them to stop poaching on British territories. An Indian aligned with the French took a shot at my ear."

"Many people believe that what Trump did in the seconds after the shot rang out likely won him the election," Director Sowell continued.

"And that was?" asked Mercy.

"Surrounded by security officers, he rose with his face bloody and raised his fist in the air shouting, 'Fight! Fight! Fight!'"

Again, they sat in silence for a bit.

"I wonder if bravery in battle relies on faith," said Tom.

"I believe that is so," said Alex. "Facing death clears the heart, and the mind."

"I once wrote that 'the tree of liberty must be refreshed from time to time with the blood of patriots and tyrants,'" said Tom.

"President Trump seems to have encountered both. Director Sowell, are you suggesting the encounter with death made Trump more religious?"

"It seems that way, yes," said the Director. "But you will be able to judge that for yourselves. I've had word that the president would like to meet you for a private dinner at the White House."

"Do you know I have never been inside?" said Ben.

"Nor I," said the General.

"It was a small and inspiring place when Abigail and I lived there," said John. "I left a message behind that I understand has since been engraved on the mantlepiece under Abraham Lincoln's portrait in the State Dining Room. 'May none but honest and wise men rule under this roof.'"

"What a moment," said Mercy, "linking our legacy to that of the current president."

"If I may observe," said Will, "unlike General Washington, I am a great fan of the Earthly Library, and I was very proud that so many Black men came to the support of President Trump. I believe he is a once-in-a-generation unifier, much like our own General."

"How kind of you, Will," said the General. "As you know, it is unthinkable that I would have succeeded without your assistance. I imagine you were elated when America ended slavery."

"Very proud, General, very proud. And when the country elected Barack Obama I was overwhelmed. Though these days, especially after that beautiful Tulsi Gabbard declassified all of those documents detailing his persecution of Trump, I wonder if he was good for the country."

"All of us who served in that lofty role wonder that of ourselves," said John.

At that moment, the food arrived. Something about the exchange of ideas across generations and some old grievances had made them hungry, and they ate heartily.

"I think we ate better than Americans do now," said Tom. "Everything was fresh from the earth, not subjected to long travel or chemical processing."

"And not so spicy!" said Mercy.

"I hear this Bobby Kennedy lad is trying to move American food production away from chemicals," said John. "He is President Kennedy's nephew."

"General, I remember how you used to complain that your camp had been taken over by women bearing laundry lines and makeshift cooking tents, slowing your troops' progress."

"I did worry about the break in discipline. But I always treasured it when Martha came to camp to be with me, so I said little."

"The Europeans made fun of that," said Ben. "They would say, '*Une armée sans armure repose sur l'amour.*' Never have I found it harder to hold my tongue."

"I am grateful to the French, but they can be such snobs. 'An army without armor relies on love'—nonsense," said Alex. "We relied on ourselves and our cause."

"And love," said Mercy.

"Our Revolution succeeded," said John. "The French Revolution descended into beheadings and mass murder by the guillotine, a disaster by any measure."

"The Jacobins enforced doctrinal purity," said Ben. "They used the guillotine not just on the royals but on allies who were not, in their view, sufficiently conformist."

"Like today's Democrat Party," said Alex.

"General, why do you think our revolution was peaceful, while theirs was violent?" asked John.

"Providence," he said. "I will make a point of mentioning this to President Trump."

"You should know, General, that some consider Trump to be the best of our presidents, or second only to you or to Lincoln," said Director Sowell. "What a thrilling conversation that will be."

"Would you like me to have your best clothes arranged, General?" said Will.

"No need, my dear friend. I've learned to manage them myself."

At that, there were smiles all around.

SCENE 10

They Scatter

Tom was delighted to see his old home, and John was equally pleased to see the place where he addressed so many letters over the fourteen years of their end-of-life correspondence.

"So this is the place where all my words landed," said John. "Think of all the letters we wrote back and forth between Quincy in Massachusetts and Monticello in Virginia, reminiscing about what we had accomplished in revolution, war, and governance."

"Two gentlemen who lived too long, trying to find peace with their memories."

"I think it was more than that. It was also a way to come to terms with our differences."

Mr. Debussy said he would pick them up in a few hours. He left to consult with several dentists, on a mission to find one who could fix the General's teeth. Mercy had suggested it after noticing the General's pain, and the Director agreed so long as they didn't tell Miss Babcock.

Tom was anxious to give John a tour of the property, but he was also curious about how the docents would describe his life. He suggested they join a group in progress. There were a few odd looks from tourists in their direction, but soon enough the guide had everyone's attention.

"Thomas Jefferson inherited this land at the age of fourteen upon his father's death," said the tour guide. "But development of the properties, the architecture of the buildings, the genius of the crops, even the layout of quarters for the one hundred thirty enslaved people who lived here at any one time—these five thousand acres were the preoccupation of forty years of Jefferson's life."

"I heard he was buried here too," said one of the tourists.

"He was. Does anyone know what his tombstone says?"

"I heard he wrote it himself."

"Yes and, ever the architect, he designed the monument too. The tombstone says:

Here was buried Thomas Jefferson
Author of the Declaration of
American Independence
of the Statute of Virginia for religious freedom
& Father of the University of Virginia.

"So far, I hear no rewrite of my biography," Tom whispered to John. "What would you like to tour first?"

"You are proudest of the grounds. Shall we start there?"

As they were about to depart, a middle-aged couple walked up and asked for Tom's autograph.

"I am merely an actor," he said, wary of the incident at the memorial.

"I figured that," said the wife, "but since chances of my meeting the real Thomas Jefferson are nil, I would delight in having the signature of someone who plays him on stage. I've always been a fan. I believe TJ has been unfairly maligned by all those Sally Hemings scholars."

"Bunch of activists," said her husband. "Everyone knows Thomas Jefferson represented the best of us, the noblest, the most righteous. They just try to sully everything."

Tom smiled then.

"Nice to be remembered so kindly and to meet Americans who think for themselves."

He signed the woman's program and handed it back to her.

"Wow," she said, "you have even perfected Jefferson's signature."

"Say, is that John Adams with you?" asked the man. "I saw on X that Trump is having dinner with actors participating in the two-hundred-fiftieth-birthday party. Is that you guys? Some influencers are spreading rumors that you're the actual Founding Fathers, brought down from Heaven for the occasion. It set off a debate among the Catholics about whether you deserved Heaven."

"On what grounds would we be excluded?" asked John.

"Did you believe in God? Some think you were moral relativists. Crazy, huh?"

"Crazy," said John. "With apologies, we must be off for the tour of the landscape."

As they walked through the gardens, more and more tourists pointed at them, and one woman glared at Tom. She turned to a girlfriend and said, "White men are all bigots, don't you think?"

When they reached the outdoors, Tom looked relieved. But John was not sure.

"Do you know what X is?"

"No idea, but I imagine it must be powerful."

"X is Elon Musk's social media platform," said a tourist who had overheard them. "He bought it to ensure our free speech."

"I rather thought that had been done earlier," said Tom.

"Ha-ha, says the guy dressed to look like the guy who wrote the Declaration."

Tom bowed at him, and the tourist left.

"I am beginning to think we will need a private tour," said John.

"And I am beginning to think this is no longer my home," said Tom. "Historians seem intent on portraying me as a plantation owner who abused his slaves. It is as if my memory and character have been snuffed out by some new political orthodoxy that measures us by their standards."

"The criticism does seem relentless," said John. "As if Satan himself took control of your soul."

"That had not occurred to me. Perhaps I should consider going to church."

"That seems a bit extreme. I went to church when I was young, but later in life I found praying in private more soothing."

"An idea to ponder."

"But first, shall we stop in the bookstore? I want to see what today's Americans are reading."

On finding the shop, they saw a man sitting at a table, autographing books. He caught John's eye.

"Mr. Adams, I presume?" he asked.

"Yes. And you are?"

"Joseph J. Ellis, a historian. I've written quite a few books on the Founding Fathers."

"This is your latest book?"

"No, but it is one of my bestsellers. My publisher thought we should issue a new edition in honor of the two hundred fiftieth anniversary."

Tom came up and stood behind John, peering at the book, *Founding Brothers.*

"You think we were brothers then?" he asked.

"You doubt it?" asked John.

They had no money, but they asked Mr. Ellis if he might gift one of the books to them.

"If you'll pose behind me and the book for a photo," he said.

As they were posing for the camera—a docent had appeared with a phone to do the honors—a crowd started to press in.

"Who are you guys anyway?" said one man, sounding a bit belligerent to Tom's ears.

"Who do you suppose us to be?" asked John.

"I say you are actors, here for the OBBR," said one man.

"Nah," said another. "There's a rumor that God sent the founders down from Heaven for our birthday party. That's what I think, that you're the real deal."

There was much gasping after that. John felt compelled to lead them away from the bookstore, somewhere they were less likely to be harassed. This turned out to be the slave quarters.

Tom noticed it first. There, in one corner, was a special exhibit on Sally Hemings.

"She was a beauty," he said. "Pale skin and long straight black hair. Sweet smile."

One female tourist hissed at Thomas Jefferson.

Tom turned to John.

"Should we notify Mr. Debussy to rescue us?"

"I believe I can use this phone to reach him."

"Tell him we're in the slave quarters."

"Awkward."

"Imagine how much faster the Revolution would have gone if we'd had these phones then."

*****

Back at the Archives, Ben offered his arm to a docent named Marybelle Austin. She roped her hand through his sleeve. Ben had shown up to tour the Archives, and Priscilla told Marybelle to keep him occupied for the morning. She had work to do, and the garrulous Dr. Franklin, well…

Once they got to the Rotunda, Marybelle explained to the guard at the entrance that she was giving a private tour to the actor who would be playing Benjamin Franklin in the OBBR.

"Good likeness," he said. "I'll get you into the line as soon as I can."

As Ben had anticipated, the room was dark and cold.

"We've had the atmospherics tested for optimum care of the documents," she said as they stood outside the entrance. "We only allow a certain number of warm bodies in at the same time."

"How many visitors do you have?"

"Roughly one million a year."

"One million Americans visit the documents every year?"

"Our website also provides reference materials for many millions more who cannot make the trip to Washington, DC. We understand that a lot of children research their school papers that way."

"My dear Miss Austin," said Ben, "that brings joy to my heart."

"People are emotional about the documents. A few years ago, two protestors upset that humans have harmed the earth snuck in undetected and threw red powder on the glass cases where the documents are kept. We arrested them and closed the museum. Americans from every state and every occupation wrote to offer to come restore them. It was touching, really."

"Miss Austin, you are talking gibberish. What has the earth done to merit protestors?"

"That, Dr. Franklin, is a long story, and if you'd like to explore it further, I can arrange to have one of the Smithsonian Museum's top scientists discuss it with you."

Ben looked unbalanced, and Marybelle wondered if she should have brought a portable chair. Just then, the guard waved to her. There was an opening in the line, and they were free to use it.

As they walked in the room, Ben noticed two large murals dominating the room.

"My goodness, there we all are," he said of the men who signed the Declaration. "Odd how often I am placed near Tom and John in these official portraits. We came from different states—Virginia, Massachusetts, Pennsylvania. Perhaps we symbolized the coming together of nation. Who was the artist? He flatters all of us."

"Barry Faulkner was born in Keene, New Hampshire, in 1881. He left Harvard University after one year to study and travel to Florence, Italy, where he worked with Dublin artist George de Forest Brush. In 1907, he won the Rome Prize Fellowship to study ancient art and architecture at the American Academy in Rome. Both murals were completed between 1934 and 1936. His last great work was completed at the age of seventy-four, when he painted a mural called *The Advent of the Coming of the Railroad*, commemorating breakthroughs in travel design."

"So he liked history," said Ben, "and invention."

"The second mural is of the writing of the Constitution."

"Delegates numbered fifty-five but it is true, as this portrait suggests, that only about half were in attendance at any one time."

"You are one of the few to be featured in both, Dr. Franklin."

They began inspecting, under glass, the Articles of Confederation, the Gettysburg Address, and the Declaration, followed by the four-page Constitution and finally the Bill of Rights.

"I wonder why Lincoln's address is here," one young man asked his female companion. "He wasn't president until almost a hundred years later."

Ben could not restrain himself.

"Young man, that becomes clear once you read the first paragraph. 'Four score and seven years ago our fathers brought forth on this continent, a new nation, conceived in Liberty, and dedicated to the proposition that all men are created equal.' See how in the second paragraph he joins the fate of the Civil War to that of the Revolutionary War, saying, 'Now we are engaged in a great civil war, testing whether that nation, or any nation so conceived and so dedicated, can long endure.' He was riding on our coattails, I suppose."

"Coattails?" asked the young man. "Ah, you must be one of those actors here for the reenactment. My name is Tony, and this is my wife, Robin."

"And this is Miss Austin," said Ben, "with the Archives staff."

"So you think Lincoln was invoking the founders to win sympathy for his war? Is that what you meant by coattails?"

"In a way, he was using America's good feelings about the Revolutionary era to make his own war more appealing. But he may have glossed over—or maybe he did not know—that in their era, the founders were controversial, especially hotheads like Sam Adams and Patrick Henry."

"Sam Adams the beer?" said Tony.

"His father was a brewer, but Sam was more of a rebel."

"I never thought of it that way," said Robin. "You must have studied much history to perform in the reenactment. Did you read *Poor Richard's Almanac*?"

"You know of it?" said Ben.

"Of course. We like historical things. Plus, it's witty."

Ben puffed up his chest a bit.

"Thank you," he said. "I was always surprised at the number of printings it went through."

"You're speaking now as Ben Franklin?"

"Yes. As you suggested, I had to study up quite a bit for this role. That book sold ten thousand copies a year from its first appearance in 1732 to 1758, when we stopped printing it."

"Why did you stop?" ask Tony.

"By then I was in politics. City council in Philadelphia, justice of peace, member of the Pennsylvania Assembly. My favorite job was deputy postmaster general of British North America, but then the nation called, and I led the Pennsylvania delegation to Albany, where I proposed a Plan of Union for the colonies, which eventually became the Articles of Confederation that you see under the glass."

Marybelle noticed that a small crowd had gathered around Dr. Franklin. She wondered if she should discourage this assemblage, where the line between reality and reenactment had long since blurred. But then she remembered that Miss Babcock had told her to keep Ben occupied for as long as possible. And he seemed to be enjoying himself.

"Is it true you liked younger women?" shouted one tourist.

"What is not to like?" said Ben.

From another corner came a French-accented voice.

"How did you convince the French to join the American Revolution?"

"*Charme et perseverance.*"

"What was Thomas Jefferson really like?"

Ben paused for a moment.

"He was actually shy about public speaking. I always thought he preferred writing, because there he could polish all his words with lofty ambition. As a speaker, well, I learned later that at this first inaugural as president, in the Senate chambers, he could hardly be heard in the first row."

By now the circle around Ben had grown so large, the guard approached Marybelle to ask her to see if she and Ben could move along to the gift shop.

"Dr. Franklin, I think we'd best move on. We seem to have attracted quite a crowd."

Even as they made their way to the gift shop, the questions kept coming, projectiles of curiosity.

"Do you think the Bill of Rights could have been stronger?"

"Why did the king insist on keeping the colonies?"

"Was John Adams a prick?"

At this Ben turned around.

"What is a prick?"

"Someone who acts big because he feels short."

"Great definition!" added someone across the room.

By now the room held perhaps 500 people, many of them pointing at Ben and whispering among themselves. Marybelle thought she heard one speculate that Ben Franklin was too knowledgeable to be an actor, and the person next to him replying that maybe he was a Franklin descendant.

At least in the gift shop the questions stopped. But Ben was so enamored of the things for sale that he tarried at every station.

And soon there was a small army following him, including one man who grabbed at his breeches, tearing them. Marybelle dug in her purse for a safety pin.

"The shop at Ford's Theater had rather banal items, but here is the weight of history. The thing is, Miss Austin, I have no currency, and I do not want to be arrested again."

"I agree we should avoid that fate," she said. "What if I paid for the items from the Archives' publicity budget?"

He wanted to get a Jefferson bobblehead to give to Tom, and he thought all of them would be amused by the pens the Archives was selling—a 250th commemorative pen that featured all of their signatures on the Declaration of Independence. There was a bobblehead of Alex, too, but Ben thought the white marble bust of him more handsome. He found books of quotations—of Tom, the General, and himself—but there was nothing from Mercy or Will.

"I hope after this reenactment, both of them become as famous as the rest of us," Ben said.

As they were walking toward the checkout counter, Ben saw a board game testing players' knowledge of the Constitution.

"We have to get this too. We can play it tonight at the Airbnb. I imagine John will win."

Marybelle blanched when she saw the total price—$345—but hoped maybe Director Sowell could take it out of his contingency funds. She'd heard that he was a big fan of these actors.

"What did you buy?" shouted one of the tourists.

"Just some curios for my fellow founders," said Ben.

One woman rushed to the cashier station.

"I want everything that he bought," she said.

"You realize that man is just an actor, right?" said her companion.

"Just in case. Because you never know."

Marybelle was relieved when they managed to escape the building. But Ben was not done buying. He spotted a vender selling hats and insisted on buying a Make America Great Again hat.

"I can wear it to the White House," he said. "Maybe President Trump will sign it for me."

As Marybelle paid twenty dollars for the hat, she worried the Director might consider it an extravagance. She was also beginning to understand why Priscilla was always complaining about headaches.

"Where would you like to go next, Dr. Franklin?" she asked. "May I take you to lunch?"

"No, thank you," he said. "Mr. Debussy and Alex should be here any minute to pick me up. I am off to a hot yoga class."

"Hot yoga?"

"Yes, we met a beautiful yoga teacher at the Jefferson Memorial, and she said we were welcome to try one of her classes. Apparently, the idea of hot yoga is to sweat all the toxins out of your body. Alex is bringing sweat pants. Ah, here is the limo now. To the morrow, Miss Austin."

And just like that, he disappeared into the traffic, leaving a number of baffled tourists behind, a few wondering what they had just seen.

SCENE 11

Playing Games

Pleading exhaustion, Mercy had asked for a quiet night at home. So that night they all met back at the Airbnb, all except Will and the General, who were happily ensconced at Mount Vernon.

"Whatever is in all those bags?"

"What an adventure I had today," said Ben. "I got a private tour of the Rotunda, where those famous documents we created are kept under glass and protected from any heat that might fade our signatures. Although I must say they have already faded quite a bit. You would not believe the crowds that pour in all the time to see them. Miss Austin from the Archives staff told me they have one million visitors a year, plus millions more via computer."

"That makes it all the more amazing how ignorant these Americans seem about their history," said John. "Did they seem intelligent?"

Ben hesitated.

"Curious, I would say. They seemed curious."

"And you went shopping afterwards?"

At that, Ben brought out his souvenirs. Alex loved his bust. Tom was horrified by his bobblehead.

"I never had the shakes," he said. "John, you've known me the longest—do you remember me shaking like that?"

"Your steadiness was impressive."

"And what is this?" asked Mercy.

"That is for you, my dear, our great champion of the Bill of Rights, a board game, called the Constitution Quest. Would you like to play?"

She squealed in delight.

"Finally, I get to test my knowledge against those who signed the document."

They played for hours, but to Ben's surprise it was not John with the greatest knowledge of the Constitution—it was Alex.

"Figures," said Ben. "The man who wrote *The Federalist Papers*."

"I thought it was interesting that the game made no distinction between the Constitution and the Bill of Rights, lumping them in together as if one," said Mercy. "If they only knew how hard we worked for those enumerated rights!"

"You know what I have always said, dear," said Ben. 'Either write something worth reading or do something worth writing.'"

"And we did both?" she asked.

"I suppose we did. I wonder what will become of this generation of Americans. They seem incapable of writing anything longer than forty-two words at a time."

"Not all of them," said John. "Today Tom and I met a writer on tour at Monticello. Fascinating man. He gave us one of his books."

"Name?"

"His name is Joseph Ellis, out of Alexandria. His book is called *Founding Brothers,* a bestseller, about us. Though it mystifies me why he started the book with the Burr-Hamilton duel."

"Because it divided American history," said Alex. "Between old traditions and new."

"Drama," said Mercy. "Every author needs drama."

"Is that why you had to exaggerate my loyalties to the Crown?" asked John.

"Perhaps," Mercy smiled.

"I forgive you, though I doubt Abigail would."

"What were you up to today, Alex?"

"A wonderful tour of the Trump Hotel and a long conversation with Eric about the golf courses he and the Trump organization are planning around the world. He offered to play a round of golf with me this weekend and teach me the game. Or if I preferred, he said, we could go hunting."

"Whatever did you tell him?"

"That I was not known for my shooting skills and would rather learn this game of golf. It was invented in Scotland in the 1740s, and as my ancestry is Scottish, this seemed apt. He bought me gear right there in the hotel gift shop, and we're to play together on Saturday. He suggested I watch a golf match on TV. Ben, do you think you could use your tech skills to arrange that?"

"I can give it a try."

Once Ben found an old championship match on the Golf Channel, the three men were entranced. Mercy went off to bed. John took out the *Founding Brothers* book he'd received at Monticello, and looked first in the index to see if he was included.

"My goodness, Tom, he devotes a full chapter to our friendship. If he only knew."

Tom did not answer. He was captivated by the game of golf.

"What a glorious vista in which to spend time outdoors. Just nature and a challenge."

"With the ball and club as proxy for more dangerous hobbies," said Alex.

"I could see the appeal to you, Alex," said John, "but it seems beneath your stature, Tom."

"I never worried about my stature as much as you think I did, John."

"Nonsense. You were always the man of ambition."

"If so, I am ambitious to see this game of golf."

"Would you like to join me?" said Alex. "I will text Eric and see if you can play too."

After a quick text, he had his answer.

"Eric said he'd be delighted to include you. He wants to know what size clothes you wear."

"Tell him I am the tallest of us, except for the General."

With that, they said goodnight and adjourned to their rooms.

The next day, Mercy rose first and went to the doorstep to get the newspaper, a habit she was finding as invigorating as a cup of coffee. This time, *The Washington Post* headline alarmed her.

HEAVENLY FOUNDERS SEEN EXPLORING CAPITAL

Videos of the actors playing the Founding Fathers made their way around town and the Internet yesterday. Before the day was out, #OurFounders was trending on social media.

Benjamin Franklin was spotted at the National Archives with a woman much his younger, looking at the documents he signed in 1776 and 1787. Thomas Jefferson and his "frenemy" John Adams were seen at Monticello, where several tourists discussed with Jefferson his affair with Sally Hemings.

Old Ebbitt's Grill reported that two gentlemen—one who looked like George Washington and the other who looked like his manservant Will Lee—were accompanied at lunch by a woman we have yet to identify. Finally, there was a report from the Trump Hotel that someone bearing a strong resemblance to a young Alexander Hamilton had lunch there.

All this comes on heels of news that President Trump is hosting the actors for the 250th reenactment at a White House dinner. Requests for tickets are pouring in nationally and internationally. Online conspiracy theorists have noted the actors' skill, popularizing the rumor that the real Founding Fathers returned from Heaven for the reenactment.

Asked about this rumor, President Trump said at a Cabinet meeting, "These are very talented actors, very talented. Where they came by their deep knowledge of our founding is not for us to know, only to celebrate. I'm just glad they are here and can't wait for their performance on July 4. In reminding us of our glorious history, they are going to Make America Great Again."

"Oh dear," said Mercy to herself. "I cannot imagine the Director will be happy about this."

"Happy about what?" asked Alex as he poured himself a cup of coffee.

Mercy handed him the newspaper, and he started laughing.

"These journalists have always been fools," he said, "always more interested in rumors and salacious gossip than the facts. I imagine you are right, Mercy—this will no doubt make Director Sowell's job harder. Ms. Babcock's too. At least we made page one."

The doorbell rang. Mercy opened it to find the General and Will Lee.

"Director Sowell asked us to join you here," he said. "My goodness, Will, look at the size of those windows."

"And the view of the Potomac. Quite a vista, General."

Mercy welcomed them, offered coffee, and showed them the Closet That Kept Everything Cold.

"If we had that during the war," the General said, "it would have preserved a lot of supplies."

"Morning, General, Will. Anything new?" asked Tom, returning to the house from his morning walk.

Alex showed him the newspaper, and he frowned.

"I fear I am better known for my relations with Sally Hemings than for the Declaration."

"Not from what I saw at the Rotunda yesterday," said Ben. "Your words are the most widely quoted in history. Also, the most influential. What has happened?"

Tom passed the paper to him. Like Alex, Ben found it vastly amusing.

"A woman much his younger!" he chuckled. "Perhaps, Tom, these Americans are not so much uninformed as they are obsessed with relations between the sexes."

"That would be nothing new," said Alex.

"May I see the paper?" asked the General, frowning.

"Dr. Franklin, do you suppose we are all being followed by these crafty journalists?" he asked.

Just then there was another knock on the door. Mercy answered it to find Director Sowell.

She escorted him in and poured his coffee.

As he sat down, he looked around the room.

"Houston, we have a problem."

"Houston?" asked Ben.

"It's a city in Texas and a long story," said Director Sowell. He told them the tale of Apollo 13, a missile to outer space launched in 1970.

"One of the oxygen tanks blew up, and the crew of Apollo Thirteen, led by Jim Lovell, reported to headquarters in Houston that they needed help to make the repair while hurtling through space. When they succeeded, the quote, 'Houston we have a problem,' become famous as a synonym for American can-do spirit, a calm assertion, as one of them said, that failure was not an option."

"And you want us to apply that American spirit to the current situation?" asked Ben.

Director Sowell nodded.

"We have a problem we had not anticipated. Now we have to figure out its solution."

"What exactly is the problem?" asked the General.

"The problem is a rumor gaining popularity that you are not actors—that you instead have been brought down from Heaven to play yourselves in our reenactment."

"As far as I know, that is correct," said John. "Otherwise, we would not be here." He said this while glancing at their magnificent view of the Potomac River, offering confirmation that they had chosen the right city for the nation's new capital.

"The next concept I have to introduce you to is public relations."

"Director!" cried Mercy.

"Fear not, Mrs. Warren. Public relations refers to a profession of people who concern themselves with influencing public opinion. Some people call it the art of propaganda. For instance, if these experts want to convince Americans to buy something, let's say a new type of coffee, they design an advertisement so clever—and this can either mean adorable or alarming or funny—that many Americans will choose that coffee."

"And what has this to do with us?" asked the General. "Surely we are not a type of coffee."

"In a way you are, sir. Because political PR, as they call it for short, applies these same strategies to people. What I'm trying to say is that we can either acknowledge you are heavenly creatures—and I can't imagine God would be pleased at this intrusion into His Kingdom—or devise a story that will protect you better than it has until now from the braying mob of the curious."

"Director Sowell, are you saying we are popular again?" asked Tom.

"I suppose that's true. There was a period of some fifty years where it was unfashionable to quote the founders, or even study them. Those who did, as you know, found you much wanting in character for keeping slaves or mistresses or large homes. Now, perhaps because of President Trump and the nation's shift politically to the conservative side, you are much in demand."

"This is divine," said Alex, and Mercy broke out into giggles.

"But, Director Sowell, we already have a protective shield," she said. "We were told to tell anyone who asked that we were actors, merely playing our roles. And so we have."

"I know, my dear, but it does not seem to be enough for these curious Americans. We need something more."

There was silence for a while as they all thought about the problem.

"Houston, I have an idea," said Ben.

Now it was Director Sowell's turn to smile.

"And what would that be, Dr. Franklin?"

Ben got up, walking to the dining room table to retrieve the game of Constitution Quest they had played the previous evening.

"We announce that we have been studying for these roles for a lifetime. Then we challenge any American who wants to match wits with us to try to beat us at this game. Then we design to miss some of the questions on purpose so that they think we are really actors again."

"That will not be difficult for me," said the General. "I have given this no thought in centuries."

"I can just say that my master was a cruel man who refused to teach me to read and who beat me senseless," said Will.

"Will, you know that is not true!" exclaimed the General.

"I know, General. But it is my observation that this generation of Americans will believe anything negative about you, as if they want to win a bet by tearing down greatness."

"Exactly why this might work," said John. "We invite them to tear us down, and we do not protest too much. They win, and we have a few days of peace to finish our work here."

"And play golf," said Alex.

"Does anyone else worry this will trivialize our achievements?" asked Tom.

"An interesting thought," said Ben. "So we have sunk to their level?"

"Or are we are meeting them where they live?" asked Alex.

"I am not keen on the idea," said Tom. "It seems to invite mockery. And I've had my fill of it already. As this was Ben's idea, perhaps we should let him—how would they put it—fly solo?"

"Capital idea," said John. "Of course, we could be in the audience to cheer you on."

"I would be happy to test my knowledge against these curious Americans," said Will.

"What about you, Alex? Do you approve of asking Ben and Will to play the contest for all of the founders, with John cheering them on from the audience?"

"Director Sowell, my calendar is filling with any number of delightful misadventures already. I am happy to defer to the eldest of us, joined by the youngest," said Alex. "But from what I've observed of the present-day Americans, I suspect you should add Mercy to the panel."

"Great idea, Alex. Mrs. Warren, would you be willing to entertain the idea?"

"I think I have already stretched the bounds of my tolerance for public speaking," said Mercy.

"Just think about it, my dear. It would be a wonderful way of introducing you to the public. Clearly, *The Washington Post* has no clue, and neither did visitors to the Rotunda yesterday."

"I can only pledge to discuss the matter in my head, and my heart, with James."

"Excellent. I've always admired his passion and good sense. In the meantime, I will confer with the Archives staff about logistics. If in your travels today you encounter any probing questions, feel free to tell the Americans about the contest. It's called creating buzz."

"Like bees?" asked Tom.

"I suppose so. It means to increase the noise and anticipation. And, Ben, I must say when I saw the bill from your shopping adventure, my eyebrows raised a bit. But now it seems the museum will be able to sell thousands of these games, a great boon to our bottom line."

"Bottom line?" said the General.

"A financial term, sir."

"I am more comfortable in the heavenly realm, or at least at church in Old Town Alexandria," said the General. "You know as a young surveyor, I actually laid out the city's streets. And whenever I was in residence at nearby Mount Vernon, Martha and I went to Christ Church there."

"I've always wanted to ask you something, General," said Tom. "I heard that it was at Wise's Tavern in Alexandria where you were first addressed as 'Mr. President' by a member of the public. Is that true? How did you receive it?"

The General nodded.

"No doubt the weight of the responsibility fell on me then. The idea that people from thirteen separate colonies marshaled a shared army and defeated a world power, and created a new country, over the course of fifteen years, for the cause of liberty—yes, I felt it intensely then."

They were all silent then.

"It does seem a miracle," said Mercy.

"Precisely why I issued the first Thanksgiving Proclamation in 1789," said the General. "As I wrote at the time—although I imagine, Alex, you helped with the words—we would have 'a day of public thanksgiving and prayer to be observed by acknowledging with grateful hearts the many signal favors of Almighty God especially by affording them an opportunity peaceably to establish a form of government for their safety and happiness... and the favorable interpositions of his Providence which we experienced in the course and conclusion of the late war—for the great degree of tranquility, union and plenty which we have since enjoyed.'"

"This plan hardly feels tranquil," said Ben, "but it could be fun."

SCENE 12
Logistics

When Priscilla heard about the contest, she wondered if she should take up drinking.

She did think the pairing of Benjamin Franklin and Will Lee genius—the best-known figure in American history paired with one of the least-known. And Director Sowell was right—if Mercy joined the panel a new generation of Americans would come to know her. She should have done this earlier, but now she would commission new items for the gift shop featuring Mercy Otis Warren and Will Lee.

She huddled with Annabelle, who had taken to introducing herself in the building as "Benjamin Franklin's much-his-younger escort."

"We could try the National Theater," said Priscilla. "It's the second oldest continuously playing theater in DC."

"Already called," said Marybelle. "Unfortunately, since DOGE started furloughing federal workers, they've been offering them free tickets, so they're mostly sold out. Plus, they only have 1,676 seats."

"What about the Kennedy Center?"

"Could work in terms of size. The Opera House seats 2,364 and the Concert Hall, 2,465. The downside is that since Trump remade the board, Democrats are boycotting the Kennedy Center."

"Are either available on weekends?"

"Yes, the Concert Hall is dark for the summer."

"And how much does it rent for?"

"The staffer I spoke to was a bit cagey. He kept asking, 'Who is this again?' as if he had never heard of the National Archives. But finally, he said that if we were a nonprofit, it would be about sixty thousand dollars. Anyway, Miss Babcock, isn't our budget for this performance unlimited?"

"I guess it is, but I hate to assume anything," said Priscilla, grabbing her calculator. "Actually, that's not too bad. If we charged a hundred dollars a seat—and even gave some away for the politically connected—we could make enough to cover the performance's unexpected needs."

"You mean like Ben Franklin's torn breeches?"

"That tourist just came up when we were in the gift shop and grabbed at Ben's clothing. Thank goodness I had a safety pin in my purse."

"At least that didn't make the papers. One problem, though. If we put the performance at the Kennedy Center, a lot of the Cabinet may want to come."

"Or even volunteer to match wits with the founders."

"Marybelle, that's a great idea! What if we change the rules? The public is invited as witnesses, and maybe they could even vote at the end about who they think won. But Ben and Will and maybe Mercy would compete not against citizens, but members of the Cabinet."

"I hope Mercy agrees to join the panel. It would give us a racial and gender rainbow."

"She's been reticent about public speaking. But can you imagine if we paired Scott Bessent against Alexander Hamilton?"

"We'd need an audience of economists to understand them! Besides, I heard Hamilton is spending his weekends with Eric Trump playing golf. Someone overheard him say that if he'd known about the game back in the day, he would have suggested to Aaron Burr that they compete with golf swings rather than pistols for their duel."

"Let me call Susie Wiles to see if she thinks any of the Cabinet secretaries would be interested."

"Miss Babcock, Wiles is the gatekeeper. Her job is to keep people away from the president. So far, she hasn't even taken our calls. I'll give you contact info for the White House social secretary. Amanda Dixon is greatly amused by this frenzy over the founders and eager to help."

"One other problem with the Kennedy Center."

"And that would be?"

"Trump loves it. He believes he rescued it from the clutches of the cultural Marxists. He loves it so much he and Melania might fly up from Palm Beach."

"If they come, it would create a lot of excitement about the reenactment. Also, it could sway Alex to give up his golf date. He told Ben he's in love with Melania."

"But I thought you wanted only Ben and Will and Mercy for the Matching of the Wits Contest."

"Maybe, or maybe we grow the pie."

With that, Priscilla picked up her phone and told another assistant to hold off distributing the press release. Director Sowell might be annoyed, but she wanted to rethink it all.

Director Sowell was too busy setting up at the DAR auditorium to take calls from the Archives. He walked Mercy past a replica of the bronze statue of her that sat outside the Barnstable County Courthouse in Massachusetts.

"I look so young and energized there," she said. "I feel neither now."

"You exude grace, my dear," he said. "They will love you."

"Perhaps they will," she said. "The question is whether a woman should be speaking in public at all, especially about political topics."

He ushered her to two white bucket chairs on the stage, where they sat and talked.

"May I tell you a story?" he asked.

She nodded.

"Have you ever heard of a woman named Lucy Stone?"

Mercy shook her head no.

"You remind me of her. Like you, she was born in Massachusetts—in West Brookfield, a few years after you passed—and like you, she was precocious, a brilliant student. She became the first woman in Massachusetts to earn a college degree."

"What college?"

"Oberlin, in Ohio, the first to offer a college education to women and Blacks."

"What year was this?"

"Lucy Stone got her bachelor's degree in 1847. After graduating, she gave her first public talk on women's rights from her brother's pulpit in Gardner, Massachusetts. The next year she became a regular speaker for abolition with William Lloyd Garrison's Massachusetts Anti-Slavery Society."

"She spoke to mixed audiences?"

"You mean to men and women together? Yes, she did."

"And how was she received?"

"Sometimes men threw Bibles or rotten fruit at her on the stage. That's how controversial it was, then, for women to speak in public. She had a close call once, but then a very strong man in the crowd, much taken by her rhetoric, lifted her to safety to evade the disrupters. The story is told that she kept lecturing, even as he swept her out of harm's way."

Mercy laughed.

"An indominable woman."

"Wait until you hear this one. In 1855, she married her husband, Henry Blackwell, and they became lifelong partners in activism, much as you and James were in the Revolution. Their causes were abolition of slavery and suffrage for women. At their wedding, she insisted that the word 'obey' be removed from their vows. And she kept her surname."

"That is astonishing. My goodness, she inherited the Revolutionary fervor."

"I would argue that she redefined it for a later generation. And that, Mrs. Warren, is what I'm asking you to do, in both writing and moderating the play, and in speaking with me at this venue, and perhaps even joining the Constitution Quest panel. Summon your courage to prove that you were always the equal of the men of your generation."

"Was she not nervous?"

"At first, yes, she was, especially while testifying before legislators."

"She spoke before Congress?"

"I'm not sure she ever spoke before Congress, but as an abolitionist and suffragist, she addressed state houses. She practiced before a circle of women, who met in a friend's parlor once a week, to rehearse public speaking. They discussed big educational, political, moral, and religious questions, as well as procedural ones, such as how to put forward motions or to offer amendments. Mostly, she said, they trained for public settings, learning to stand and speak."

"How very inspiring. Could you summon her? I'd enjoy talking to her."

"I fear I have exhausted the Lord's patience with how many souls I have claimed so far."

"Yes, I noticed James Madison never made it. We are quite an assemblage, are we not?"

Director Sowell smiled.

"The proudest of my life. Truly an honor."

"The chairs are comfortable. And those seats in the auditorium, they will be full of people?"

"We are oversold. It will be standing room only. Of course, we will continue the fiction that you are an actress who has mastered the life and letters of Mercy Otis Warren. But I suspect many in the audience will be as easily swayed as I was, eager to believe that you are visiting from above."

"How I should prepare?"

Director Sowell smiled and pulled from his briefcase a book, *Lucy Stone: An Unapologetic Life* by Sally G. McMillen. He handed it to Mercy.

"You'll enjoy this book. Miss McMillen argues that Lucy Stone has been forgotten by history because she parted company from its more famous nineteenth-century advocates, Susan B. Anthony and Elizabeth Cady Stanton."

"Why?"

"After the Civil War, Anthony and Stanton campaigned throughout the country against the Fifteenth Amendment, the one that freed the slaves, giving them rights of citizenship. They argued that if Congress didn't give women the vote at the same time, they would oppose the vote for former slaves. Lucy Stone was a staunch abolitionist who believed women would win the vote next. She wanted in no way to impede the victory of the freed slaves."

Mercy was quiet.

"I wonder if we who objected to the Constitution without a Bill of Rights were also castigated by the elites. They dubbed us Anti-Federalists. They favored a strong central government, while we advocated a federal system that honored state and individual rights."

"You are right about that and about the comparison to the women's suffrage leaders. Miss Anthony and Mrs. Stanton were firebrands given to inflammatory talk, so the newspapers doted on them. Miss Stone was a diligent worker, who ran her own suffrage newspaper in Boston, influenced by Quakers pushing for the abolition of slavery. She was quieter, principled."

"My dissident friends, as the Federalists also called us, were hardly quiet. But they were patriots, especially when they roared. My goodness—James told me that Patrick Henry could and often did rattle the rafters in the Virginia Assembly."

"So I've heard."

"Thank you, Director Sowell," said Mercy. "An opportunity to speak before a group of people who care about history and share a personal connection to our Revolutionary roots is a marvel. But I wonder. Do you think a hereditary organization is somehow at odds with our Revolutionary spirit of democracy? After all, we rebelled against the monarchy."

"Interesting point," said Director Sowell. "I would argue that appreciating history through family connections is not the same as passing wealth to only the first sons."

He took Mercy's arm and escorted her to their waiting car for the ride back to the Archives.

"Director Sowell," she said, "you've given me an idea about act two of our play."

"Yes?"

"As you know the second act is about the war, those eight years where a ragtag army fought, often barefoot and without enough food, for our rights."

Director Sowell nodded.

"I was thinking about how to narrate a war with access to neither guns nor soldiers. But today, you have given me an idea. What if I proposed to the General that we sit in two chairs, much like the DAR has assembled here, and I interview him about the war. He could recap what he thought were the pivotal turning points, the close calls and the providential turns, the reaction of the troops to hearing the Declaration of Independence read aloud, and their near-mutiny over provisions, his represented requests to Congress, and the insults he endured from England."

"I wonder if the General would ever say anything negative about Congress."

"The General is very diplomatic, is he not?"

"Ask him. See what he says."

Mercy smiled.

"I shall consider the literary advantages and also discuss them with Miss Babcock."

"Always a wise idea, my dear, always a wise idea. I'm off to a meeting with her myself. Shall I drop you in Georgetown first?"

She nodded.

****

At the Archives, the Director went straight to his office for the meeting. Priscilla was waiting, yellow pad in hand.

"Refreshing to see someone is still using those pads amid all the high tech," he said.

"An old habit from my father."

When they had first planned this reenactment more than two years before, Director Sowell warned Priscilla that many people might find it credible that these actors had traveled from Heaven to reprise their earthly roles. She feared he was about to make the institution look foolish and insisted they keep it a secret. He deferred. Now, Priscilla thought perhaps he had been right. Given that Vice President Vance and half the Cabinet were strong believers in Jesus Christ and Heaven, perhaps it shouldn't have surprised her. But the White House social director told her interest was so high they might have to move the dinner from the Lincoln Dining Room to the East Room, the largest room in the building, but only because the Big Beautiful Ballroom had not yet been completed. The Archives, too, were inundated with requests for invitations. Clergy from every Christian denomination, Revolutionary-era historians, eighth grade students, foreign leaders, Moms for Liberty—she was hard-pressed to think of a category not covered.

The Director had asked for her recommendations on how to handle the influx of requests.

"What do you think of an online contest?" she said. "Invite all those who want to attend to submit a written essay on their favorite Founding Father—or Mother—and what they would say to them if lucky enough to meet them backstage after the performance."

"Seems labor intensive, making more work for our already-taxed staff. Plus these days, everyone will just ask Grok to write their essays. What if we took applications on our X page, where people could post their requests in online videos? Followers could vote on the best, maybe ten?"

"Might work. But the main problem is how we are going to accommodate all the people who want to see the OBBR. It's not like past years, when we just hired a Thomas Jefferson reenactor to read the Declaration of Independence on the steps of our balcony."

"I've been thinking about that too. I know we planned to do the reenactment in our auditorium. But what if we moved it to steps of the Archives, broadcast to an overflow crowd on the Smithsonian Mall? We could put up sound systems and huge TV screens for those who find themselves far from our building. And invite anyone who wants to come."

"Director Sowell, have you forgotten the Capitol Fourth, the annual concert with fireworks on the east side of the Capitol? Hard to imagine two competing events the same day on the Mall."

"We could do ours in the morning. We could even serve breakfast foods that would have been familiar to the founders—that young Director of the Indian Museum might have some ideas—and the actors could wander around, table hopping, answering questions from Americans."

"A *breakfast*. With *tables and chairs*. At the *Mall.* The logistics, the traffic. Oh, my God."

"Try not to take the Lord's name in vain, my dear."

"Sorry. But I cannot possibly manage the play and this, well this, *mass invasion* of our space."

"I believe you have forgotten who we work for. But I agree completely on the need of a separate staff. Yours will be more than occupied by producing the play."

"We don't have room for thousands of people on the steps of the Archives. And I don't know if you noticed, but the Fourth of July falls on a Saturday this year. A Saturday!"

"I'm aware," the Director said, leaning back in his chair. "And I've already talked to the head of the Smithsonian about letting our audience spill onto the grassy area of the Mall."

Priscilla felt faint again. The Director seemed oblivious to the challenges—what would they do for bathrooms, who would offer first aid care, how many more staffers could she manage, what if the visitors crowding on the Archives' steps wanted to see the documents in the Rotunda?

She sighed. If she was going to criticize his idea, she needed an alternative plan.

"If we keep the performance in our auditorium," she suggested, "it will make be easier to stage the play, the acoustics will be better, and we'll have all the necessary bathrooms for the crowds."

He thought for a moment.

"You may be right. Perhaps an outdoor picnic might be too ambitious. Your suggestion does avoid the sore sights and smells of porta potties marring the entrance of our majestic building. But I still think we should set up large-screen TVs on the Mall for the overflow. Your thoughts?"

"Let me muse on that."

"Miss Babcock, one more thing." His tone was gentle. "You are doing a great job on this production. But I believe after this celebration is over, you should take a vacation. Walk the Freedom Trail in Boston where the patriots first rebelled. Or visit the Jamestown Church in Virginia, now a museum, where the Puritans came for religious freedom. Or see Independence Hall in Philadelphia, where the Constitution was born. Or even go to Nevis in the Caribbean to retrace Alexander Hamilton's footsteps. The itinerary is yours to plan. The Archives will subsidize it. I just want you to return excited about American history again."

Priscilla pursed her lips and left his office in a huff. Insulting, she thought. She was working harder than ever and now had to take grief from her boss for not being more excited about it.

But...a paid vacation? To a destination of her choice? Maybe the Director was right. Maybe she did need to replenish her connection to the country's history instead of its politics. By the time she returned to the stage, an unwitting smile played on the corners of her lips.

That smile managed to last even as she watched Mercy tussling with the actors invited to audition as soldiers in the Continental Army.

"Do you mean to tell me we have to walk in this fake snow barefoot?" one actor complained.

"Yes, sir, such is the assignment."

"And where are our uniforms? These clothes are ripped and nasty."

"Yeah," agreed another. "I've done other Revolutionary reenactments where actors get to wear those cool three-cornered hats and natty uniforms."

"And the slop we're supposed to eat—what's in that? I'm a vegan."

"Gentlemen, we are hoping to recount the war as it was, not as it is portrayed on the screen. The patriots who won our freedom fought from their hearts, not from their stomachs or their vanity."

"I'm calling my agent," said one of them. "I didn't sign up to portray a second-class citizen."

"You mean to tell me our patriots had to fight without shoes or proper food?" asked one of the actors. "Wow, I had no idea. Sign me up! It would be my honor to portray them."

Mercy smiled.

"Welcome to the play. Here, a copy of the script and a rifle. The gun is real, but has no ammunition. I have no idea why. Something about a man named Alec Baldwin. Your name?"

"Joe," he said. "I'm just an average American Joe."

Mercy smiled.

"Actually, American Joe, you are a gift from Heaven."

There were just a few more desertions before they had a full contingent of soldiers, and even enough musicians for a fife and drum marching corps.

"It does seem odd that we let the musicians dress in fancy costume but not the soldiers," Mercy said to Priscilla, who smiled.

"Americans have come to expect the fife and drum marching corps at every Fourth of July, so we provide one."

"Another example of the contest over memory, between those of us who lived through the Revolution and those of us who prefer to remember it as they imagined it."

"Perhaps it belongs to both."

SCENE 13

DOGE and the Dentist

"You will not believe what just happened," Ben said as he limped into the kitchen for coffee the next morning.

"You have found a doctor to treat your yoga wounds?" asked Alex.

Ben winced.

"I could never have imagined that stretching my limbs in a sauna would result in chronic back pain. Mrs. Blackett suggested I take a few days off. As if I would ever go back! Of course, the sight of all those women of all colors and sizes in those skimpy costumes—well, it almost made the injury tolerable. But, no, that is not the news I wanted to share."

"Do tell," said Alex.

Sipping on his coffee, Ben said, "Just now I had a text from Elon Musk."

"How did he get your number?" asked Mercy.

"What an interesting question. Actually, I have no idea how that works, but these Americans do seem to have a lot of numbers."

"Elon Musk, the richest man on the planet, texted you? Count me jealous," said Alex.

"Remind me who he is," said Tom, as he and John walked in from their walk along the Potomac.

"He builds rocket ships and rescues stranded astronauts," gushed Alex. "He builds electric cars that run on electricity and can be driven by computer. He is developing neurological implants to help paralyzed people walk again. He campaigned for Trump because he thought the republic was in danger. In short, I guess you could say he's the Benjamin Franklin of his day."

Ben smiled.

"Thank you, my friend, but I think he just wants to show us what he has done to rein in government spending," said Ben. "He no longer lives here—he and President Trump had a falling-out last year—but he said he would fly in for our visit. He saw the piece in *The Washington Post* about us wandering about and wants us to visit DOGE headquarters."

"DOGE?" said Tom.

"For goodness sake, my dear friend, really you should keep up with the news," said John.

"Why spend my time on that? The newspapers are so insufferably biased."

"You should know. You employed that scuzzy James Callender to write scurrilous things about me during the 1800 election and about the General after his death!" said John.

"John, Tom hired Mr. Callender to write scandalous things about me too," said Alex. "Callender disclosed my affair with Maria Reynolds, which wounded my wife, Eliza, and almost ruined my career. But I never talk about it with the Man from Monticello because, well, we all did what we thought we had to do to birth this nation. None of us were innocents in the newspaper wars."

"Treason!" said John. "That scandalmonger Callender savaged me for going to war with France. He was guilty of treason! He is why I had to enact the Alien and Sedition Acts."

"A terrible mistake, John, the worst of your presidency," said Tom. "Thanks to your overreaction, I won the election. And on my first day in the White House, I had to pardon Callender."

"If I may interject, I'd like to come to John's rescue on the question of the Alien and Sedition Act," said Alex. "As you know, I came to this country as an immigrant, and in the 1790s, I supported immigration to help bolster the workforce. But by the end of the decade, with the threat of French Revolutionary violence spreading to our shores, I changed course."

"You changed your mind after I called for open immigration," said Tom.

"And look at our nation now," said Alex. "Mexican flags flying, immigrants speaking no English, and many of those driving big trucks on the highways without comprehension of the traffic signs. I said then and repeat now, 'The safety of a republic depends on a common national sentiment and love of country.' The Alien Act had its flaws, but at least it extended the period of naturalization, allowing for assimilation of those already here and deportation of those who should not have been admitted."

"I wonder if Lin-Manuel Miranda knows this about you," said Tom. "Maybe the play should have centered more on me."

"Hubris keeps wounding you, Tom," said John. "If you had met Callender's bribe terms, making him port collector in Richmond, he would not have disclosed your affair with Sally Hemings."

"Because thieves have honor? No, he would have disclosed it sooner or later. I never disputed it, although it amuses me to see some historians try to cloud my paternity by suggesting my brother Randolph was the paramour. One thing the historians seem unaware of is that Sally loved me. I brought her to Paris during my diplomatic mission to watch over my daughter. She could have sought freedom in France, where slavery was outlawed. She chose to come home with us."

"Gentlemen, gentlemen, please!" said Ben. "Why are we talking about old newspaper wounds and pesky issues of paternity when we are being invited to witness the most remarkable new technology toppling government corruption?"

"Why is this important?" asked John.

"Two reasons. One, President Trump asked Elon Musk to end waste in federal spending. So far, they've eliminated two hundred million dollars. And two, to do this work, Elon has assembled a team of high-tech experts who are marshaling their computer talents to the task. These men—and I think one deaf woman—are not using pencils, poring over reams of paper, adding up numbers on an old abacus. They're using computer technology, which provides answers faster than man. They dress casually and take funny nicknames, and—is Mercy still sleeping?"

"No, she left for early church service," said John.

"In that case," Ben said conspiratorially, "I can tell you that one of Elon's brainiac techies calls himself Big Balls."

Alex and Tom both laughed at that.

"Imagine boasting about that out loud," said Tom.

"Why would they want to meet with us?" asked Alex. "I was known in my day for financial prowess, but I cannot imagine I could teach them anything they do not know. And they hardly seem like the types who would believe we are visiting from Heaven."

"True, most inventors trust their instincts more than God's," said Ben. "Maybe they reached out to me because Elon wants to discuss the process of discovery."

"The only thing I ever invented was our country, and I had help," said John. "I will suggest to Mercy that we skip this one—I hate to think of her mingling with those crude ruffians."

Ben nodded.

"I will reach out to Mount Vernon and see if they care to join us."

The DOGE crew invited the founders to visit that afternoon. Mercy and John were preoccupied with the script. Mount Vernon, it turned out, was preoccupied with George Washington's teeth.

"Has word leaked about this dental appointment?" the General asked Director Sowell, after he and Will were escorted to the Director's office at the Archives, overlooking the Mall with its 550-foot-tall obelisk honoring the toothache-plagued president.

"No one aside from you the founders and the dentist. And me and Mr. Debussy, of course."

"I have been afflicted with teeth problems since those camp dinners, when I kept biting into walnuts without any thought of injury. I tried to keep these issues as private as possible, as I knew it would dim my reputation among my men. The enemy too."

"I'm sorry to tell you, sir, that schoolchildren know little else about you, except for the story of how, at the age of six, you chopped down a cherry tree with your hatchet, only to tell your angry father, 'I cannot lie, I did cut it with my hatchet.' The story goes that at that point your father, Augustine, embraced you and declared that your honesty was worth more than a thousand trees."

The General winced.

"How I wish that were true."

"You have no idea how many teachers and parents have tried to convince children that this story is but a fable. Something about it seems to appeal to the American imagination. Perhaps every generation needs its heroes."

"That is flattering. Why do they know me for my false teeth?"

"Perhaps because having such a visible flaw makes you more human, more approachable."

"And still I hesitate. During the war, I wrote a letter to my French dentist, Jean-Pierre Le Mayeur. It was intercepted by the British. We heard that all those Red Coat officers mocked me."

"You were angry, as I recall," said Will.

"I will emphasize to all the need for secrecy. I must say when Mrs. Warren brought this request to my attention, I did not know what to make of it. After all, I thought, why would the General need teeth in Heaven?"

The General smiled, and the Director could see at once the problem—there were no teeth on one side of his mouth, leaving his face lopsided.

"True, no doubt true. But as Will can tell you, this irritant has been mine for a long time. If today's dentists have figured out how to fix the problem, I owe it to my painful memories to open my mouth once again."

"I think that prudent, as we have rewritten the reenactment in ways that may require you to open your mouth quite a bit," said the Director.

"How have you changed the script?"

"You led our Revolutionary War for eight years. It's a big canvas. So, Mrs. Warren suggested we put two chairs on the stage and let her interview you about the military highs and lows, the lack of healthy food and pay for your men, the haughtiness of the British, and the inventiveness of your strategies about your command, your challenges, your triumphs."

"My dear Mr. Sowell, I would rather have all my teeth pulled at once! I spent the eight years of my command and the eight years of my presidency appeasing various factions in the military and political wings of our new nation. No, sir, I do not care to reopen those issues. John Adams would be angry if I accuse Congress of being weak, Thomas Jefferson would bristle anew that I did not delegate more authority to him as my secretary of state, and even Mrs. Warren might be unhappy with my stewardship of the Constitutional Convention. No, sir, no, I say—with respect, no. And if I have to return to Heaven to avoid this fate, so I will do."

The Director held up his hands in surrender.

"Heavens, no," he said. "We will return to the original script."

The General sat back. He looked tired.

"Here's another question. We were thinking about announcing to the American people an essay contest called How History Would Have Changed if George Washington Had Better Teeth. The winner would win a free trip for his or her entire family to visit DC for the reenactment, all expenses paid, and meet you in person. And we could slip in a line about your having found a new dentist who might, finally, be able to address the problem."

"It is so much fun to be an American nowadays," said Will. "I keep telling audiences that they have it so good now, but where I see opportunity, they see discrimination. I fear Americans have become perpetual victims, especially many of African descent."

"Some are, yes, well put," said the Director. "But at this museum we present the heritage that makes us an exceptional people. Americans first, ethnicity second."

"Mrs. Warren—she will not be angry if I decline an on-stage interview?"

"General, Mrs. Warren is a very talented writer. She will find a way to weave the story in somehow. But you will still star in the play, as needed?"

The General looked surprised.

"Oh he will," said Will, smiling. "After all, it was his play."

Mr. Debussy arrived and escorted them to the car, where Ben, Alex, and Tom were all waiting.

"This is quite a delegation to escort me to my dental appointment."

"Actually, General, I'd like to drop the others off at DOGE before taking you to your dental appointment. If that meets with your approval."

"Yes, certainly. I have Will at my side."

"General, would you mind if I joined the Elon Musk meeting?" Will asked.

"I would not mind in the least. I have faced this dental agony alone for a long time. I see no reason to burden you with it. You can tell me later about these DOGE fellows."

Commissioned by the Director to find a dentist for the General, Mr. Debussy had outdone himself. Most dentists he'd consulted said dentures would take weeks. Nuvia Dental Implants in Alexandria promised to have the patient smiling within twenty-four hours. Today's visit was for taking X-rays of the General's mouth, and selecting the most natural color teeth. He would bring the General back for surgery tomorrow. Hopefully Will could be with him then.

Meanwhile, at DOGE, Elon greeted them at the door.

"Welcome to my brothel," he said.

Tom looked alarmed.

"A joke," said Elon quickly. "Kidding."

Once inside—and to Ben, the interior looked like a much larger version of the Houston space station they had spotted at the Air and Space Museum—techie Antonio Gracias walked them through some of the agency's most astonishing discoveries.

"This is my favorite," he said, pointing to a digital chart projected onto a screen on the back wall. With columns for each year, the chart showed that over a five-year period, from 2021 to 2024, some 5.5 million immigrants had entered the US illegally and received Social Security numbers.

"Is that the same as receiving text numbers?" asked Ben.

Antonio looked at Elon, who shrugged.

"Social Security was enacted in 1935, at the height of a severe economic depression," Elon explained. "President Franklin Delano Roosevelt called it a safeguard 'against the hazards and vicissitudes of life.' It was aimed at older Americans, a cushion to assist them in retirement."

"Government was not formed to erase debt," said Tom, "though I must say, my farms at Monticello might have benefitted from such generosity."

"I have to disagree," said Alex. "You could make a case that the central government was formed precisely to assume the debts of the states, to give them—what Mr. Musk called a cushion."

"Perhaps," said Elon, "but now we have so much debt we are in danger of bankruptcy."

"Was Franklin Roosevelt a Democrat?" asked Will.

Elon nodded.

"As you can see, once you start a government program, it is difficult to stop. And what alarmed us here is that many of these 5.5 million people were illegal migrants who used their new Social Security numbers to obtain Medicaid benefits—those are for poor people of any age—and to acquire what we call a voter ID card. We believe millions used those to vote in 2024."

"You mean foreigners voting in our elections?" asked Alex. "I seem to recall in the early days it was the states who decided whether they wanted foreign residents to vote or not."

"Interesting history, but how did you find all this?" asked Ben.

Elon smiled.

"Ah, the tech question."

He motioned to a young man wearing tight jeans and a button-down shirt.

"This is Edward Coristine," Elon said. "You may have heard of him. He goes by Big Balls."

Ben laughed uproariously.

"This is the guy I was telling you all about."

"This is not something we boasted of back in the day," said Tom.

"Where can you acquire pants that fit so tightly?" asked Will.

"Just ask for slim fit," said Edward. "Every brand makes them."

"So how does this work?" asked Ben. "How do you find waste, fraud, and abuse?"

"Show him USAID," said Elon. "Epic!"

Edward signed on to his computer, and they all gathered to look over his shoulder.

"They call this a spreadsheet," he explained. "We asked the computer to search for the word 'transgender.' That's like the guy that Ben misgendered at Madame Tussauds."

"You know about my arrest?" asked Ben.

"We thought it was hilarious," said Elon. "I personally am looking forward to the trial."

"Anyway, we also asked the computer to search for 'diversity equity and inclusion' and 'climate change.' Those are code words for the woke crowd who tried to turn the country toward communism. This federal agency—the US Agency for International Development—"

"Why does the United States have an agency for international development?" asked Tom.

"Excellent question," said Gracias. "I guess the answer is no one noticed what they were doing."

"And what were they doing?" asked Will.

"We found they were spending $2 million for 'sex-change' procedures in Guatemala, $1.5 million to fund DEI projects in Serbia, $70,000 for a DEI musical in Ireland, $47,000 for a transgender opera in Colombia, $32,000 for a transgender comic book in Peru, $2.5 million for EV cars in Vietnam, $1 million to help disabled people in Tajikistan, $61 million to send condoms to countries around the world, mostly to Africa, and $2.1 billion in humanitarian aid to a terrorist group in Gaza—and that was after Hamas attacked Israel on October 7, 2023.

"Plus all the media that hate us—*Politico* got thirty-four million dollars, *The New York Times* got fifty million dollars, *Reuters* got three hundred million dollars—USAID was sending them lots of money too."

Tom looked pensive.

"Do you mean the government was subsidizing news organizations to criticize the government?"

"I knew there was a reason you were my favorite Founding Father!" said Gracias. "With apologies, Dr. Franklin."

"None needed," said Ben, smiling. "I think we understand Edward's nickname now. It takes courage to face the enemies of government, especially when they are embedded within."

"You should know Edward also fought back against a group of teenage thugs who almost killed him," said Elon. "He was in the hospital with a concussion when Trump decided to send in the National Guard to patrol the streets of DC. The city is safe again."

"All that wasted government spending makes me think the US has become too rich for its own good," said Alex. "I fought to put custom duties and excise tariffs on foreign goods to pay down our war debt. Now the US Treasury is in danger of paying more in interest than it takes in!"

"The debt exploded under President Biden, who printed money we didn't have. Our debt is now suffocating us," said Elon. "I've heard you called the original tariff guy, Alex. Treasury Secretary Bessent and his team might welcome your ideas. Shall I set up a meeting?"

"Did you just call him Alex?"

"If you can be Big Balls, Edward, I don't know why he can't be Alex."

"Perhaps," said America's first treasury secretary, "perhaps I can be both."

They all laughed at that. Edward and Gracias outfitted them with DOGE paraphernalia—hats, pins, T-shirts, and hoodies.

As they were trying on the gear, Elon touched Ben's elbow.

"A private word?"

"Certainly."

Elon led Ben to a modest office without windows.

As the others oohed over the latest findings of waste at EPA, HHS, and Agriculture, the two giants of invention across the centuries huddled in conversation. They emerged after an intense conversation, and the founders prepared to leave DOGE headquarters.

Once they were safely in Mr. Debussy's car, Alex asked Ben what happened inside the room.

"One of those most electric conversations of my life," said Ben. "We discussed the printing press and penicillin, the wheel and indoor plumbing, the light bulb and the telephone, the advent of concrete and nails. We talked about the intersection of creativity and science and the imprint of man on nature. Also, he wants me to fly to Texas to see his robots. Apparently, they can do all human chores—he even trained them to do the Trump dance. And, finally, he wants to hire me."

"Elon Musk wants to hire Benjamin Franklin?" asked Alex.

"Of course," said Will. "Genius attracts genius."

"Ben, are we not due back in Heaven after the birthday celebration?"

Ben smiled.

"Elon said he thought I could stay as Josiah Folger. And he wants to get me a new lawyer."

"You would not use John to represent you in court?" asked Alex.

"Elon thinks I need a lawyer to argue that pronouns are protected speech, under the Bill of Rights and its First Amendment, and the liberation clause of the Declaration of Independence."

Ben looked at Tom, who looked stunned, then smiled.

"And to think we used that document to declare a revolution."

SCENE 14

Kennedy Center 1

"What are you ladies up to?" asked the Director as he sat down to join Priscilla and Annabelle. "Are you planning the contest or reviewing the General's teeth essays? Suddenly our building seems to be pulsing. I don't remember when there was so much excitement about our history."

"Speaking of history," said Priscilla from her desk, her voice showing disapproval, "I understand you arranged to fix the General's teeth."

"He wanted to look like everyone else," said the Director, sitting across from her.

"This isn't California!" Priscilla said, raising her voice. Even as the words left her mouth, she realized she was not supposed to yell at her boss. But the metaphor was so apt—as if Malibu's vapid values had drifted east to infect the political class—she couldn't stop herself from gilding it. "What's next, new boobs for Mercy? Shall we buy elevator shoes for Alex? How about some trendy Dior specs for Ben? And, hey, what about a Ralph Lauren makeover for Will?"

"Miss Babcock, please calm down. Your tirade is not good for my blood pressure, or your headaches. I think Will has already discovered Ralph Lauren. But your comparison of DC's faux airs to California's celebrity chic is spot-on hilarious. You've no doubt heard the line that Washington is Hollywood for ugly people."

"Yes, I've heard the line. The only thing I remember discussing about George Washington's dentures is the contest we did about how better teeth might have changed his life. Which, by the way, was a big hit in elementary schools. Entire classrooms sent submissions. So now, after we've managed to teach children a bit about our history, you want to change the script."

"Speaking of the script, how is it going? Are rehearsals on track to resume soon?"

Despite herself, Priscilla relaxed. "I must say Mrs. Warren is quite the wordsmith. I gave her some scripts to read of a more contemporary style that featured narrators—*Shawshank Redemption* was her favorite—and she seems to have adapted nicely, both to the rhythm of current language and the idea of moderating the story herself. Rehearsals next week."

"And ticket sales?"

"Sold out as soon as they were posted. Plus, there's a brisk resale business going on. *The Washington Post* says hotels in DC are virtually sold out, suggesting many are coming from out of town. And, speaking of Jeff Bezos, he wants two tickets in your box."

The Director was silent for a minute.

"My box? I trust you assured him that the Archives has no such elite seating."

"I did, but I held back the row of seats where you usually sit, smack in the middle. Even at that, you might have to turn away some requests. Vice President Vance is bringing his family—Usha and the three kids. Lara and Eric Trump are bringing their two children. As for Elon Musk, we keep hearing that he is bringing seven of his thirteen children and two of their mothers. Baron Trump is coming, too, along with his parents. We have seats for all of them."

The Director smiled.

"We are popular again. We are a hot ticket."

"The Kennedy Center event sold out, too, with about a hundred standing room tickets left. I offered them to students at American, Georgetown, George Washington, and Howard."

"Any backlash?"

"Yes," said Annabelle, "we received protests at being excluded from University of Virginia, founded by Thomas Jefferson, and from Harvard, on grounds that many of the nation's founders, including John Adams, were graduates."

"And panelists for the contest?"

"I heard Karoline Leavitt wanted to test her wits against them, but President Trump talked her out of it," said Annabelle. "I mean, if she missed one question, the media would ridicule her."

"Probably true. I heard that Stephen Miller and Sebastian Gorka were also itching to join the debate, and that would have been dynamic," said Priscilla. "But the White House said no to all."

"Gorka would have been formidable," said Annabelle. "Funny how sometimes expats from Britain know more about our history than those of us born here."

"Hardly a tribute to the Archives' ability to teach," said Priscilla.

"If we survive this holiday," said the Director, "we will have inspired much learning."

With the Cabinet opting to sit in the audience, Priscilla and Annabelle had selected the best of the essay entrants, who were flying in from all over the country to match wits with the founders. Her favorite essay was from an eighty-three-year-old constitutional scholar from Princeton named Dr. Augustine who was confident he could beat Ben. Priscilla thought this unlikely, as Franklin had been in attendance at the sessions of the Constitutional Convention in 1787 that very hot summer in Philadelphia where fifty-five delegates gathered from the thirteen states to craft a new foundational document. But she reminded Ben that the goal was for the founders to lose.

Annabelle's favorite applicant was a twelve-year-old boy named Timmy McIntyre from South Bend, Indiana, who had just started studying the Founding Fathers in school but vowed to work hard because he wanted to meet famous people visiting from Heaven.

"You have created a marvelous opportunity for Americans to experience history in person."

The Director was beaming. A rare sight, in Priscilla's experience.

"We are sticking to the story that these are mere actors, but from the mail we are receiving, many people seem to have heard about, and accepted, the rumors of their arrival from Heaven."

"Who would have thought that possible?" said the Director, winking at Priscilla. "Maybe it's because of all the talk of interplanetary travel among the tech titans. Maybe that makes the Other Realm seems more accessible. How will the contest work?"

"Like an old game show," said Annabelle. "Two panels of three people each, free to confer with each other before answering a question. But they'll only have thirty seconds per answer."

"Ah, so Mercy has agreed to participate?"

"Yes, thanks to your gentle persuasion," said Priscilla. "She keeps talking about Lucy Stone."

"And you have recruited a team of citizens to match wits with them?"

"Two panels. We've tried to balance them by geography, race, age, and sex. But so many people applied that we thought it better to form two teams, both battling separate panels of founders."

"You mean there's to be a second panel of founders?"

"Yes, John was miffed at being excluded from the first one, and we moved Mercy to that panel, putting Alex in the first one. Tom was reluctant, but I told him the public would not be satisfied unless they saw the author of the Declaration, the father of our democracy. OK with you?"

"If it's OK with the founders, it is with me. And how is the General's Teeth Contest going?"

"Some of the funniest comments I've ever received in this building!" said Priscilla. "One little girl from California had a traumatic encounter with a dentist after her mother raised her on soy milk instead of calcium-enriched regular milk. She said she plans to get a new set of teeth at least every two hundred fifty years and thinks George Washington should too. On a more serious note, there was the man from Beaumont, Texas, a retired veteran, who said if Washington had not been in constant pain, he would not have been as brave in war."

"I liked that one," said Annabelle, "though I was touched at how many people said it would not have mattered at all, that a brave and daring general would be undeterred by such trivial details."

"Have you selected the winner?"

"Still a work in progress. There's also dentist in Delray Beach, Florida, who has volunteered to make the General a new set of teeth free of charge. Dr. Spodak said, 'Teeth make the person. If Washington had such teeth earlier, he might have won the Revolutionary War faster.'"

"I imagine the General would agree with that sentiment," said the Director. "By the way, I know he demurred earlier, but if the president is attending, I'd like to offer the General a ticket again. Can you imagine the publicity, the reaction, if George Washington sits next to Donald Trump?"

Priscilla had been musing a lot about these actors, wondering if they could actually be heaven-sent. It still seemed unlikely—after all, it wasn't your body that went to Heaven, but your soul. Still, there was something affecting about them, something, well, eighteenth century.

"And to think I fought you on bringing these actors in for the reenactment."

"Understandable," said the Director. "Many would have been more dubious and less polite."

The day of the contest dawned gorgeous—blue skies, clouds like white powder buffs and nary a raindrop anywhere. Forecasters were, however, predicting a scorching day, with the heat index topping 100 degrees Fahrenheit. No matter. Crowds started lining up on the Potomac side of the Kennedy Center in the morning. An enterprising local network reporter approached a couple eating a breakfast of homemade bread with natural almond butter.

"No jam?" the reporter teased.

"No jam," said the woman. "Bobby Kennedy taught us to avoid sugar."

"Why are you in line so early?"

"We are big fans of Alexander Hamilton," said the man. "I believe he was the smartest of all the founders, and I want to see if he measures up to reputation."

By noon, three people had fainted in the hot sun and had to be treated for heat stroke.

At 1:00 p.m., doors opened for ticketed guests, with those on the wait list invited to mingle in the lobby. The audience was like a who's who of Washington, sprinkled with bold-name celebrities. Lin-Manuel Miranda, author of the Broadway sensation *Hamilton*, had finally relented over Trump's moves to refurbish the Kennedy Center in both décor and substance, allowing his play to embark on an epic run there. Dallas Jenkins, whose TV show *The Chosen* was the most popular series ever produced about the life of Jesus Christ, had badgered Kennedy Center Chairman Ric Grenell for tickets. It seemed like a number of the cast—including Jonathan Roumie, who played Jesus—were with him.

Network cameras stood ready to broadcast the event, including C-SPAN, Right Side Broadcasting Network, and Elon Musk's new Starlink Affair. No one from the left-wing cables—MSNBC or CNN—or alphabet networks had requested space. Word was they were all too broke.

At 2:00 p.m., the Director strode on stage to introduce the panelists and the rules of the game.

"This has been a project of intense planning by our staff, who verified the answers. In my view, this is a real contest between the intent of the founders and the understandings of the current generation. We are thrilled to have you here. Are you all ready to watch history being made?"

"Yes," screamed the audience, as one little girl yelled out, "Mom, it's just like the National Spelling Bee!" The audience laughed.

"Our moderator for this first panel will be Joseph J. Ellis, a historian whose work focuses on the lives and times of the Founding Fathers of the United States. Please welcome Professor Ellis."

"Thank you, Dr. Sowell, and thank you to the audience for your enthusiasm for this event. I once offered a promising student an autographed copy of one of my books if she would enroll in my class at Mount Holyoke. It is reassuring to see our history is still of interest without bribes."

After a few obligatory laughs, he began the introductions.

"In our first panel, Benjamin Franklin, Will Lee, and Alexander Hamilton will represent the Founders Team. Please help me welcome them. Gentlemen?"

As soon as the three of them took the stage, there was a roar from the audience, with a few gasps of recognition. Dr. Ellis introduced them, though they all took issue with his introductions. Ben protested that Ellis had nowhere mentioned his experiments with electricity. Will wanted to be remember as the General's valet, not just staff. And Alex corrected him about his heritage.

"As you know, Dr. Ellis, I am a Scotsman by heritage. Nevis was an accident of birth."

Ellis nodded but corrected nothing.

"Now allow me to introduce our Citizens Team: Dr. Theodore Augustine, an emeritus scholar in constitutional law from Princeton; Timmy McIntyre, a twelve-year-old from South Bend, Indiana, who has been studying the Founding Fathers in school; and Julia Collins, from Wilmette, Illinois, a twenty-day winner who in 2014 earned $428,000 on the quiz show *Jeopardy!*"

The audience cheered.

"Here are the rules. After I begin reading each question, the teams can buzz in if they think they know the answer."

"So we are to confer first?" asked Dr. Augustine.

"At the risk of annoying your teammates, yes, perhaps that would be advisable. You might want to designate one panelist to push the button, on accord of the others."

A sprinkle of laughter came from the audience. Priscilla thought it more of a nervous reaction.

"We will start with the easiest questions and work our way forward. The questions will be worth one point each. Panelists, are you ready?"

They all nodded, except for Ben, who more or less grunted.

"First question. Who said, 'Give Me Liberty or Give Me Death'?"

The Citizens rang in first. Timmy McIntyre, who was controlling the button, knew that it was Patrick Henry, and the other two nodded their approval. At the Founders Table, Will was manning the button, but Ben Franklin had fallen asleep, making it difficult to win his assent.

"Dr. Ellis, do you think we could procure some coffee?" asked Alex. "I fear Dr. Franklin is sleepy from the summer heat."

"If Dr. Franklin gets some coffee, I would like some too," said Dr. Augustine. "We are comparable in age, it seems."

"Yes, of course. Would anyone else like coffee?"

No one did, and Dr. Ellis decided to continue the contest, as neither side was advantaged by its elderly contestants.

"Second question. Who said, "There, I guess King George will be able to read that without his spectacles'?"

"John Hancock," yelled out Timmy McIntyre.

"Press your button, son!"

"Did I get it right?"

The audience was laughing.

"Third question. Who was on the Committee of Five that was assigned to write the Declaration of Independence?"

"It was me!" said Ben Franklin, who had been roused by insults to his age and pushed the button himself. "Along with John Adams, Thomas Jefferson, Roger Sherman, and Robert Livingston. We had to pull from each of the major colonies. Massachusetts, Virginia, Pennsylvania, Connecticut, and New York were all represented."

"Excellent," said Dr. Ellis.

Alex interjected. "To be clear, Mr. Jefferson wrote the document. The committee only edited it."

"Yes, of course, but just for the record," Ben added, "it was I who suggested changing Jefferson's language, in the original draft, from 'we hold these truths to be sacred and undeniable, that all men are created equal…' to 'we hold these truths to be self-evident.'"

"Because you didn't want to involve the Lord?" asked Dr. Augustine.

"A damnable accusation, if familiar," said Ben. "I believed in religion's morals, and I often said during the Revolution that 'rebellion to tyrants was obedience to God.'"

Priscilla thought Ellis looked harried, as if a classroom of unruly students had suddenly discovered that wet paper towels made good projectiles.

"Gentlemen, while we appreciate the depth you bring to the discussion, please limit yourselves to the questions at hand."

"Let them speak!" yelled a man from the audience. "We didn't come to hear some pointy-headed elitist professor. We want to hear from the founders!"

A rumble of agreement came from the crowd. "We want the founders! We want the founders!"

Priscilla thought it hysterical. Somehow Dr. Ellis regained the floor.

"Panelists, ready for the fourth question? This is a difficult one, in my opinion, as historians are themselves divided, so you might want to wait until I have read all the options. Ready?"

"Wide awake," said Ben. "The coffee is excellent."

"Why was slavery not outlawed in the Constitution? Was it because, one, the Southern states would have balked at signing it; two, some founders were slave owners, and it would have hurt them economically; three, to avoid further angering the British; or, four, all of the above?'

At the Citizens table, Dr. Augustine seemed to be arguing with Julia Collins, who favored answer one while he insisted on two. At the Founders Table, Will had frozen over the button, prompting Alex to reach over and push it.

"Number four," he said.

"Alex, how we could have angered King George any more than we already had by declaring our independence?" Ben asked. "Surely you remember how he turned his back on John and Tom as they presented their credentials?"

"A stunning moment in world history," Alex agreed.

Ellis looked toward the Citizens' table, and Julia Collins pressed the button saying, "The Southern states."

"Correct."

"Question five: After the war, who said, 'They had the splendor, we the advantage'?"

At the Founders table, Ben was conferring with Alex, but they couldn't remember which of Washington's generals had offered the assessment. Will smiled and said to Alex, "You may have been his aide-de-camp," he said, loud enough for the audience to hear, "but I was his valet, and I knew his secrets." The audience laughed. Will pressed their button. "General Nathanael Greene."

"Correct," said Dr. Ellis.

The RSBN cameras panned up to the presidents' box, where George Washington, sitting next to President Trump, was beaming, clapping loudly for Will's correct answer. *The money shot,* thought Priscilla. The Director will be very happy. She wondered where he had gone to, but she assumed he was sitting next to some famous people in the presidential box.

"Question six: Who was Mercy Otis Warren?"

Will smiled at Ben and Alex and pressed the button.

"A poet, a playwright, a patriot. She was also a commentator who argued that we couldn't have a Constitution without a Bill of Rights because it would make the central government too big at the expense of the states and the public."

"Smart woman," yelled a voice in the balcony, easily recognizable as Elon Musk. It was greeted with much laughter and a few boos.

"Question seven: General Cornwallis surrendered at Yorktown, Virginia, because, one, his troops were outnumbered; two, the French navy had joined the fight; three, George Washington had outsmarted him; or four, all of the above."

Both teams rang in at the same time with the correct answer—"all of the above"—and Ellis awarded them half a point.

"Finally, teams, last question, who wrote, 'The American war is over, but this is far from being the case with the American Revolution'? Was it John Adams, Thomas Paine, Dr. Benjamin Rush, or Mercy Otis Warren?'"

Both teams seemed deep in conversation. Julia Collins finally persuaded a very stubborn Dr. Augustine that it was Dr.

Benjamin Rush, and the Citizens Team won the final question, winning the contest, 4.5 to 3.5.

"May I say something?" asked Alex.

Oh dear, thought Priscilla. Dr. Ellis nodded in his direction.

"Since we arrived here some weeks ago, we have all been impressed, I think it is fair to say, by how seriously Americans take this idea that our Constitution is a lasting foundational document that guides our laws. So, on behalf of the Founders Team, and perhaps also the Citizens Team, we would like to salute you, the public, for caring about this nation we fought for and created."

He stood and began to clap, and the audience stood and applauded in return, and Priscilla sat pinching herself in disbelief. And they still had one more panel to go!

Before the next panel could convene, Priscilla's phone flashed a new text message. She ran out of the hall with the speed of a gazelle. Director Sowell had been taken to the ER at George Washington University Hospital.

SCENE 15

Kennedy Center 2

Priscilla entered the Director's hospital room just as the second panel was coming on the TV screen installed above his bed. He looked happy, though he was connected by wire to various monitors. Probably she looked worse—security was so tight around the hospital that Mr. Debussy could only get her to Washington Circle, and she had to run the last distance.

"Don't worry, I'm fine," he said. "Just a tad too much excitement."

"What do the doctors say?"

"Little. In the meantime, how are things at the Kennedy Center?"

"The reports I got suggested we managed the transition with few bumps. One couple from Indiana refused to leave their seats, insisting they were sure their tickets were for both sessions. We had about two dozen no-shows for the second session, maybe the weather, and this allowed us to seat the spillover crowd that had been waiting in the lobby—and, from what I hear, running up a big bar tab while watching on those large TV screens we put up." But none of that was why she'd come. "The doctors have said nothing?"

"One of them keeps coming in to watch the debate," said the Director. "Dr. Chopra said he finds it invigorating. So far, he's told me nothing about my case."

"What happened?"

"It was when Alex was thanking the audience. I started to sweat and feel light-headed. I think I was overwhelmed by a sense of what I was witnessing—people long dead speaking to the living. Then I blacked out, and the next thing I knew, I was in a hospital bed. Did you know this is where President Reagan came when he was shot?"

"Yes, I did. But something tells me Reagan got more attention than you are receiving. Let me go find someone who can answer some questions."

"The only questions I want to hear are those for the next panel."

Applause was even louder for the second panels. Tom, Mercy, and John would face off against a Citizens panel of Abram Coblentz, an Amish farmer from Pennsylvania famous for making a wooden set of the Founding Fathers; Nikki Reed, a Hollywood actress who played Betsy Ross in the Fox TV series *Sleepy Hollow*; and Sam Turner, a Detroit autoworker whose ancestor of many generations, John Brown, led a slave rebellion in 1831, presaging the Civil War.

The new moderator was Ned Ryun, a scholar of the Revolution, and a conservative. Tom had insisted in a meeting with the Director that he would not appear with Joseph Ellis as moderator, calling him a closet Federalist.

"He called me an American sphinx!" Tom had complained to the Director.

"Perhaps an attempt to humanize you for contemporary audiences," said the Director. "He saw you as neither liberal nor conservative, privileged nor populist."

"But by definition, a sphinx is a creature from Greek mythology said to have a human's head and a lion's body. Was I really that inscrutable?"

"Of course not, Tom. In any event, you are certainly entitled to a moderator more in keeping with your political views."

The Director suggested Ned Ryun and gave Tom one of his books—*Restoring Our Republic*.

"I think you'll enjoy it, especially the chapter on the danger of judicial activism."

Ryun introduced the Citizens Panel first. Turned out the Amish farmer from Pennsylvania had a wry sense of humor—"The founders were hardly wooden," he said, "I just made them that way because it's the only material I know how to carve." Nikki Reed looked glamorous in her low-cut green gown, though she conceded to a reporter that Betsy Ross, seamstress who stitched an early version of the American flag, would not have worn such an outfit. As for Sam Turner, descendant of the slave that lit a spark to the Civil War, he came wearing a business suit—and a MAGA hat.

Again, as happened with the first panels, the Founders were introduced to thunderous applause and much excitement. Mercy got a huge round of applause, which seemed to annoy John.

Ned Ryun had devised a different set of rules that were looser, more conducive to debate. In a planning meeting, Priscilla had argued that Ryun's style would make scoring more difficult. But she thought it might appeal to the panelists—and the audience—more. She had given her OK.

She came back into the Director's hospital room with Dr. Chopra in tow. She asked a medical question when both men shushed her.

"Question one: Why was Benedict Arnold, the great traitor to the American cause, never hanged?"

Mercy had control of the buzzer on the Founders team. "He escaped," she said.

"Correct," said Ned Ryun. "Although some historians wonder why the Americans did not ask for him to be repatriated as a condition of the Treaty of Paris that ended the war."

"The British were eager to settle the affair quickly," said John. "I was there you know. The specter of a new nation overwhelming the greatest fighting force in the world was simply too embarrassing. They wanted to put the defeat behind them, perhaps to fight another day. We wanted them to recognize US independence and accept boundaries that would allow us to expand to the west. Once they agreed to both, we pocketed our victory."

"Reasonable," said Sam Turner. "But how did he escape?"

"Perhaps we can discuss that with General Washington at a later time," said Ryun. "In the meantime, question two: Who said, 'If men were angels, no government would be necessary'?"

"My friend James Madison," said Tom, putting his hand on Mercy's to buzz in.

"Correct," said Ned Ryun.

"I liked my quote better," said John.

"Yeah, me too," said Abram Coblentz. "The one where you said, 'Our Constitution was made only for a moral and religious people. It is wholly inadequate to the government of any other.'"

"Cool," said Sam Turner. "I'm going to tell that one to my pastor."

Tom whispered a reminder to Mercy and John that they were supposed to lose the contest.

"Gentlemen, and ladies, this is proving an exciting conversation. Let's move on to question three: Why did Alexander Hamilton engage in a fatal duel with Aaron Burr?"

Nikki Reed buzzed in for the Citizens team.

"Manhood," she said. Lots of whoops and hollers of agreement came from the audience, and up in the gallery, Alex wore a wide grin.

"Yes, we'll accept that. Dueling was considered a way for men to prove their virtue."

"I was expecting more questions about the Constitution," said Mercy.

"The Constitution was only as good as those of us who relied on it to govern," said Tom.

"Touché," said Nikki, seeming to flirt with the affable Mr. Jefferson, who smiled back.

Ned Ryun looked uncomfortable with all the chemistry flying between one of the Citizens and one of the Founders.

"Question four: Why were Americans so upset about the Tea Tax?"

"I got this," said Sam Turner as he put his hand on top of Nikki's and rang in. "They were big tea drinkers, and they didn't like that East Indian Company's monopoly. Plus—the way it went down during the Tea Party, man that was a wild scene, with the Indians and all those angry Americans. If Trump had been there, he would have slapped tariffs on everyone!"

The audience howled. Up in the balcony, President Trump smiled and waved.

"Actually, we learned to make our own herbal teas," said Mercy. "My James liked ours better."

"Of course," said John. "James Warren was a patriot. Abigail and I were great friends of the Warren family until, well, Mercy knifed me in the back."

"I merely called you a monarchist," said Mercy. "You wrote a book about the virtues of the British bicameral legislature. And you wanted to call our new president 'Your Excellency.'"

"I like the sound of that," Trump yelled from the balcony. More laughter.

"Question five: Who was Sam Adams?"

Almost at once, several voices rang out in unison.

"My cousin!" said John.

"My friend," said Mercy.

"A badass," said Abram.

"Contestants, can I remind you to ring in? Perhaps we can ask each of you who shouted an answer to make your case. Then we can let the audience decide which is the best one. Let's start with Mr. Adams. Make the case for your cousin."

"My uncle was a brewer, and Sam grew up inhaling the hustle and bustle of business. He also inherited his father's anger about the British suppression of the Land Bank he founded to help colonial artisans and manufacturers. They were both passionate about the Revolution, and Sam convinced John Hancock, the wealthiest man in Boston, to support his Sons of Liberty, who began the fight toward independence."

"I never thought of him as a troublemaker," said Mercy. "He was passionate, though. He often made the case for independence at meetings in our parlor, and mind you, at the beginning there were a lot of Tories among us, loyalists to the Crown. He had fire in his eyes and in his belly."

"Mr. Coblentz?"

"The Sons of Liberty, the Tea Party, the Boston Massacre, Lexington and Concord—these were the seeds of our Revolution. Without Sam Adams—without his stockpiling weapons and using guerrilla fighting tactics—we might all have British accents. Besides, he made a great beer!"

The audience roared its approval. The Founders team was all smiles, even after Ned Ryun awarded the points to the Citizens.

"Question six: Why did Mercy Otis Warren have to publish her commentary under a pen name?"

Ironically, the Citizens Team buzzed in first.

"She was a girl," said Turner. "I mean, come on."

"It's a little more complicated than that," said Nikki. "Mrs. Warren, women weren't allowed to comment on politics in those days, were they?"

Mercy nodded. "Politics was considered the purview of men," she said. "So, if women wanted to discuss political issues, they had to do so behind the cover of a pen name."

"We should have never given you the vote!" called out a male voice in the audience, to laughter.

"Actually, your big mistake was giving us an education," said Mercy. "After the war, women were asked to become a Republican Motherhood, to raise a new generation of Americans in the virtues of the Revolution. We argued that to do that, we needed to be literate and educated. Soon women were being tutored at home and later went off to college, like the men."

"You mean you weren't all trad wives?" asked Nikki.

"That is one of my regrets about the wording of the Declaration of Independence," said Tom. "I should have written, 'All *people* are created equal.' And we should have banned slavery."

"Why was the Declaration silent on slavery?" asked Sam Turner.

"I had it in the original draft—you can view it at the Archives—but the Continental Congress took it out because they were afraid Southern colonies would desert the cause of independence otherwise. It saddens me that we had to wait almost a hundred years to put it right."

The audience was on its feet, and Ned Ryun awarded the points to the Citizens. The Founders were losing four to two.

"Question seven: What was the most contentious fight during the Constitutional Convention?"

Sam Turner pushed Nikki's hand down on the buzzer.

"The Three-Fifths Rule," he said. "See, the Southern states were mad that only free men counted toward the size of a congressional delegation. But they didn't want to acknowledge slaves were people too. So they agreed on compromise. Everybody was happy. Except the slaves, of course."

"The size of the congressional delegations was one of the most contentious we faced," agreed John. "Intense debates lasted for two weeks. I heard the crisis was so bad that the General almost despaired of seeing a favorable outcome. That's why he was so adamant about keeping the proceedings secret. He didn't want anyone to know how close to failure Congress came."

"Mr. Jefferson," said Ned Ryun. "Have you any thoughts on this?"

"I am overwhelmed by the setting, as Alex was. We are debating the facts and impacts of the Revolution by those who profess to have been there and those who studied us in school. It is daunting. It's also becoming clear that they know more than we do."

The Opera House exploded in laughter and catcalls—you could sense the jubilance, even via the TV screen in the Director's hospital room. Priscilla thought the implication lingered—were these actors, or had they really come down from Heaven to debate American citizens?

"Very well, let's move on the last question, which will decide the contest. This topic allows for many interpretations, so we will let all six panelists opine on their views, and let the audience select the victor. Question eight: Who or what won the American Revolution? Mrs. Warren, as you wrote the war's first history, I'll call on you first."

Mercy: "The people, a groundswell of emotion from everyday Americans that they did not want to be taxed and then not represented in Parliament, that they didn't want Red Coats patrolling the streets of their cities, or commandeering their homes and supplies, taking their homes and women at will, forcing men to fight. Why were the British here? It was a people's revolution."

John: "I agree with that. We had been educated, many of us at Harvard, and expected to be treated like civilized adults. Instead, the British were arrogant and haughty, and treated us with much cruelty. If you read a lot of history, that is always a recipe ripe for rebellion."

Nikki: "Mercy, didn't the women have a lot to do with winning the war?"

Mercy: "Oh my, yes. We held spinning parties to weave fabric from our own local materials, so we didn't have to import British cloth. I guess you could say that's another reason we won, because the war made us economically self-sustaining and united all of us in winning. We all liked pretty British goods, of course, but it felt wonderful to do our part for the country."

Sam: "I have a different idea. We were always a nation on the move. Men took their families and everything they owned and grew the country. It's in our DNA. We were destined to grow, west and south and even north. As men and their families resettled the continent—people of real grit—our population exploded, even as the British one was shrinking. That's it."

Abram: "I do read a lot of history, and I believe we were destined to win."

"Mr. Jefferson, I'll give you the last word."

"In some sense, I agree with Abram," said Tom. "Ours was always a nation of the faithful. Many of those who sacrificed all to immigrate to the New World came for religious freedom. The whole culture was infused with the moral order of the ancient Hebrews, the Ten Commandments. But in the colonial era, many of us were also much influenced by the political philosophy of the Greeks and Romans, as interpreted by the Enlightenment writers."

Someone in the audience started applauding.

"Fans of the Enlightenment," Tom said, smiling. "We succeeded, in war and in governance, generation after generation, because the culture respected both God and man. French philosopher Alexis de Tocqueville noticed this in 1835, when he toured our young country and wrote a book called *Democracy in America.* In it, he wrote that 'liberty cannot be established without morality, nor morality without faith.' He thought we were hurt by excessive individualism, egalitarianism, and materialism. But I believe those are our jewels, and the reason we've lasted for two hundred fifty years. We are of many cultures, made into one by our enterprise and, as Mr. Turner put it, our grit."

Watching on TV, Priscilla would not have believed it if she hadn't seen it with her own eyes, but an audience at the Kennedy Center, stood then and applauded, including all the panelists. Tom looked embarrassed, but finally he rose, too, and waved to the crowd. They roared at him, and then, when Nikki came over and kissed him on the cheek—well, they went crazy with glee.

SCENE 16

The White House Dinner

First Lady Melania Trump had decorated the East Room in shades of gold, befitting the golden era her husband had declared and the founders had ushered in. She regretted that the size of the guest list precluded using the more intimate State Dining Room, with Abraham Lincoln peering down in wonder and deep thought. And even at that, so many had claimed an invitation she had to use round tables seating ten each, which she feared would hamper conversation.

But at least in the East Room she had a bigger canvas. Her décor was so breathtaking most gasped on entering the room—glittering in gold, everywhere gold and white and more gold.

"I predicted a Golden Era, but our wonderful First Lady made it come to life," President Trump said as he stood to greet Founders, Citizens, and every self-important person who had managed an invitation. "Before we begin, I've asked the Reverend Franklin Graham to pray over us."

The son of the Reverend Billy Graham, Franklin was tall like his father but not as famous, known more for philanthropy than pulpits. Bowing his head in prayer, he began:

> Our dear father, who art in Heaven, thank you for the company we keep tonight, for the nation that our founders created, nurtured by the generations of patriotic Americans who followed in their footsteps. Thank you for watching over this nation, for protecting its freedoms and its sovereignty, for making it the oldest Republic in the world. We thank you, too, for the bounty in this room—the beautiful décor, the plentiful food, the magnificent company. Truly, Lord, we are blessed. In humility and gratitude, with hearts full of wonder, we join to say, Amen.

A chorus of amens circled the room. And then, it seemed, everyone began talking at once. As the wait staff, dressed in white jackets, began serving the meal, the Director, released from the hospital several days before with a warning to curb his activities, looked around in awe.

"Spectacular, isn't it?" he said to the woman on his left, a historian from Hillsdale College.

"Unrivaled," she said. "I hear you were its instigator."

"More of a cog in the wheel. But even that is honor enough for me."

The first course was a gorgeous green gazpacho make of yellow tomatoes, cilantro, and cucumber—smoothed with blended sunflower seeds to give it a creamy texture, plated on the

Abraham Lincoln China pattern and served with an American Riesling from Colorado.

At the president's table, Donald Trump sat flanked by George Washington and Thomas Jefferson. Photographers had a field day. As is protocol, the president stood to give the first toast.

Glass in hand, he waited for the room to quiet and then began.

"President Kennedy held a dinner in 1962 for that year's Nobel Prize winners, calling them 'the most extraordinary collection of talent, of human knowledge, that has ever been gathered at the White House—with the possible exception of when Thomas Jefferson dined alone.'

"Tonight, we have not only Thomas Jefferson but all the Founding Fathers, and one of the Founding Mothers—what a pleasure to meet you, Mrs. Warren! I hear that without you and other critics they called deplorables, we wouldn't have a Bill of Rights. No free speech. No guns. Deplorables, imagine that! Everyone wanted to come to this dinner—historians, politicians, diplomats, tech gurus, foreign leaders, and corporate tycoons. The press wanted to come, but we said no. Isn't that right, Karoline? Isn't she the greatest? I bet all the founders wish they could have had a press manager as good as Karoline. Think how our history would have changed!

"So I would like to toast our celebrated guests, representing the greatest generation of political talent ever assembled. The founders blessed us with the Constitution, the Bill of Rights, and a legacy of reaching for the stars. They created the ideal on which we still stand—freedom to pursue our dreams. There's been a lot of speculation about whether they are incredibly well-informed actors or sent from a heavenly perch. Ever since Butler, I've believed fervently in God. Either way, whether they are actors or characters returned from Heaven to help us celebrate our two hundred fiftieth birthday, let us salute them. To the founders!"

All across the ballroom, guests clicked their glasses and said, "To the founders!"

Then Trump said, "And I would be remiss if I did not credit our beautiful First Lady for the breathtaking elegance of this room. We have the aesthetic glitter of her décor and the intellectual glitter of our visitors. What a great combination, not seen since Jefferson dined here alone."

There was much laughter as Trump sat down. That's when General Washington stood up.

"I raise my glass to thank the White House, and the team at the National Archives that is hosting us, and the Americans we have met during our journey here. Speaking for my fellow Revolutionaries, I'd like to say that we fought hard to create this nation, but few of us could have imagined it would have lasted two hundred fifty years. In my day I often said that Americans accustomed to freedom must be led, not driven. Thank you, President Trump, for your leadership. And to current generation of Americans, so patriotic and optimistic, we are grateful. To you!"

As a ripple of laughter, applause, and cheers broke out across the ballroom. Melania was about to signal the wait staff to serve the main course when suddenly Benjamin Franklin stood to speak.

"And I raise my glass to celebrate why I think we have lasted for two hundred fifty years. I was the most famous scientist of my day, and I was always proud of the inventions I created. What a privilege it is for me to come back two hundred fifty years later to discover a new generation of Americans has reimagined the world with its new creations—these hand-held smartphones and those self-driving vehicles and airplanes that defy gravity and even spaceships that circle the globe and land back on Earth safely. To today's inventors, I salute you, for saving the republic. To creativity!"

There was silence at first, guests unsure how Trump would feel about a veiled toast to his once best friend, now frenemy Elon Musk, though their alliance improved after Elon gave two hundred twenty-six million dollars to the GOP for the 2026 midterms. Finally, Trump stood and raised his glass, saying "To the inventors." Melania signaled for the main course—pasture-raised bison meat, with scalloped potatoes and julienned carrots. This time she served it on the Reagan State China service, similar in its red-and-white design to Lincoln's, pairing the dish with a pinot noir.

Soon, many guests were table-hopping, seeking autographs from the founders or asking their advice about how to navigate life. Priscilla was so thrilled to have been invited as a guest that she walked the room as if in a trance, overhearing snatches of conversation between the near-famous and the historically so. She was glad she had opted for flats.

"What makes a happy life is ambition," Ben told one guest. "It's hard to achieve anything without that. As Adam Smith wrote in *The Wealth of Nations,* governments cannot create innovation. You could even make a case that it is best governments not fund it, as such money tends to cloud creativity. If you are to remain a great country, and I believe you will, it will be because you never stop innovating, never stop reinventing yourselves—or the nation."

Pete Hegseth was deep in conversation with George Washington about the Revolutionary-era battle in Princeton, where the secretary of the newly renamed War Department had gone to college.

"How did you manage to rout the British?"

"We suffered a lot of defeats in 1776, and I knew I needed something bold. The British smirked at the very idea that our amateur army could defeat the greatest fighting force in history. No doubt you've heard of how I led our troops across the Delaware River on Christmas Eve."

"And in prayer," said the secretary.

The General smiled.

"I did kneel down and pray, and I am pleased so many remember that. We surprised Hessian troops in Trenton and took many prisoners—Lieutenant General Hamilton took charge of their capture and told me most were hungover from drink. By January 3, we turned north to Princeton, with forty-five hundred troops to their twelve hundred. I ordered one battery to attack the British at William Clarke's farmhouse from one direction, as I led into battle against Cornwallis from the other."

"Amazing you still remember the troop strengths," said Hegseth.

"Something a commander never forgets."

"True. I led men in combat in Iraq in 2005. I can see them still and count them too."

"Mr. Secretary, I've been wanting to ask you a question as well. I've always thought that operational surprise was a tremendous advantage in warfare. Alex, who is far more in touch with earthly matters than I, recently briefed me on the US military's takeout of Iran's nuclear capability. What an operation—flights of thirty-six hours, buster bombing with pinprick accuracy on a moonless night, refueling planes and firing Tomahawk missiles. An extraordinary performance. How do you explain—no leaks, no military response, complete silence?"

"Well, Mr. President, if I told you I'd have to kill you."

Both broke into wide smiles.

Meanwhile, Alex was deep in conversation with Treasury Secretary Scott Bessent. Priscilla wasn't sure she heard correctly, but she thought she heard the treasury secretary mention mutiny. And Alex responded by telling him a story about George Washington's top commanders.

"It was toward the end of the war. They had put up with bad food and unsanitary conditions, done everything the nation had asked of them, and they had never been paid. They met to write a letter of protest to Congress. The General heard about their meeting and asked to speak. They were respectful, though not warm. He pulled from his pocket his remarks. Then he pulled his bifocals from another pocket and began to read. In that moment, I believe, those generals saw a man with white hair and fading vision, who had given his all for the fight, and who had grown old by their sides."

Bessent smiled.

"And you think I should try that with the Federal Reserve board members?"

They both laughed.

"Remember one more thing. What I learned from life is that the fiery and destructive passion for war is much more powerful in the human heart than the sweet sentiments of peace."

"Ah, so you don't think they will jump at the chance to retire?"

Next she saw Breitbart's Matt Boyle talking to Supreme Court Justice Clarence Thomas about whether the nine justices believed these founders were actors or heavenly sent.

"I believe the court is split five to four, with Chief Justice Roberts siding with the court's four female justices in the opinion that these people are actors."

"And you?"

"I am only a Supreme Court justice. Far be it from me to question God's plan."

This being DC, Priscilla noticed a lot of business transactions taking place across the East Room. Secretary of State Marco Rubio was lobbying South Carolina's Lindsey Graham to stop funding Ukraine. Deputy Chief of Staff Stephen Miller agreed to an interview with podcaster Theo Von. She thought she heard Border Czar Tom Homan threaten to deport a congresswoman.

Priscilla kept walking the room. At the head table, she saw Tom huddled with President Trump.

"I hear you think I'm the best president since you lived here."

Tom smiled.

"You know what you and I have in common?" asked Trump. "The media hates us. I blow up a ship coming from Venezuela with narcotics, eleven gang members killed. And the media howls about how I robbed these criminals of due process."

"They have been howling a long time," said Tom. "During the Barbary Wars, I sent the Navy and Marines to the Mediterranean to suppress Muslim pirates and slavers trying to block US shipping lines. An uproar from the press. Fortunately, Congress, backed me up."

Priscilla thought she heard something about #MeToo, but as they were at the head table and pressed head-to-head, almost whispering, she couldn't get close enough to be sure.

"I'm trying to save you from those wolves who want to sully your reputation because of Sally Hemings," said Trump quietly. "Let me tell you something. I've had my share of dalliances, but I could not have possibly slept with all my accusers."

"Mr. President, I inherited Sally, my wife's half-sister, from my father-in-law, John Wayles."

"Busy plantation owner, huh? Doesn't matter. Just stay strong. The Fake News wants to make everything about sex and race. But what you and the other founders did was magnificent. I don't want you to absorb all this guilt. We have a team of historians who are working hard on your case. I promise you, those revisionists at the National Park Service will not win. And the young people are being drawn into our circle because they want to Make America Great Again."

Priscilla thought Tom looked ashen, but she wasn't sure. She walked up to him and asked if he would autograph the menu for the Archives' records, if only to cheer him up. It seemed to work.

"Mixing ancient history and contemporary politics again, are we?" he said, smiling.

Next, Trump turned to the General.

"President Washington, I've been wanting to ask you a question," he said. "I've read that early in your first term, you had many protestors out in the streets, tar and feathering tax collectors. Mine don't care about paying taxes—they're all rich. They protest so they look virtuous to their party."

"Ah yes, the whiskey tax. Congress passed it, and I signed it, to pay our war debt from the Revolution. But it was unpopular with farmers in western Pennsylvania. They were accustomed to distilling their own rye, barley, wheat, and corn to make whiskey. They did not much like the government taking a cut. So I rallied a militia of thirteen thousand men and shut down the rebellion."

"And did that work?"

"Yes, but I regretted it later. I should have sent one of my generals, keeping the two functions—the political and the military—separate. I understand these days there is a very strict compartmentalization, and I believe that is a good idea. But I will say this, Mr. President—and I do not recommend it—but I must say it got everyone's attention."

The two presidents smiled at each other.

"I heard you organized a mighty parade for the day the Army turned two hundred fifty years old," the General said. "Nothing better for morale."

Trump looked at Washington as if seeing him for the first time.

"You were our first president," Trump said. "I suspect you will go down as the only president ever elected unanimously by the Electoral College. But now I realize you were also the savviest, understanding that symbolism was as important as substance. Yes, that mighty parade sent a message, to friends and enemies, especially Iran and Israel. But its real purpose was to build esprit de corps, to make our soldiers feel more united around a mission, and more appreciated."

The General beamed. "Well done, Mr. President, well done."

"Thank you. You were my lodestar. And now, I'm off to dance with the First Lady."

Guests oohed at the dessert of custard tart with raspberries and blueberries, a nod to the French role in providing critical military prowess to the American cause. President Trump led First Lady Melania to the front of the room, where a wooden floor had been set up for dancing. As they did in 2025 at an inaugural ball, they danced to Elvis Presley's rendition of "Glory, Glory Hallelujah."

After Vice President J. D. Vance and his wife, Usha, joined them on the dance floor, Alex made his move. Boldly, he tapped on President Trump's shoulder and asked to dance with Melania. Trump said, "Hell no." After slinking back to his table, Tom greeted him with a smile.

"It seems your pride is always defeating you," said Tom.

"I'd rather die trying to do something bold than die wondering if I could have."

"A fitting epitaph. And yet what most know you for now is the rap music in that play."

Alex smiled.

"Do you know my favorite lyric? 'History has its eyes on me.' I suppose that's how we all felt, was it not, as if we had the eyes of history on us?"

Tom nodded.

"Lately, I've been reading the works of a French author named Emile Zola. He wrote that it is the obligation of every writer to 'live out loud.' And that is what we did, Alex, you and me and the others. We wrote a new country into existence, never shy of expressing our opinions or daring our critics. If history had its eyes on us, it's because we lived out loud."

Just then an usher came up and tapped Alex on his shoulder.

"The First Lady has agreed to dance with you," he said.

Alex nearly jumped from his seat and reached the stage just as Trump was relinquishing his wife.

"Be more careful than you were with Burr," said Trump. "I'm a good shot too."

The band played the title song from *Hamilton* as Alex took Melania in his dancing arms. He looked like—well, like he had died and gone to Heaven. Except that in contemplating the First Lady's beauty, and being in its proximity, Alex had not calculated Melania's height. He was five foot seven. She was four inches taller. In addition, she was wearing heels, with the result that when Alex reached for her waist, he found himself staring directly into her bosom. He jerked his head upward to meet her eyes, a position that only emphasized the dilemma posed by his stature.

"So how was it?" asked Tom when Alex returned to their table.

"Sublime."

But the evening's real surprise came when Will Lee went up to Vice President J. D. Vance and asked if he could dance with Usha. The band played a song from country singer Christina Perri called "A Thousand Years" about a love that could last longer than the United States of America.

Suddenly, people were standing, clapping, smiling. Mercy looked at John. He was crying.

"I don't believe I've ever seen you cry before," she said. "Whatever is the matter?"

"Do you remember when we hoped the British would honor our request for rights as citizens? We were so naive then, so sure they would accede to our arguments. Anyway, I was."

"I think we were all stunned into sensibility at the Boston Massacre. It had never occurred to me before then that they would kill us because we asked for rights of citizenship."

"I suppose that is always how rebellions begin, in the shock of dueling expectations. And now, look at this splendor, at this intersection of history and politics, at this couple dancing across the generations, one born of Indian ancestry, the other of slavery, both Americans, proud and free."

"And the tears?"

"I know I railed against too much democracy, but now I am overwhelmed. I've seen enough to know we did good work here. Time for me to go home. This America is too spicy for me. I will talk to Director Sowell. He can hire an actor to play me in the OBBR, and I can return to Heaven and to Abigail, and follow events in the Earthly Library without bearing witness in person."

"But who will help me finish the play? You have been an able partner."

"I have given that some thought," said John, smiling. "I suggest you team up with the man of the hour."

"The man of the hour?"

"Alexander Hamilton."

"My goodness, you want me, who opposed the Constitution as written, to write it with the man who was the document's greatest defender, the author of most of *The Federalist Papers*?"

"I believe they call it poetic justice."

The next morning, John and Mercy met with Director Sowell. He nodded on hearing their news. He was not surprised of John's request to return to Heaven. Of all the founders, for all his study, John seemed the least acclimated to modern life, or anyway the least healed over his history.

"I've no idea how to return you to your heavenly perch," said the Director.

"I imagine I can handle that," said John.

But when the Director heard about the switch in authorship, a partnership between Mercy the critic and Alex the defender, he laughed.

"That should make the final act a document of great passion," he said.

"Actually, I asked Alex about it this morning, and he laughed too. But I think John is right, such a collaboration should make for some, what do they call it now, literary fireworks?"

On reaffirming that John really wanted to leave, the Director agreed to engage actor Henry Thomas—if interested. Then he suggested a farewell dinner for the original heavenly cast.

"I suggest we dine in Old Town Alexandria at Gadsby's Tavern, where they have been serving guests in an elegant colonial dining room since 1770. Will and the general can join us there, and afterward, Will can return to the Georgetown Airbnb to take over your room."

"He would leave the General's side?" asked John.

"In the last few days, Will Lee has become a new man," said the Director. "He seems to want to experience life as a contemporary American, not as a figure of history. And I believe he is taking pleasure from being recognized. People who remember his performance at the Kennedy Center ask to pose with him for a photo. Those enchanted by his dance with Usha Vance at the White House shake his hand and ask what it was like. It is, in short, much more like Heaven."

"Was that your plan all along, to tempt us with earthly pleasures as a reward for our achievements as founders?" she asked with a smile.

"I'm not sure I anticipated that—no one could have predicted how historic and modern influences would combust this way. But it does please me greatly, Mrs. Warren. It does indeed."

PART III

The Constitution

"The American war is over, but this is far from being the case with the American revolution."

—Dr. Benjamin Rush, 1787

SCENE 17

DAR

For the speech, Priscilla suggested Mercy wear a navy pantsuit with white trim—"A classic look," she said. Mercy thought the outfit handsome, though she doubted it would get as many compliments as she received for the satin embroidered gown she made for her wedding in 1754.

Sitting in a big white chair, alone on the stage except for Ben Franklin, who was subbing for Director Sowell, she was nervous. But as she looked out at the vast audience, she was grateful. All these women, by their membership announcing a pride and interest in history, many of them bringing their menfolk—the validation of it all made her smile. Tom and Alex had clashed in politics after the Revolution—the Republican who loved personal liberty and the Federalist who understood government power—but they were sitting together in the audience, united in their admiration for her. Separately, each had called her a genius. She smiled at them. She thought her two Jameses—brother James Otis Jr. and husband James Warren—would be proud.

"I know you were expecting the director of the National Archives, our esteemed Thomas Sowell," Ben said on introducing himself. "Doctors have advised him to moderate his schedule, and as I was a delegate at the Constitutional Convention, it seemed a natural substitution.

"As you may have surmised, I am the actor playing Benjamin Franklin in the upcoming One Big Beautiful Reenactment. In that role, my path in life often crossed with that of Mrs. Warren's writings, and I am honored to be here to find out, essentially, why no one knows who she is."

There was laughter at this.

"I want to start with the question of legacy," said Ben. "Later we will hear about the beginning—your upbringing, the unique circumstances that led to your education and writing career, your passion for the Revolution and disdain for the monarchists. But for now, I want to begin at the ending: Why do you think you are not better known in the eyes of history?"

"I have thought about that question much since my arrival. After all, I wrote passionately in favor of a Bill of Rights, and I wrote the first history of the Revolution. I am rarely mentioned."

"I've noticed. But why?"

"The historians who write about the founding tend to disparage the war as not really revolutionary, unlike the bloodier French Revolution. I did not fit their narrative. It still astonishes me we defeated the greatest empire in the world. I do not agree with those second-guessing chroniclers who dispute the motives of the founders, arguing the war was fought to protect their wealth or their right to own slaves. The war was fought to protect our liberty."

Tom was on his feet, leading a chorus of applause. Mercy blushed.

"It seems we have started in the right place," said Ben. "Let us go back to the beginning."

They talked about her growing-up years in Barnstable, Massachusetts, near Cape Cod, and about how her older brother had encouraged her mind and convinced their father—called the colonel for his role in the Indian Wars—that Mercy should also be allowed to learn with her brothers. Their tutor was their uncle, Jonathan Russell, a reverend and a teacher of the classics.

"I was encouraged to read English, but not Greek or Latin. That was reserved for boys preparing for college. I read the great English authors—Shakespeare and Pope and Milton."

"Did you have a favorite?"

"My favorite book was Sir Walter Raleigh's *History of the World,* which he began writing while imprisoned in the Tower of London. Apparently, he had annoyed the queen by secretly marrying one of her ladies in waiting without Elizabeth's permission."

One man shouted, "God bless the queen." A few giggles came from the audience.

Mercy smiled. "In any event, something in the lessons, something in the reading, made me yearn to express myself, and I began to write."

"At one point you, and the Otis family and Warrens, were all staunch loyalists. What happened? What turned you against the Crown?"

"I can answer that question in one word: Hutchinson."

"Thomas Hutchinson, the Crown's royal governor of Massachusetts."

Mercy nodded.

"Parliament passed all kinds of bills levying taxes on the colonies. Hutchinson carried them out with zeal, against the grain of public opinion. In 1765, the Stamp Act for the first time taxed us directly—not the thirteen colonial governments but the people who lived there—for everything printed in the colonies—including pamphlets protesting the Stamp Act!"

"Why do you think the Stamp Act was such a lightning rod, if you'll excuse the expression?"

There were a few laughs in the audience at this mention of Ben's great experiment.

"I sometimes think the problem was one of perspective. We colonists thought of ourselves as British citizens, due all the rights and courtesies of citizenship. They thought of us as British subjects obliged to obey. No one knows this better than you, Dr. Franklin."

"Ah, yes, you refer to my trip to London."

Turning to the audience, he added, "The Commonwealth of Pennsylvania sent me to convince Parliament to repeal the Stamp Act. Three hours as a witness before some of the most hostile men of power was even more nauseating than the sea voyage. It was all very humbling."

Some in the audience laughed. Mercy smiled.

"When Dr. Franklin came home from London with a Stamp Act repeal in his pocket, there was much joy and pride. Until then, we had been thirteen colonies with our own industries, our own customs, and, later, our own constitutions. That is when, I believe, we became a nation, when we saw that we had more power standing together than we did as thirteen separate entities."

"One thing I learned on that trip was that we had only a few friends in Parliament. One of these was Isaac Barré. He called us 'Sons of Liberty actuated by principles of true English liberty, carving British colonies out of an uncultivated and inhospitable country.' Sam Adams adopted the name for his rebellious militia."

"Yes, they created a flag of their own, saying 'No Taxation Without Representation.' After the Tea Act was enacted in 1773, they organized a protest. Hutchinson refused permission for ships in Boston Harbor to depart without off-loading their tea. Sons of Liberty responded with the Tea Party. When Boston dumped the tea, it electrified colonies as far away as Virginia and South Carolina, which also had ports. After all, if the British could attack colonists in Boston, might not they be next? Two years later, at Lexington and Concord, Sons of Liberty became a real army."

"Historians believe the Sons of Liberty met in the Warren parlor so Mrs. Warren could attend."

She laughed then, and it made her blush.

"Goodness, that never occurred to me! Perhaps James did offer our parlor because he knew of my passion for politics and wanted me to be able to attend. What a dear man. And how lovely of today's historians to teach me something I did not know!"

"I remember your husband as a very serious patriot."

Mercy looked down, and tears formed at the corners of her eyes.

"During the war, we were often apart. He was quartermaster to the Continental Army. I saved our letters, which passed to our great, great grandson Charles Warren, who became a historian. Charles must have published them because they are all over the internet now."

There was laughter at this from the audience.

"I remember one letter where he wrote from Boston, 'This day I have read one Excellent Sermon & heard two others. What next can I do better than write to a Saint?'"

Some in the audience sighed. One woman shouted, "What did you write back?"

"I wrote something like, 'If there were more men on the Continent of your spirit, we might sooner defy the power of Britain.' I guess I was political even in my love letters."

"And were you joining the mobs by paper, hurling rhetorical slings into the public square?"

"Only indirectly, Dr. Franklin. By then I was raising our children—James and I had five children in ten years, and they were all boys!" There were groans in the room. "I wrote some plays and poems objecting to royal authority in the colonies in philosophical terms but always under cover of a pen name. I certainly I did not take up my pen again until the Constitutional Convention in 1787, when I wrote a blistering pamphlet, *Observations on the New Constitution* under the pen name 'a Columbian Patriot.' That is when I joined the debate over the war and its meaning."

"I remember you enraged a lot of people. Whatever did you say?"

"The Federalists, led by George Washington and Alexander Hamilton,"—here she smiled at Alex—"they were proud they had created a system of checks and balances—spreading power among the executive, legislative, and judicial branches. It was Montesquieu's great idea, and the men who wrote our Constitution thought it would protect the republic, as each branch would police the others. I saw it as a dangerous experiment that could topple the very liberties we fought for in the Revolution. I remember writing, 'The glorious fabric of liberty is shaken to its foundation.' That might be another reason history has forgotten me. Florid language."

Some in the audience laughed.

"Dr. Franklin, I am sure you remember the ratification debate was fierce—Massachusetts almost rejected the document, as did Virginia. New York went along only because a majority of states had already approved it. But you would not know it from my prose. I cited the Roman Empire and the French Enlightenment and begged the states to reject the document. Without a bill of rights, I feared, the men and women who fought the war would be forgotten, and the central government would become big and oppressive, choking citizens of their breath."

"And now? What do you think now?"

"I had a long discussion of this with President Trump recently at the White House. He is surely a Federalist, believing in the sanctity of the presidency. But he agrees that the dissidents were smart to worry about the rights of the states and the citizens, the very taproot of our nation's soul. After all, when Mr. Jefferson's Declaration of Independence called for 'the consent of the governed,' surely he meant that the people must influence the government."

"I know that you have only recently encountered contemporary America, but I wanted to ask for your thoughts on the status of women. Do you think feminism has liberated them?"

"Ah, you saved the thorn for last," she smiled. "It is marvelous, and unexpected, to see women in positions of power and acclaim. That is a tribute to their brains and the freedom America has afforded them to use them. But the nation's social fabric, in my observation, has frayed. We were raised to believe in God, family, and country. Now, it seems, society is organized around self-indulgence, and children are taught that their feelings are more important than their morals. I find it fascinating that girls and women are encouraged to pursue athletic careers—something unheard of to my generation—but horrifying that men are allowed to compete against them. And I suspect that if we privileged God and family, where all pitch in for the sake of the whole, over feminism, where it seems each woman is for herself, our society would more often wear a smile."

"Goddamned MAGA!" screamed one man. "You're just a Christian nationalist!"

Security escorted him out.

"No one has ever called me those before," said Mercy. "Whatever do they mean?"

"They mean you're speaking the truth!" called a man's voice from the audience.

A funny thing happened then. Several people rose and began to clap, then more and more, until Mercy Otis Warren received a standing ovation. She stood, waved, and bowed.

"This might be a good time for audience questions," said Ben. "We have microphones set up in each aisle, and if you line up, I will call on you in the order of your arrival. Yes, please, the woman in the purple suit."

"My name is Shannon Zingle. I'm an optometrist from Franklin, Tennessee, outside Nashville, which was named for you, Dr. Franklin. I'm curious, Mrs. Warren, have you had a chance on this visit to talk to Vice President Vance? Would you call him a Federalist?"

Now it was Ben's chance to laugh.

"As you Americans like to say, that is delicious," he said. "Mrs. Warren?"

"I, too, think this question poses an interesting dilemma. Like President Trump, yes, I think Vice President Vance believes in a national government. But given his background—coming up in the Appalachian part of the country that was mired in poverty because of federal policies—I have no doubt he is also keen to protect the states and citizens from an intrusive central government. The Constitutional Convention came down to a war between the big states and the small, between the urban leaders and the farmers, between Federalists who lobbied to make the central government strong and the Dissidents who wanted to keep power in the hands of the states. Maybe Trump has managed to combine the hopes of the all the founders. And maybe Vance will too."

He scanned the audience. "Next question. The woman in gray."

"Mrs. Warren, how are you?"

"I am fine, ma'am. Everyone on earth calls me Mercy now."

"After hearing about your love for your husband, James, I think I'll stick with Mrs. Warren."

Mercy smiled.

"My name is Karen Farmer, and I'm from Detroit, Michigan. I was the first Black woman ever to be admitted to the DAR. I was able to trace my heritage to Private William Hood of Erie, Pennsylvania, who served during the Revolutionary War. My question to you is, why do you think the Constitutional Convention did not abolish slavery?"

"I have pondered this question deeply. In his draft of the Declaration of Independence, my friend Thomas Jefferson wrote in his list of grievances that King George had forced on us a barbaric trade in human beings. In those days, the whole world was guilty—the Dutch, the Persians, the East Africans, even our own Native Americans. All made money from slavery. It does seem as if the Constitutional Convention was a perfect venue for America to announce that it was not only freeing itself from the shackles of oppression by another nation but from the savagery of slavery. But as my friend Alexander Hamilton has noted, the thirteen colonies would not have held together as a nation without slavery—which was the economic engine of both North and South. President Lincoln famously said, 'This Government cannot endure, permanently half *slave* and half *free.*' So from the Stamp Act in the 1760s to the Civil War in the 1860s, it took a hundred years for America to do right by all its citizens. And I, for one, am grateful we finally did."

Karen nodded and sat down.

"We have time for one final question. Yes, the lady in pink."

"You are due soon?" asked Mercy.

"In two weeks, but I didn't want to miss this event. My name is Erica Gonzales, from Alexandria, Virginia. Two questions for you. First, if my baby is a girl, may I name her Mercy?"

Gasps of wonder and some applause greeted this announcement.

"I would be honored," said Mercy.

"My second question is similar to the last. Why do you think it took so long for women to get the vote?"

"This is a difficult one for me, because I never thought the vote was as important as moral influence. My friend Abigail Adams was much more interested in the franchise than I. She even wrote her husband, John Adams, not to 'forget the ladies' in writing the Massachusetts state constitution. If the men writing the laws did forget the ladies, Abigail predicted, they would 'foment a rebellion.' She was right, I think. They did rebel, and now they have the vote. But my brother, my father, and my husband all respected my views and even wrote them into their own pronouncements. I did not mind writing under a pen name because I knew I would have more authority that way. I was long passed from the Earth before any of my writings—even the eyewitness history of the Revolution—was credited to me. But I was not alone. Like me, Alexander Hamilton, James Madison, and John Jay wrote *The Federalist Papers* under the pen name Publius, a Roman aristocrat who helped overthrow the monarchy in favor of the Roman Republic. They were not credited with authorship until after the flames were extinguished, the debate long settled. We had power long before we had the vote. Yes, the vote for women added the honor of full citizenship. But always we had influence."

"I have a question," said Ben. "What do you consider your most important contribution?"

Mercy looked pained.

"Is that really for me to say?"

"Shall I answer it for you?"

She nodded.

"I believe your greatest gift to the nation was to call John Adams a monarchist."

"Dr. Franklin, why would you say such a thing?"

"Because his presidency never recovered, and neither did his reputation. Justifiably."

A man in the audience yelled, "At least he was a man of God. Why on earth did you people take religion out of the Constitution?"

"Dr. Franklin?"

"You are right," Ben said. "The Declaration pins its call for independence with Britain not on man but on God. The very words, 'endowed by their Creator with certain inalienable rights,' suggest a God-centered framework. But we who wrote the Constitution had a different task. We were trying to craft a blueprint for governance, 'to form a more perfect Union, establish justice, ensure domestic tranquility, provide for the common defense, promote the general welfare, and secure the blessings of liberty.'"

Mercy nodded.

"I remember that Rhode Island, founded by Puritans, was so upset that the new Constitution did not explicitly protect religious freedom they did not join the union for than a year after the Constitution was ratified."

"Yes, some of my fellow delegates in the Constitutional Convention kept calling the state 'Rogue Island.' Soon after he was sworn in, President Washington, wrote a letter to the Touro Synagogue in Newport in 1790, assuring them the government would not interfere with individuals in matters of conscience and belief. You could say God was not in the text, but in our hearts."

Applause boomed in the auditorium, at least in many parts of it. Ben thanked the DAR for the invitation, and Mercy for agreeing to participate. Tom and Alex came up and gushed.

"How did it feel?" asked Tom.

"I am still not sure what James would say about my taking such a public role. It seems—I am not sure how to put it—a bridge beyond our times."

"Exactly!" said Alex. "That is the gift we have been given with this unexpected journey to the America of our future, to live in the twenty-first century. I believe your husband and your brother would both be thrilled that you had come out behind your pen names to claim your place in history, on a par with men on a public stage."

As they exited, Mercy and Tom overheard a conversation from a couple leaving the event.

"How impressive was that actress," said the woman. "To have memorized all those details."

"That was no actress," said the man. "Nothing has convinced me more than this event that these so-called actors are here on loan from Heaven. And what a gift that is."

The woman looked up at him, a look of astonishment on her face.

"You're kidding, right?"

"I've never felt anything more deeply—other than when I met you. We who are beneficiaries of God shining his light on this nation are connected to her. And we need to honor her."

"But how?"

"Perhaps we should go to church on Sunday."

He kissed her then, and they disappeared into the crowd.

Mercy smiled, looked at Tom and said, "For my next trick I will convert you."

SCENE 18

Tom's Library

Once he moved into the Airbnb, Will took advantage of every opportunity to sample everything that his roommates and Georgetown had to offer. He accompanied Tom on his long walks every morning. As part of his transition from Mount Vernon, he also asked Ben for tech advice.

"Dr. Franklin, can you teach me to use social media?" said Will. "I want to write a blog."

"Only if you call me Ben."

"I doubt I will be able to do that. But I would be happy to thank you in my first post."

They sat together at the dining room table near the window. Ben demonstrated how to set up an account on X, Instagram, and TikTok. He pulled up Grok, which made an emoji of Will's image.

"There are a lot of Will Lees," said Ben. "Do you want to be @WillLee1776?"

Will thought for a while, then smiled.

"What about @TheOriginalWillLee?"

Ben smiled.

They worked together for a few hours. By the time they were done, Will knew how to post items on the three platforms, monitor the internet for content, and make friends and followers.

"I notice you seem to write long," said Ben.

"Funny—I who was once a slave with no education."

"That might be a great angle for your first post. But I wonder, would you also like me to set up a blog on Substack for you."

"Substack?"

"A platform for serious writers. Sometimes they refer to is as long-form journalism."

"Yes to Substack. I may not have been a Founding Father, but I sometimes feel like I was schooled by those who were. It amuses me how much I enjoy writing."

They titled his blog *The Original Will Lee*. Ben cleaned out the laptop John had left behind and installed Will's passwords. From that moment, Will seemed to come to life, not as a figure of history but on modern terms, as a man smack in the middle of a tech revolution.

"This writing assignment has enlivened you," said Mercy.

"How so?"

"You seem more outgoing. Before, it was as if you were standing on the General's shoulders for a better view. Now you seem much taller, more your own man."

"I like that."

He wrote about his transition from being a slave for George Washington to being a guest at Donald Trump's White House. He admonished the Black Congressional Caucus for banning Republican members. He wrote about his visit to the Martin Luther King Jr. Memorial with the civil rights leader's niece, Alveda King, and their conversation about the content of a man's character being more important than the color of his skin. He wrote about Supreme Court Justice Antonin Scalia's view that much of the 1960s civil rights legislation had been subverted, "from a guarantee that race or sex *will not* be the basis for discrimination" to a promise that they "*often will.*" To his surprise, and Ben's, within weeks, he had 250,000 followers.

"My personal liberation," he said to Tom one day as they were walking.

"If only mine were as easy," Tom said. "I seem to have a cloud over my head on Earth. Many Americans think less of me for having had relations with Sally Hemings. And maybe they are right. But I was thirty-nine when my Martha died, and she made me promise, on her deathbed, not to take a new wife. She did not want our children raised, as she was, by a stepmother."

"My first wife died too. Margaret was a free Black woman in Philadelphia, who worked as a paid seamstress and washerwoman for the General's household there. During the war, I would see her when she cooked for Continental Army officers. The General was not keen on our marriage but acquiesced because I had served him with fidelity for so long. I suspect he feared I might escape from slavery to Canada with her. I never had the chance. She died on her way to Mount Vernon."

"I am sorry for your loss," said Tom. "Tell me something. What was it like to be a slave for George Washington?"

Will was silent for a long time.

"I was a house servant, on account of my being born of an enslaved woman and a white plantation owner, so I was shielded. There were hardships—family separations were the worst—and there were moments of laughter and song. But do you know the hardest part?"

Tom shook his head.

"Listening to you Whites talk of freedom, declaring that all men are born equal. I heard one speaker say the colonists were like slaves under the boot of British tyranny. It made me hopeful that Whites would sympathize with our plight. But they thought freedom applied only to them."

The silence was even longer then. Finally, Tom spoke.

"Since my arrival here, I have given this matter much thought. My parents and grandparents, who came to this country from Britain, brought the memory of servants and slaves with them. It was part of my inheritance too. It seemed normal to me. But I knew it was wrong. That is why I slammed King George for importing it here, in the Declaration's first draft. Slavery had no business here. As you and Alex so poignantly noted, slavery was inconsistent with our values. Now I wonder if it would have been better to fight our Civil War at the beginning."

"Alex says you could never have created this country, at least economically, without the South. As Lincoln said, we could not long survive half slave and half free. But maybe not enough people thought like that at first. Maybe it took time to build consensus."

"The abolitionists, here and in Britain, often mocked us for it. Samuel Johnson, a great writer, once asked, 'How is it that we hear the loudest yelps for liberty among drivers of Negroes?'"

"The essential question," agreed Will. "John's wife also opined on this, did she not?"

"She did. Abigail wrote him a letter. He showed it to me. As I recall, she called it 'a most iniquitous scheme to fight ourselves for what we are daily robbing and plundering from those who have as good a right to freedom as we have.' She was a spirited woman."

They walked in silence for a bit. Then, Tom said, "I feel a need for coffee. How about you?"

"I know just the place," said Will. "I found it the other day, and it is on Thomas Jefferson Street!"

"Name?"

"Baked and Wired. I was looking for a place to find both coffee and an internet connection."

"You are a man of many talents."

Once they had ordered—a latte for Will, black coffee for Tom—they sat. Will eyed the pastries, each looking more delicious than the last.

"Pastry?" asked Tom.

"They look good, but I've noticed a few pounds creeping up on my body. I have an image now."

"How did you manage to attract so many—what do they call them—followers?"

"How did you?"

"I have never written a blog."

"I meant back in the day. After you wrote the Declaration."

"My authorship of that document was not widely known during my lifetime. It was written into history after my death in 1826. I had left instructions for it to be mentioned on my tombstone, and historians came to credit me. But if this news attracted followers, I would not have known."

"What a crime!" said Will. "In my view your Declaration was the most sublime, the most elegant, the most important piece of paper ever produced, ever!"

"In spite of what Mercy calls our original sin?"

"Yes, despite that. Surely you know how many slaves resonated to your message that 'all men are created equal.' Mum Bett won her freedom from similar words in the Massachusetts

Constitution. Several slaves signed up to fight in the Continental Army—the General frowned on the idea, but I saw them, volunteering for the very promise of freedom, just the idea of it."

"John always worried that freedom was contagious, that it would light a fire under all the people who felt themselves oppressed—slaves, savages, women, even children."

"It did, it seems to me. But it also created a habit. Feeling oppressed is something these Americans today enjoy. It angers me because I knew real oppression. They have no idea."

"You think they should be more grateful?"

"Of course. This whole movement for reparations disturbs me greatly. As Director Sowell likes to say, those who toiled under slavery truly suffered. But their descendants were lucky to be born in this country, with all its riches and opportunities. Their ancestors' burdens accrue to their benefit. They just have to embrace it, to exploit their chances at a great life."

"Small comfort for the slave."

"Which makes his journey such a privilege for me. By the way, may I quote you in my blog?"

"May I see it before you hit the—what do they call it—the send button?"

"Of course. I will have it to you soon."

"Are you coming to the Library of Congress with us today? There is a luncheon in my honor, something of a reunion with the books I gifted to that institution so many years ago."

"I had not responded yet, as I still hesitate to presume the company of the founders. But if you think I would be welcome…"

"I know you would be. I will ask the Library staff to set an additional seat for the luncheon."

Will smiled.

"After all those tables I set, I must admit it is nice to have someone else set a place for me."

The General had opted to stay in Mount Vernon, where the docents had asked him to lead one of the garden tours—and Ben had gone to the Air and Space Museum Center at Dulles Airport, to attend a lecture and special screening of a movie called *Those Marvelous Wright Brothers*.

The rest put on their modern clothes and asked Mr. Debussy to blast the air-conditioning in his car. They were greeted at the Library's front door by Acting Librarian of Congress Todd Blanche, installed by Trump after he fired the previous librarian of Congress, Carla Hayden, for continuing to fund diversity programs at the library after his executive order against them.

"Welcome to the Thomas Jefferson building," Todd said, reaching to shake Tom's hands. "It is an honor to have all of you here. We have arranged a private tour for you, led by our most knowledgeable guide, a man named Emery Woods."

"Good thing Ben is not here," Mercy whispered to Will, who nodded in agreement.

Emery Woods turned out to be a man with a deep voice and a keen interest in art and history. Which, as Will later observed in his blog, was a necessary combination for this tour.

"We begin outside, so forgive me for putting you in the heat a bit longer."

"Even better that Ben is not here," Will whispered to Mercy, who smiled.

"This is the most elaborate Beaux-Arts structure in the United States, a nod to the optimism and exuberance of the Gilded Age. Beaux-Arts architecture flourished in the last quarter of the nineteenth century and exploded in popularity in America when it was showcased at the World's Columbian Exposition in

Chicago in 1893. The first Library of Congress was opened in 1800, inside the US Capitol, but this building was constructed between 1890 and 1897 and magnificently restored a hundred years later. Its dome was originally gilded with twenty-three-carat gold leaf, but that was changed after Congress complained that it dimmed its own dome."

"Who is that figure in the fountain?" asked Mercy.

Emery gave her a dubious eye. Like most at the Library, he had heard that some believed these actors might actually be their characters, visiting from Heaven. But he was a tactile person, fascinated by objects, resonating to reality. It unsteadied him to think he was giving a tour of the Jefferson Building to Thomas Jefferson. So he decided to just assume they were actors. He would assess the other question later, in private, perhaps with a glass of chardonnay.

"Neptune, the Roman god of fresh water. Unless there are further questions, I can deliver you back inside to the air-conditioning."

Once inside, he said, "This is the largest library in the world, with nearly twenty-six million books in its collections. Every book published in the United States is here, and more published elsewhere."

When Emery stopped at the Gutenberg Bible. Tom sucked in his breath. All his life, Tom had hungered for books as others hunger for food, sometimes going into debt to acquire them. Now he stood before the first book to roll off a printing press instead of from a monk's quill pen.

"There are only a few Gutenberg Bibles in the world," said Chris. "Even more remarkable, ours was purchased in 1930, at the start of the Great Depression that flattened America economically, and still Congress wanted to make this purchase."

"If Andrew Jackson had not abolished the Second National Bank, perhaps we would have been spared the periodic banking collapse," said Alex.

"Sir, I don't know if you're aware of this, but the Library of Congress holds the largest collection of Alexander Hamilton's writings—from *The Federalist Papers* to his classic *Report on the Manufactures* in 1791 to, sadly, the last letter he wrote to his wife, Eliza, before his duel."

"May I see that?"

The letter was under glass. Alex bent down to see it. Mercy took his arm and began to read.

> This letter, my very dear Eliza, will not be delivered to you, unless I shall first have terminated my earthly career. If it had been possible for me to have avoided the interview, my love for you and my precious children would have been alone a decisive motive. But it was not possible, without sacrifices which would have rendered me unworthy of your esteem. I need not tell you of the pangs I feel, from the idea of quitting you and exposing you to the anguish which I know you would feel. Nor could I dwell on the topic lest it should unman me.
>
> Adieu best of wives and best of Women. Embrace all my darling Children for me.
>
> Ever yours
>
> A H
> July 4, 1804

Tom offered Alex an embrace, a first for both.

The Reading Room was, as Emery had promised, magnificent. Books lined every wall, and desks of polished wood offered readers space to work under the light of green library lamps. There was a hushed reverence in the room, as if everyone was aware of the sanctity of the space, the nobility of its purpose. And the ceiling, so high and elegant, was breathtaking.

Next Emery accompanied them to the Rare Books and Special Collections room, where Jefferson's collection was displayed behind glass walls. Tom noticed a speaker's lectern and seats filling up with people. But as always, his attention was drawn to the books.

"So many books!" said Will.

"How did you collect them all?" asked Alex.

"While in Paris as a diplomat, I snuck away, during the afternoons, visiting all the principal bookstores, turning over every book with my own hands. I bought everything I could that related to America but also everything that was rare and valuable in science, politics and the arts."

"In this collection," said Emery, "we have copies of very rare items—including forty volumes by Marcus Cicero."

"My favorite classical philosopher," said Tom.

"Mr. Jefferson also left us his much-underlined copy of *The Federalist*."

"That I would like to see," said Alex, "if only to see which ones interested him."

"All of them, Alex, all of them. After all, I had to figure out how to counter them."

Alex smiled.

"Ladies and gentlemen, please take your seats," said the librarian of Congress, as he stood at the front of a room filled with donors, public officials, and other guests.

"We are here today to honor the legacy of the man who left us this extraordinary collection, Thomas Jefferson, and to thank Jerry Jones, whose generous family foundation has allowed us to reassemble as much of Jefferson's original collection as possible. I imagine most of you have heard the story, but I want to repeat it here for posterity's sake. Congress created a library in 1800, for its own research needs, but when, during the War of 1812, the British burned it down, we lost the entire set of books. Thomas Jefferson offered us his 6,487-book collection, which we purchased for twenty-four thousand dollars. I asked my staff to calculate how much that would be worth and it turns out his books were so valuable it would have cost us half a million dollars today.

"There was some pushback—one congressman called it 'an exorbitant expenditure for a dubious hobby'—but Mr. Jefferson, who had always said he could not live without books, replied that Congress should not live without them either. As he wrote to us, 'There is no subject to which a member of Congress may not have need to refer.'"

Tom smiled.

"In 1851 there was another fire—the British had nothing to do with this one—and it destroyed two thirds of the Jefferson volumes. Ever since, we have tried as an institution to find copies of the works he wanted to pass down to us. And no entity has done more in that effort than the Gene and Jerry Jones Family Foundation. They have committed resources and talent to the hunt for vintage books that had once lined Thomas Jefferson's bookshelves. Whenever we heard from an archivist or a rare book collector, I would call Jerry Jones and his first question was, "How much money do you need?" No equivocation, no quibbling. This is a man, a family, who revere the legacy we honor today. Jerry, I wonder if you would like to come up and say a few words?"

Jones had a big smile on his face as he approached the microphone.

"When you're the owner of the Dallas Cowboys football team, you get a surprising amount of pushback," he began. "Players, coaches, and fans don't necessarily quiet their opinions in deference to mine. I suppose that's what our founders bequeathed us—a sort of messy right to free speech. No matter how many Superbowl rings I win, this will always be my proudest achievement. Because," and here he looked at Tom, "Thomas Jefferson gave eloquent voice to the instincts of an ambitious people who hated tyranny. We owe him everything."

Applause was thunderous, many in standing ovation.

Todd Blanche returned to the microphone, encouraging all the guests and patrons to head to the luncheon to be held on the second-floor mezzanine.

"Wow, great table décor," said Will, as he eyed the gold-bordered chinaware and crystal glasses.

Before Tom sat down, he was approached by a man who introduced himself as Clyde Hemings Jefferson.

"I'm Eston's sixth great-grandson," he said. "This is my wife, Clarisse."

Tom greeted them.

"You look a little like Eston," he said. "When did the family take my name?"

"During the Civil War. Our ancestors thought your name might save us from slave catchers."

"I hope it helped," said Tom. "I am honored."

"Don't worry about the naysayers, Mr. Jefferson," said Clarisse. "We are very proud of our link to you, one of the most important men in history."

"What my wife hasn't told you is that we named our oldest son Thomas," said Clyde. "He is threatening to read through your entire collection."

"Tell him to start with Cicero. It will set up the rest," said Tom. "And thank you for introducing yourselves. You do me proud."

Will took their photos. He thought he saw a tear in the corner of Tom's eyes.

Once everyone was seated, Blanche rose to speak. But Alex came up and whispered to him.

Blanche nodded.

"The gentleman to my right has asked to make the first toast," he said.

A hush fell on the room. Alex rose, glass in hand.

"I know many of you think we are but actors here for the Big Beautiful Reenactment. And some may even be open to the idea that we are the spirits of the men and women we represent. Either way, as you know, Mr. Jefferson and I were not the best of friends in life. Certainly, over the National Bank, and in our party affiliations, we were on opposite sides of many debates. But I want to say publicly here how much of a debt we owe to the man who collected all these books. What an impressive gift it was for Mr. Jefferson to collect and for Mr. Jones to preserve. So. I'd like to raise a glass—as I put my dueler's gun down—to honor the Man from Monticello."

Tom raised his glass and smiled at Alex.

Later, Tom and Alex stayed up until midnight talking. Some of their earlier disagreements had hardened into conviction. But many were surprisingly amenable to healing.

The next day, *The Original Will Lee* published a blog post about events at the Library of Congress and what they said about America's heritage. The post drew one million views.

SCENE 19
Protests

Priscilla was asleep, that deep space of dreams, when suddenly her phone wakened her.

"Miss Babcock, this is Jim in security. I'm afraid there's a problem at the Archives."

"What kind of problem?" Something told her she would need coffee for this conversation. She put the phone on speaker and walked to the kitchen to make her morning Nespresso.

"Protestors have descended on the museum. They are blocking every entrance."

"What are they protesting?"

"Trump. The Founding Fathers. ICE. I saw one sign that read 'We Want Our History Back.'"

"Oh dear," said Priscilla, who generally sympathized with civil rights protests and had even marched in the women's march herself after Trump's first election. But now she was horrified. How would the actors get into the building for rehearsals? Would protestors turn into a mob that would destroy the nation's foundational documents? Would the OBBR have to be canceled?

"Have you contacted the Director?"

"He was not answering his phone. My supervisor thought you would be the right person to call because of the OBBR and all."

"Yes, thank you. Do they seem violent? Is there a danger they will break through the barriers to damage the place?"

"We are concerned," said Jim. "We have requested reinforcements, but that order would have to come from the White House. We are reaching out to them now. One option is the National Guard. Another is the military. Either way, we feel we need to clear the place."

"Oh, my goodness. Thank you for letting me know. I'll call the Director."

He answered on the seventh ring, sounding groggy and distant.

She briefed him on everything she knew.

"Sounds like our security team is on it. Not sure what more we can do."

"But, Mr. Director, do you want the National Guard to clear the protestors from the entrances? The optics, that our heritage is under military control, might not be the image you want to convey."

"That's the president's call, Miss Babcock. And he has a good sense of history. I understand what you are saying—that we don't want to make martyrs of these ahistorical, well-funded social justice faux warriors. But neither do we want to leave unprotected our most precious inheritance from the founders. You were right to call, and you are right to infer that I catch up on my sleep some other time. I'll get in touch with the White House now and ask for a meeting."

Priscilla paused a moment to see if he would invite her to join such a meeting, but he did not. Maybe someday, if she were promoted to the Director's role, she could sit in on such history.

"Do you think we should cancel the rehearsals?"

"When were they scheduled for?"

"Today at 10 a.m."

"That would be prudent. Much will depend on whether the White House decides to clear the streets immediately or let the hooligans bellow for a few hours until their lungs give out. I'll call you when we have a decision."

Her first call was to Mercy at the Airbnb, where the founders were having breakfast, except for Tom, who was out for his morning walk, and the General of course, at Mount Vernon.

"Oh dear," she said, "how unfortunate."

Priscilla could hear the men in the background asking her what was going on.

"Mrs. Warren, do you know how to put me on the speaker?"

"No, Miss Babcock, but I suspect Ben does."

She handed her iPhone to Ben, and within seconds, they could all hear one another. Priscilla briefed them and told them not to come to the building until she advised that all was well.

Ben looked irritated.

"With all due respect, Miss Babcock, we have never run from a fight in our lives. You could even argue that we best known for charging into the fire, even when the odds were against us."

"Yes, of course, Dr. Franklin, and it is a reputation you have earned proudly. But I'm afraid we cannot risk your safety. You are too precious to the nation and to this performance."

"I seem to recall something in Tom's Declaration about the pursuit of happiness," said Ben. "And I'd like to say it would make me happy to mingle among the protestors, to talk reason to these uninformed Americans, to appeal, as President Lincoln might say, to their better angels."

"Normally, I would agree with you. But these protestors are paid by outside groups to carry signs designed for them, with messages that reflect the group's agenda. The protestors may or may not agree with the cause they are promoting. They are paid actors in a performance of their own."

As she said this, Priscilla thought back to all the protests of the last few years. How naive she had been to think them organic.

"What a terrible commentary on our political discourse!" said Alex. "Maybe the culture should embrace anew the art of dueling. Honor is something to take pride in, to defend."

"At the very least, honor is not something to sell for money," said Will. "I would like to give these protestors a piece of my mind too. They have no idea how lucky they are to be Americans."

Priscilla rubbed her eyes, aware that she was getting nowhere.

"I'll tell you what. I'll let the Director know of your desire to, well, interact with the protestors. Can you sit tight, at least for the morning, until I confer with him?"

"I suppose we can," said Mercy. "Though I have not known boys to sit for that long."

After Priscilla hung up, they contemplated how to spend the day.

"How about we go to the American History Museum?"

"It would be amusing if we learned something new," said Mercy.

"Exactly what I have enjoyed most about this visit," said Alex. A faraway look entered his eyes. "That and the company of beautiful women."

"Where are we going?" Tom asked as he came in from his walk along the Potomac.

"I will call Uber," said Ben. "I imagine Mr. Debussy is busy with the Director at the White House."

"I gather we are not going to rehearsals?"

"Not yet, although I plan to ask the Uber driver to drive us by the Archives so we can at least see the protests from a distance."

"What are they protesting?"

"Us," said Mercy. "They claim we're on the wrong side of history."

"We are the British now?"

Ben smiled.

"Can you request a large van?" asked Alex. "We'll need the room, and it might protect us from the riffraff."

Ben sat in front with the driver, Tom and Will sat in the row behind them, Mercy and Alex in back.

"A good thing John has already departed," said Tom. "I can just hear him making some snarky remark about the 'seditionists.'"

"From what Miss Babcock told us, these are less seditionists than hired actors," said Mercy. "The import of John's patriotism would probably be lost on them."

"I for one am glad the General is not here," said Will. "He would definitely call out the troops."

Ben told the driver they were going to the American History Museum but would like to pass the Archives on their way.

"The roads are closed on account of the protests," said the driver, a man named Mohammed.

"We're visiting from out of town," said Mercy. "We only want to see their signs."

The driver sighed, saying, "I'll get you as close as I can."

Mohammed came to a checkpoint at Ninth Street NW and Constitution Avenue. He leaned out to seek permission for a quick drive-through. The policeman poked his head in the car. Ben paled.

"Sergeant Bilk, how nice to see you again," he said, with false cheerfulness.

"You again! I should have known your type. Always looking for trouble, aren't you?"

"In three centuries, no one has ever reacted to me as you have, sir. I am here with friends, most of whom you met at the Wax Museum weeks past. We want to look at the protestors' signs."

The sergeant looked in the back, disapproval written on his face.

"Technically, this road is not yet blocked. We're waiting on word from the White House. I suppose I can allow you to drive from here, along Constitution Avenue, if you exit at Seventh Street. I'll call ahead to the detail there and tell them to allow you through. But if I see so much as an arm hanging out this car window, you are all going to jail, and this time, I'll add terrorism charges so you will be there for a very long time. Not you, driver—you just make sure you get them safely out of this zone."

With that, Mohammed rolled up his windows and proceeded slowly along Constitution Avenue.

"Sergeant Bilk reminds me of Governor Hutchinson," said Mercy. "Always spewing hatred."

Will, Alex, and Ben pulled out their phones and began to take pictures of the protestors.

"Look at that sign—'Mexico for the Mexicans.' I wonder what that means?" asked Tom.

"Maybe the Mexicans here want their land back, like the Indians," said Will.

"When did we acquire Mexican lands?" asked Tom.

"It was before the Civil War," said Alex. "Mexico went to war with us, we won, and in the treaty after the war, we paid them fifteen million dollars for California, Texas, and the states in between."

"Civil unrest is the worst kind," said Ben. "It suggests that the nation is not well. As I often said, 'Only a virtuous people is capable of freedom.'"

"I always worried about that too," said Tom. "It is always the spirit of a people that preserves a republic in vigor. Degeneracy killed the Roman Empire."

"Is that what you think happened, that the people have turned corrupt?" asked Mercy. "That is what John always said, too, that the government we created would only work for a moral people."

"Calvin Coolidge too," said Alex. "He was one of the accidental presidents, a vice president who became chief executive after President Harding died in 1923."

"I read that he had a wry sense of humor," said Tom.

"He did," said Alex. "They called him Silent Cal because he spoke little. A woman sat down beside him at a White House dinner and told him she had bet a friend that she could get him to say three words. He replied, 'You lose.'"

"He was a great fan of ours," said Ben. "He once said that we live in an age of science and of accumulation of material things but added, 'These did not create our Declaration. Our Declaration created them. If we are to maintain the great heritage which has been bequeathed to us, we must be like-minded as the fathers who created it.'"

"I wonder why this Calvin Coolidge is not better known," said Mercy.

"Maybe because he held his tongue," said Tom.

"I do not understand how these protestors could hate their own country so," said Will. "This country may have not been born free, but it became so because of righteous reformers."

"Ben is right to say that the nation is not well," said Alex. "If you watch the TV news, it seems like most blue cities—those who did not vote for Trump—are regularly in flames, with paid agitators throwing bombs and homeless people sleeping on the streets."

"Precisely why Trump has the National Guard patrolling DC," said Ben.

"Look at that sign," said Tom. "'The 1619 Project Lives.' Anyone know what that means?"

"There was an effort about five years ago to convince Americans that the first colonialists landed not in 1620, escaping Europe for religious freedom, but in 1619, for slavery," said Will.

"Are we never to stop being punished for having slaves?" said Tom. "Do Americans not know that Africans invented slavery, a global phenomenon with roots deep in antiquity?"

"It does not look like they know much about our history at all," said Alex. "Look at that sign, 'No More Taxpayer Funds for White Colonizer History.' Is that what we have been reduced to—colonizers? We who fought against the powers that tried to colonize us? No wonder God brought us down from Heaven. We must be here to educate them, to set them straight."

Mohammed's eyes, visible in the rear-view mirror, narrowed.

"A figure of speech," Alex added hastily.

"Look at that sign," said Mercy. "'The Founders Were the Patriarchy.' Ooh, and that one, 'End White Privilege, Finish the Revolution.' If they only knew how hard we fought for our rights."

"Or how close we came to being hanged for treason," said Ben. "My goodness, they are hanging Director Sowell in effigy."

"Is he on fire?" said Will.

"It appears so. Can you hear what they're saying? I hesitate to inspire Sergeant Bilk's wrath by opening a window to hear better."

"I think they are saying, 'No Trump! No KKK! No Fascist USA!'" said Tom.

"Maybe they inherited protesting from us," said Mercy.

Suddenly, the van started shaking.

"People are pounding on our vehicle," said Will. "They look angry."

Mohammed sped up, trying to lose the protestors.

"I think it's time we got out of here," he said.

"Long since," said Mercy. "Maybe we should never have come."

Just then, a protestor shouted 'Down with the Founders' and lobbed a Molotov cocktail at a police car. It exploded and crashed in the roof of the car in front of theirs.

As Mohammed tried to speed up, protestors blocked the path, their numbers increasing.

"Hey, it's those actors here for that stupid reenactment," screamed a woman. "Get 'em!"

They were surrounded. Mohammed could not move forward without running anyone over.

"You stole our history," screamed one woman with purple hair. "Trump is a Nazi. He's Hitler. He's using you to hide his homophobia and racism. You should be ashamed!"

"Trans is my founder," said a man wearing a wig and a sequined dress.

"What a travesty," said Tom. "We protested tyranny. They are protesting their own privilege."

"A brilliant point," said Alex. "Perhaps we made the country too wealthy."

"Maybe you were too empowering," said Will. "Seems to me these people are spoiled."

The car started to tilt. Mercy plowed into Alex, who caught her. Ben shook his fist at one protestor with a sign that said "Benjamin Franklin Is a Transphobe."

Sirens rang out. Units from the DC Metropolitan Police descended on the scene, pulling protestors off the van, putting them in handcuffs and forcing them into a police wagon.

"It seems like the police need more muscle," said Alex. "They are treating them so gently."

"I would give them a good beating if I could," said Mercy, "like naughty children."

"That's what the British said of us, remember?" said Ben.

Just then one protestor yanked open the back door handle. Mercy screamed, and Alex pulled her as far toward the opposite door as he could. The protestor grabbed Will by the shoulders, pulling him from the vehicle. Soon Will and his assailant were surrounded by a circle of protestors.

"Go home where you came from, you Oreo. We don't want your kind here," said one.

"And what's with the fancy clothes? Think you're special, huh?" said another.

With that, the first protestor punched Will in the face. Police officers swarmed the area and pulled the attacker off Will's body. Another arrested the assailant. A third got Will back in the car.

Sergeant Bilk knocked angrily on the driver's door, signaling frantically that Mohammed should exit Constitution Avenue. Motorcycle policemen gave protective escort.

There was silence for a long time once the car exited from the scene.

"You OK, Will?" asked Ben.

"Nothing feels broken, though I may have a black eye. It pleases me to know what side I am on."

"Do you think they are really Americans?" said Ben. "Would Americans be this upset at the founding?"

"Surely this is but a small number of them. Look how kind and welcoming people were toward us at the Kennedy Center, the White House, and the Library of Congress," said Mercy. "Maybe there are two Americas—one that shares our principles and one that does not."

"Now that we are safely out of the zone of danger, Mohammed, would you mind if I opened my window?" asked Ben.

"I wouldn't recommend that, sir. It's ninety-six degrees out today. I'll crank up the air-conditioning."

"I told the General this was a swamp, but he was infatuated with the idea of putting the capital in the tropics," grumbled Alex.

The museum was only a few blocks away. Mohammed had to navigate a few blocked streets but managed to deliver them without further injury.

"We would never have navigated without you," said Ben. "Thank you."

Mohammed smiled. "Now I just hope Uber will compensate me for the damage to my car."

"Let the Archives know if they do not," said Ben.

"Lunch first?" said Will. "I'd like a chance to relax over food and calm my nerves."

"I will not be joining you for lunch," Alex said. "I am off for lunch with the lovely Mrs. Blackett."

Ben smiled.

"I wondered why you looked so sporting."

"I did too," said Mercy. "I bet my James would have loved clothes like that."

"Eric Trump was my fashion adviser. He said you can never go wrong with khakis, a white shirt, and a navy blazer."

"Be careful," said Ben. "Remember what happened the last time you took up with a married lady."

"We are just having lunch, Ben," said Alex. "I plan to admire her beauty, enjoy her company, and return faithfully to Eliza above. Ah, my Lyft has arrived."

Mercy asked the men to follow her, stopping at something called Men's Restroom.

"Before we eat lunch, Ben, you and Tom should go into this parlor and tend to Will's injury," she said. "Make sure the eye is cleaned with water. Use your handkerchief to pat it gently. I will wait for you here."

To her surprise, they were in the Room Where Men Rest for some time, as lots of men came in and out. When they finally emerged, Will's eye injury was covered with a mask of some sort.

"What happened?" she asked when they emerged.

"Apparently history does not stop at the restroom door," said Tom.

"We were recognized," said Will.

"When men heard what happened, they condemned the rioters and flew into action," said Ben. "One said his wife always carried a first aid kit when they travel, so he left and got it from her. This mask on Will's eye is called a Band-Aid, and apparently everyone in America has them!"

Will smiled.

"Nothing restored my faith in America more than that crowd of men all helping to fix my eye. But now, I am hungry!"

The cafeteria was enormous, and as it was not yet noon, they had plenty of time to scout out their choices and settle at a nice sunny table near the windows, from which they enjoyed a view of Washington's Monument.

"I am glad the General was not with us," said Will. "He would have been furious. He had clear rules of military engagement. He believed unruly protests would not serve the cause. Few seem to know this, but he did a fair amount of disciplining—even ordering the hanging of deserters."

Ben's phone rang.

"Miss Babcock," he said. "I will put you on speaker."

"Are you OK?" Priscilla's voice asked. "I heard what happened this morning."

"None the worse for wear," said Ben, "though saddened by what we saw."

"Where are you now?"

"American History Museum. Will wanted to sample what astronauts eat in space."

"I am glad you are out of danger. Will, someone told me you were injured. Are you OK?"

"I am restored by the kindness of strangers in applying—they called it first aid—to my eye. And to the anger of many in the Room Where Men Rest when they heard what happened."

Priscilla wasn't sure she understood everything Will said, but she was gratified that he sounded better—at least well enough to attempt to eat that dreadful freeze-dried food.

"Any update on our plans?" asked Ben.

"I've just gotten off the phone with the Director, who's been at the White House all day. The security team has a game plan, which I am not authorized to disclose. However, I can say we are hoping to resume rehearsals in a day or two. I'll let the rest of the cast know."

"I would like to call the General," said Will. "He may be upset when he hears what happened to me. I'd like to reassure him that I am well."

"Of course.

"Do you know if Mr. Debussy will be available to pick us up from the museum in a few hours?" asked Ben. "Speaking for myself, I'd rather not get in an Uber again anytime soon."

"I'll arrange that," said Priscilla.

After lunch, they decided to tour separately and meet up in an hour at the recently restored American flag—tattered in the War of 1812.

Happily, Mr. Debussy was waiting out front when they emerged.

After they piled in, he asked them how they liked the museum.

"Rather an insult," said Ben. "The exhibits merely touched the surface of their subjects. One of them said my lightning rod discovery was 'tainted by oppression.'"

"Tainted by oppression?" asked Tom. "No respect for history, nor even any recounting of history. Just allegiance to a narrative."

"I just looked up the Smithsonian," said Will. "Up popped this executive order that President Trump signed last year."

"What does it say?" asked Mercy.

"'Once widely respected as a symbol of American excellence and a global icon of cultural achievement, the Smithsonian Institution has, in recent years, come under the influence of a divisive, race-centered ideology,'" Will read.

"Any examples?" asked Tom.

"Apparently, at the National Museum of African American History here in the capital, one exhibit proclaims that 'hard work, individualism and the nuclear family are all aspects of white culture.' And at another museum, a video portrays as Jesus a man named George Floyd, a drug addict and career criminal whose death at the hands of police caused riots in 2020."

"A reinvention, much like mine at Monticello and at my memorial."

"Makes me think about history," said Will. "Abolitionists from the early 1800s on wanted to end slavery. They believed, both races, in uplift, in reaching down to raise up the slave population, to teach them to read, to help them thrive. It seems almost as if the current generation of reformers wants to keep them ignorant."

"Eric Trump calls them race hustlers," said Tom. "He told Alex they use American guilt over slavery to unfairly punish white people. Some of these so-called reformers even want current taxpayers to pay reparations to the Blacks, whether their ancestors were slaves or not."

"Are there no Blacks standing up to protest this injustice to White Americans?" asked Will.

Tom smiled.

"Have you met Director Sowell?"

SCENE 20

Arlington Cemetery

Alex borrowed Eric Trump's car—Eric had taught him, and he wanted to test his driving skills. He picked up Ben at the Airbnb, then drove out to Mount Vernon to collect the General.

"Where are the others?" asked the General.

"Mercy is busy with the script. And Tom demurred because little Tommy Blackett has invited him to come to his elementary school for Bring a Hero to Class Day."

The General smiled.

"And Will?"

"Will said he wanted to try the Metro, so Priscilla is showing him the procedures. But he had warned they might be a few minutes late because he wanted to write another blog post first."

"A literary star is born," said the General. "I suppose I should have known. He was a marvel at organizing my papers."

Ben stirred in his seat.

"Alex, you are a better driver than most of our Uber hires," he said.

"Thank you," said Alex. "Perhaps I should act as your guide. We are driving to Arlington Cemetery, which did not open until the Civil War. So many were dying that the Union confiscated two hundred acres of land from Robert E. Lee's estate for a military cemetery."

"I've heard about General Lee—a West Point graduate who resigned the Union cause to lead the Confederate Army for his native Virginia," said the General. "I am related to him by marriage. I think it was Martha's great granddaughter, Mary Anna Custis, who married him. And somewhere I read that they were third cousins, so maybe, through Martha, I am family to him too."

"Their home was originally built by your and Martha's grandson, George Washington Custis, as a memorial to you. Nowadays it is a museum, still looking down at all those Civil War dead."

At the cemetery, Will and Priscilla were waiting for them.

As soon as she had heard about this part of their itinerary, Priscilla asked to be included. Her grandfather, who died in the Vietnam War before she was born, was buried there. She knew him mostly from family lore, from photos—everyone thought she looked just like him—and from the love in her mother's eyes when she spoke of her father.

"How did you get here so soon?" asked the General.

"Priscilla and I took the Metro. It runs underground at high speed. Except when you get to the cemetery, it is above ground, as if the sun was blessing your visit."

"Will was recognized," said Priscilla. "A young lady asked for his autograph."

"Sometimes I think you are the most adaptable of all of us," the General said to Will.

Captain Marjorie Taylor received them in the lobby. The General looked shocked.

"How long have women been fighting in our wars?" he asked.

"Since World War I. It was an unpopular war, fought by the great empires of Europe, and there was a lot isolationist sentiment here that America should stay out of it. Recruitment stalled. So, in 1917, Secretary of the Navy Josephus Daniels allowed women to enroll in the US Naval Reserve Force. Loretta Walsh was the first. She had to sew her own uniform—she took a man's uniform and tailored it. By the time the war ended, twelve thousand women were in the military, the government sewing their uniforms. To date, some three million women have served in the armed services."

"But most of their jobs were away from the battlefield?" asked the General.

"Yes," said Captain Taylor. "And now that the Trump Pentagon has reinforced uniform standards for combat roles, it's even rarer to find a woman on the front lines."

"I forgot how big the cemetery is," said Priscilla.

"Arlington National Cemetery is the final resting place for more than four hundred thousand service members and dependents, an equal number who are here by dint of achievement in politics, art, entertainment, or sport. The cemetery currently covers six hundred acres, with plans for expansion to the south. We draw more than three million visitors a year, with thirty funerals on weekdays."

"Is that a tribute to the popularity of these grounds or to the explosion of our population?" asked Alex.

"Or our frequent entanglement in wars?" said the General.

"All of the above, I suppose," said the captain. "We're stopping first at the Tomb of the Unknown Soldier. As you can imagine, through the ages, one of the consequences of warfare has been large numbers of unidentified dead. Prior to the Civil War, unidentified remains were often buried in mass graves. Here at Arlington, we honor those unidentified soldiers with this tomb. As you can see, there is a twenty-four-hour-a-day honor guard protecting them in death."

"Why do we privilege the unknown?" asked Ben.

"Secretary of Defense Pete Hegseth talked about this on Memorial Day last year." She dug into her pocket for her notes. "I wanted to read you his quote directly because I find it inspiring. He said, 'In America, with our great experiment in self-government, it is fitting that the most honored and closely guarded tomb in the land is that of an anonymous soldier of unknown rank. It is uniquely American that we honor anonymous sacrifice above worldly greatness.'"

Priscilla teared up, thinking about the grandfather she never knew.

"Where are the Vietnam veterans buried?" she asked.

"Their graves are dotted throughout the cemetery, depending on when they died. The one I know about is Corporal Mark D. Marshall, killed in 1969. He's in Section Fifty-One. He was killed in action while serving in Quang Nam, Vietnam. His decorations include the Purple Heart."

Priscilla made a mental note to return to Section Fifty-One.

"Do you have any graves from the Revolutionary War?" asked Will.

"Eleven veterans of the American Revolutionary War are buried in Sections One and Two. These men did not die in battle; all died years or even decades after the war. Originally buried elsewhere, their remains were disinterred and then brought to Arlington for reburial early in the twentieth century. As far as

I know, other than these patriots, the earliest marked graves we have here are from the War of 1812. They were discovered at Washington Barracks and reburied here almost a century later. Next, I'd like to take you to our most visited gravesite."

"Captain Taylor, would you mind if we sat for a bit?" asked Ben. "I am recovering from yoga."

"What he means is that when the lovely Mrs. Blackett instructed us to do the warrior's pose in hot yoga, Dr. Franklin neglected to bend his knee, and this sprained his back," said Alex.

"For your information, Alex, I hurt my back trying to get a better look at the girl next to me."

The captain found them a lovely spot underneath a cover of trees and offered travel water bottles. She looked like she could have welcomed a break too, but she remained standing.

"Interesting, about the female soldiers," said the General. "Remember the soldier who cut off her hair and disguised herself in a uniform? We only discovered her identity as Deborah Sampson after she was wounded the third time, an injury to the chest. Quite a shock to me."

"Given how poorly our army was clothed, I am not surprised she managed it," said Alex. "The one I remember was Margaret Corbin, who took over her husband's cannon after he was killed in the Battle of Fort Washington. She was the first woman to receive a war pension from Treasury."

"I heard about another one," said Will. "Her name was Nancy Hart. Apparently, she was a tall, gangly woman with red hair and a face scarred by smallpox. I imagine life was difficult for her. But she was a real patriot in northeast Georgia backcountry. When British soldiers barged into her home, demanding that she cook for them, she agreed. They put their rifles along the walls and sat down to eat. After they had consumed food and drink, she grabbed one of their guns and opened fire. She killed two and held the rest captive until her husband arrived."

"I never heard that one," said Alex. "American grit in action."

Captain Taylor had reached into her bag for a bottle of water. Now she had positioned herself against a tree to steady her posture. Alex thought she looked pale.

"Are we taxing your patience?"

"It's more that you are taxing my imagination," she said. "I was told you were actors here to perform in the OBBR. But your knowledge about history is profound."

"And you wonder if we are time travelers," said Will.

Captain Taylor looked at him in shock.

Priscilla sympathized with her. She was starting to wonder too. If these people were really sent from Heaven, perhaps she should start going to church again. Just in case. And the way they all talked about the founding was making her more patriotic.

The captain cleared her throat and continued with her prepared script.

"When President Kennedy was assassinated in 1963, he was only forty-six, young and handsome, with a beautiful family and a call to 'ask not what your country can do for you but ask what you can do for your country.' The Kennedys captured the nation's imagination. Rather than take him home to Massachusetts, First Lady Jacqueline Kennedy requested he be buried at here, to make his gravesite more accessible to the public. In the first three years after his death, more than sixteen million visited. Cemetery officials and members of the Kennedy family decided to build a larger and more suitable site on these grounds. It was completed in 1967, and Mrs. Kennedy lit an eternal flame at its center. She was laid to rest next to her husband in 1994."

"When you die young, perhaps you are more appreciated," said Ben. "What do you think, Alex?"

"I was forty-eight years old when Aaron Burr killed me, and I understand my funeral was enormous. I was interred at Trinity Church in New York, very near to Wall Street, the heart of my financial world, where I had a lot of associates and friends. A huge procession moved through the streets, my hat and sword on top of the coffin. Following the caisson carrying the casket was a riderless horse, a gray horse with backward-facing boots in the stirrups. I read later that I was the first American to be afforded this honor. So maybe you are right, Ben."

"And at the gravesite?" asked the General.

"It is a four-columned white marble affair. I think the shock of my death—in a duel at so young an age—prompted Trinity Church to sing my praises in the highest notes. They called me a 'patriot of incorruptible integrity, a soldier of approved valor, and a statesman of consummate wisdom whose talents and virtues will be admired by grateful posterity long after this marble molders into dust.'"

"Believe it or not, my inscription is very plain," said the General. "It is on the grounds of Mount Vernon and reads 'Within this enclosure rest the remains of Genl. George Washington.'"

"But you had that majestic send-off by Major General Henry Lee at your funeral that followed you into history. 'First in war, first in peace, first in the hearts of his countrymen,'" said Alex.

"All the rest is commentary," said Ben.

"Ben, do you know that your funeral was massive?" said Alex. "Some twenty thousand people poured into the streets of Philadelphia, in a city of twenty-eight thousand, more than had ever marched before! Printers and inventors, philosophers and candlemakers, librarians and postmasters. In France, the

National Assembly proclaimed three days of mourning, calling you an inventor of electricity and of nation, someone 'able to restrain thunderbolts and tyrants.' You were our first international star."

"How delightful," said Ben. "Was that Count Mirabeau?"

"I believe it was. Of course, in England, they were less admiring. Acknowledging the arc of your life, from journeyman printer to diplomatic envoy, one London magazine said you created the 'world's first laboratory for the self-made man.' But when it came to the rebellion against the king, that same journal called you 'one of the most dangerous enemies this country ever had.'"

Ben laughed aloud.

"That is as much as I could have hoped for."

The General looked pensive.

"I suppose I should take this moment, Dr. Franklin, to apologize for not attending your funeral. I felt that as the nation's first president, I should avoid venerating the founders for fear of encouraging or signaling a monarchy."

"I understand, General."

"That is why I directed the Cabinet not to wear black armbands for a month in your honor, although France did, and so did Tom. I did not want to make marble statues of us founders."

"And yet that is what has happened, although lately some Americans have toppled you from your perches," said Will. "I wonder, if you founders had not been there—with your passion and your knowledge, your curiosity about the world and fear of its evils—would this nation be what it is?"

There was a silence then.

"A nation has a history and a memory of itself," said Ben. "Perhaps the latter is more potent."

"What about you, Will?" asked Alex. "Where are you buried?"

Will looked at the general, who was not smiling.

"At Mount Vernon with my general," he said, "in the slave portion of the cemetery."

"Unmarked?" asked Ben.

"I imagine," said Will.

They were silent for a time. Priscilla wondered how this actor could have known that.

"If you want to be reburied at Arlington Cemetery," said the general, "I will see what I can do to have you exhumed and interred here. What do you think, Captain Taylor?"

"I have contact information," she said, her voice shaky. "Rules for admission are very strict."

"You doubt my influence could get him in?" asked the general.

Captain Taylor cleared her throat.

"I thought we would next visit the gravesite of Pierre Charles L'Enfant, a soldier in the Continental Army who later designed Washington, DC. He died in 1825 and was originally buried at a friend's farm in Maryland. Almost a century later, at the urging of both French and US officials, he was reinterred here."

"A great man," said the general. "I first met him when he made some pencil portraits of me. And he drew eight plates, as we called them, detailing camp and troop formations, to train the men."

"I recall he served in the war too," said Will.

"He was wounded at the Siege of Savannah and was taken prisoner of war after we surrendered Charleston, South Carolina," said the general. "I managed to arrange a prisoner swap, and he served with me until the end of the war."

"You also hired L'Enfant to build the capital city as I recall," said Will.

"His was a grand vision, to make of this city a majestic site, in the manner of Paris and Rome. But he proved temperamental, and I had to let him go." The general looked intently at L'Enfant's gravesite. "It warms my heart he has been given a place of honor here. He loved this country—when he first arrived, he changed his name to Peter to fit in better."

"We had quite a few Frenchmen fighting with us."

"The Marquis de Lafayette gambled his life to join our fight," said the general. "The French king had forbidden his men to fight for America. Risking his life, Lafayette, at nineteen, left his pregnant wife, traveling in disguise as a woman to avoid detection. His contributions were immeasurable."

"Is he buried here too?" asked Priscilla.

"I am unaware," said the general. "Ben, do you know where he is buried?"

"He is buried in Picpus Cemetery in Paris, under soil from Bunker Hill, his grave marked by an American flag that is continuously maintained in honor of his role in our war."

"As I recall, General, he was like a son to you," said Will.

"Yes. He fought under me at Valley Forge and his leadership was pivotal at securing victory at Yorktown, along with Alex. After the war we corresponded regularly. Lafayette stayed with me at Mount Vernon on his visits to the United States."

"You are being modest," said Alex. "I recall he named his son Georges Washington Lafayette."

The General nodded. Alex thought he saw a tear in his eyes.

Will noticed Ben breathing hard, so he took his arm. Captain Taylor noticed too.

She led them to the lobby, where they could sit and cool off. They all gathered around rows of computers as the captain showed Priscilla how to look up where her grandfather was buried. She vowed to come back to visit him after the OBBR. Will looked up African Americans buried at Arlington. Ben sat quietly, wiping his forehead with her handkerchief. Then the captain escorted them to the entrance, where Alex's car was parked. After they piled in, Ben spoke first.

"Who could have thought death would be so exhausting?"

"And so meaningful," said the General.

"Yes," said Will. "It makes me wonder if death is really about reputation."

"Brilliant," said Alex. "And here, at this intersection of military history and national memory, one million souls marry their reputations to the nation's."

"I wonder, Alex, if we could swing by the Pentagon next," said the General.

"I hear it is quite a process to get inside that building without an appointment," he said.

"Outside is a memorial to the people who died on September 11, 2001, the worst terrorist attack in this country's history. Two airplanes, seized by terrorists, flew into the Twin Towers in New York, huge office buildings that toppled to the ground like pancakes. American Airlines Flight 77 hit the Pentagon, killing one hundred eighty-four people. No need to enter the building. I'd like to see the memorial."

When they arrived, a docent explained that illuminated benches were arranged according to the victims' ages, from Dana Falkenberg, age three, to John Yamnicky Sr., aged seventy-one. On the plane, all sixty-four perished, including the captain, Charles F. Burlingame III, a graduate of the US Naval Academy. Another one hundred nineteen people were killed inside the Pentagon, many burned to death.

The General asked her to point out the captain's bench. He knelt down in prayer, Alex at his side. Will and Ben took photos. Priscilla thought to herself that no actor would have made this stop.

Also—this too was a new thought—she recalled how much of a role war had played in US history. She would talk to the gift shop director about including more memorabilia from wars.

Back in the car, the General said, "Violence breeds more of the same, it seems."

"Biblical," said Will, "as if straight from the Gospel."

SCENE 21

Floating Through the Skies

One day, Miss Babcock called to let them know, as requested, that she had arranged for a charter airplane and offered a ride to all the founders who wanted to explore the skies. Mercy and Alex declined—saying they were too busy with the script—but the others were all onboard.

Captain Sully would fly them to Philadelphia for the day, where they could revisit some of the great landmarks of their political careers, including Independence Hall where both the Declaration of Independence and the US Constitution were crafted. Ben was thrilled.

"A reunion of sorts," he said.

"Yes, with our history," said Tom.

They donned their colonial best—except for Will, who had dressed in his Ralph Lauren. Mr. Debussy drove them to the city's General Aviation Terminal, near Reagan National Airport.

"How lucky you are," he said. "Most often you have to pass through a busy airport and clear security before you can board an airplane. Captain Sully will notify us of your estimated return this evening, and I will be here to pick you up, eager to hear of your trip."

"Welcome to your first flight," said Captain Sully. Outfitted in his pilot's uniform and hat, he shook hands all around. "This is one of the Gulfstream G650s—as efficient and luxurious as most of the business executives who regularly fly them."

Once onboard, a handsome woman in a fitted suit greeted them. Will couldn't stop looking at her.

"This is our stewardess, Marilyn Houston, and she'll be assisting you in any way you need during our flight," said Sully.

"As in Houston we have a problem?" Ben asked her.

"No," she said, smiling. "But do let me know if you need anything. The flight to Philadelphia takes less than an hour. A choice of movies and news channels are on board for your flying pleasure. We will be serving breakfast, choice of French toast or hot oatmeal."

"While we're flying?" asked Ben. "Is that advisable?

"Don't worry, Dr. Franklin. I'm fairly adept with the plates," said Marilyn.

Sully then gave them all a tour of the cockpit.

"It's pretty simple really. This instrument is called the yoke. Lower it and the nose goes down. That's for when we land. For now, I will pull it back so we can lift off. Once we're in the air, if I want to move the plane's position in the sky, I turn it to the right or left and the wings follow my cue. I can also use these thrust levers to climb to cruising altitude."

"And what are those things on the floor?" asked Ben.

"Those are the rudder pedals, to align the plane with the runway."

"And this will work you think?"

Sully laughed.

"Not to worry, Dr. Franklin. I've done this thousands of times. Most of the time we put it on autopilot anyway."

"Autopilot? If you're not driving the plane, who is?"

"A computer."

Ben blanched.

"And God has given us a beautiful, sunny day. Sometimes in the rain it can be a little dicey."

"Dicey?"

"Like throwing dice in a game of chance."

Ashen, Ben returned to his seat, where Marilyn showed him how to buckle his seatbelt. He gazed at her with affection.

"If we lose pressure, these automatic masks will drop from the ceiling. Put them on, pull the cord, and breathe."

"What is in them?" asked Ben.

"Oxygen," she said.

"I have no doubt we are in good hands," said Will, looking admirably at Marilyn.

"Ben, I have never known you to be so reluctant," said Tom.

"Maybe, I am just a terra firma guy," said Ben. "I never liked sea voyages either."

"I find it all marvelous," said the General. "Miss Houston, could you ask the captain if I might ride in the cockpit with him?"

"Certainly," she said.

"The General wants to ride with me?" said Sully. "Perfect."

Once the General was buckled in, the captain went on microphone to announce their departure.

"This is Captain Sully. I'm honored today to be joined in the cockpit by George Washington, the father of our country. We are traveling to Philadelphia, covering one hundred six nautical miles. I'm taking the scenic route, but we'll be there within the hour. Until then, relax and enjoy your flight."

Marilyn sat down and buckled herself in, the engines roared, and the plane tilted up to the skies. Ben closed his eyes and clutched the armrests. Sully tilted the airplane to give them a better view out the right window. His voice boomed over the plane's intercom.

"Our flight path follows the Potomac River, to minimize sound disruption to residents," he announced. "If you look out the windows to your right, you can see how all the memorials look from the skies. Sometimes I think I could find the white marble of Capitol, the Washington Monument, the Jefferson Memorial, and the Lincoln Memorial in the dark."

"Gracious," said Ben. "I wonder if Philadelphia's landmarks will gleam like that."

"We will know within the hour," said Tom.

Once they had reached cruising altitude, Ben began to relax.

"My, my," he said as the plane lifted off. "It is as if we are floating through the clouds."

Marilyn showed him how to download TV shows, and he and Tom, sitting together, decided to watch a PBS documentary on Albert Einstein. Ben was enthralled, Tom not so much.

"May I pick the show for the return flight?" asked Tom.

"Yes, maybe something with a love interest."

"I was thinking about Lincoln or the Civil War."

After the General left to serve as copilot, Will asked Marilyn to join him.

"Honored," she said. "I'm a big fan. In fact, you're the reason I volunteered for this flight."

"You read my blog?"

"Everyone does." She pulled out her phone. "Let's take a selfie so I can share it with friends."

They spent the flight talking about ancestral roots and family histories. At one point, when Marilyn had to leave her seat to attend to duties, Tom leaned over and winked.

"Good taste," he said. "If Alex were here, he could lend you his navy blazer."

"That's OK, Tom. I assume my Ralph Lauren line will be up to the task."

They both smiled.

"It will be strange to walk through Independence Hall again, will it not?" Tom asked Ben.

"I have been wondering that myself. Will I feel sentimental?"

"Nostalgic anyway."

On descent, as Captain Sully tilted the plane, they could see modern skyscrapers and several huge fields for playing sports.

"I suppose Independence Hall is too small to see from the skies," mused Ben.

"But to stand on the spot where the nation was founded, that will be impressive," said Tom.

Marilyn instructed them to buckle up for the landing.

"Could you show me again?" asked Ben, which made Will laugh out loud.

On landing in Philadelphia, the General rejoined them in the cabin.

"Sublime from the front window. On the flight home, Captain Sully said he will let me fly."

"We followed your lead once before, and that worked out well," said Ben.

Before leaving the cabin, the General turned to Captain Sully and Marilyn Houston and asked if they would like to join them on the tour. Marilyn looked thrilled, but the captain demurred.

"I have to stay with the aircraft to handle refueling, coordinate with ground crews, and ensure the plane is ready for departure when you return," said the captain. "But Ms. Houston, you may go."

"But what about cleaning the cabin?" she asked.

"I imagine I could handle that."

"Thank you, Captain," she said.

"Actually," Will said to Marilyn, "I suggest the three of us stay behind. I can help with the cleanup, and then I can treat you both to lunch. You have been so kind."

"Try City Tavern," said Ben, "if it is still there."

"I remember it well," said the General. "We used the quarters above the tavern to house soldiers in 1777. And on my journey from Mount Vernon to New York for the presidential inauguration in 1789, I stopped in Philadelphia, where City Tavern hosted a banquet for me."

"I believe it's still there," said Captain Sully. "It was run by a famous chef for many years, but now I understand it is under the management of the US Park Service."

"The Park Service is running a restaurant?" asked Tom. "Meddling at will."

"Perhaps we can meet you there after we tour Independence Hall," said the General.

"A great idea," said Sully. "We will book a table for six."

A limousine greeted Ben, Tom, and the General at the bottom of the plane. The driver was named Saul, and he wore a hat much like Captain Sully's. Unlike Mr. Debussy, he did not offer interesting tidbits as they drove. But on arrival he did give Tom his business card.

"Text or call whenever you would like to be picked up for the return trip to the airport," he said.

"Thank you," said Tom. "That offers us a sense of freedom, liberating us from logistics."

"My pleasure," he said, dropping them off at Independence Hall, which in their day had been known as the Pennsylvania State House.

"On 520 Chestnut Street," said Ben. "Right around the corner from my home."

"The grounds are beautiful," said Tom. "It is as if they constructed a park around our history."

"It looks smaller than I remembered," said the General.

Once inside, they were greeted by a docent named Emily Positano.

"Miss Babcock asked me to give you a tour of Independence Hall, the better to prepare you for your roles in the upcoming birthday reenactment," she said.

"This building is a World Heritage Site. Built between 1732 and 1753. Here delegates to the Second Continental Congress met from 1775 to 1783, and later a new generation met to draft the US Constitution. The Declaration of Independence was adopted here on July 4, 1776, and the Constitution was drafted and sent to the states for ratification from this space in September 1787. We proudly call this the birthplace of our nation, of our proudest foundational documents."

"Are we allowed to enter the rooms where those debates took place?" asked Tom.

"Certainly," said the docent, looking puzzled.

"No one was allowed in during the convention," said Ben. "I mean, that is what I've read."

The General looked amused.

"Still annoyed by my closed-window policy?" he whispered to Ben.

"How many visitors do you have each year?" asked Ben.

"At Independence Hall, we have about half a million, but to the surrounding park and visitor center, we receive about four million each year. Of course, traffic spikes on the Fourth of July."

"Increases?" asked Tom.

"Yes," said Emily, a bit flustered. Were these actors staying in character to annoy her?

"The red brick exterior is Georgian style, and we have preserved the furnishings inside to reflect some of the eighteenth-century furnishings of the day."

As soon as they walked in the Assembly Room, the General smiled.

"The 'Rising Sun' chair," he said. "Imagine that, Ben, still here."

Ben smiled. Tom, who had been serving as an American diplomat in Paris during the Constitutional Convention, looked puzzled.

"We finished our deliberations after four long months," said Ben. "The room was hot and stifling. Tempers flared for months over such arcane questions as how many citizens each congressman should represent. After he was elected president of the Convention, the General sat at the front of the room, on a chair on which was painted a sun. There were times when I wondered if we would ever succeed. When we did, I rose to make a speech."

"I will never forget Dr. Franklin's words," said the General.

Ben recited, "'I have often looked at that picture behind the president without being able to tell whether it was rising or setting. But now at length I have the happiness to know that it is a rising and not a setting sun.'"

Must be method actors, Emily thought.

"I will leave you to your wanderings for ten minutes," she said. "We have another tour coming through after that so I will return then to point you toward the gardens and the Liberty Bell that once stood outside this building. No sitting on the furniture please."

She left, and Tom said, "Let us take a moment to stand in silence and inhale our history."

"I am tempted again to sit in my chair, to activate those memories," said Ben.

"Please do not do that, Ben," said the General. "We cannot afford for you to be arrested again."

"I remember this room from the Continental Congress, where I presented my Declaration," said Tom. "How was it different for the Constitutional Convention?"

"It was sweltering, and the General would not allow us to open windows for fear our conversation would be overheard."

"To preserve the sanctity of our deliberations," said the General.

"I assume slavery was the main sticking point," said Tom.

"One of them," said Ben. "The central tension in my view was between the localists, who wanted to keep power in the hands of citizens, represented by James Madison and his Virginia Plan, and the commercial interests, who wanted a monarch, as outlined in the New Jersey Plan."

"Who defended a monarchy?" asked Tom.

"Your friend Alexander Hamilton," said Ben. "Alex was recognized and spoke, for six hours. He talked about the tendency of local governments to subvert the central government. He cited the Greek republics and Charlemagne's empire, dropping offhand references to Aristotle, Cicero, and Montesquieu, weaving in the histories of Sparta, Athens, Thebes, Rome, and Carthage. At the root of his argument was that an elected monarch was little different than an elected executive."

"He might have prevailed if more delegates were of his mind," said the General. "Oddly, public opinion swung his way only after the central government was created."

"You mean only after you had been sworn in as president," said Tom.

"When I spoke, I often rose on behalf of ordinary people," said Ben. "I remember one day warning the convention not to adopt measures that would 'depress the virtue and public spirit of our common people.' I reminded them that during the war, American seamen who were captured refused to board the enemy's ships, as British seamen did regularly when we captured them."

"I always thought that was one of your better speeches," said the General.

"I reminded them, Tom, that this difference arose because of the different manner in which ordinary people were treated in America and Britain. And I said that loyalty, and love of country, was too precious a gift for any new nation to throw away if it wished to survive."

"A question of national identity," said Tom.

"Yes," said the General. "True, the slavery dilemma kept coming up in different ways, but I think you are both right that the core issue was who we were going to become."

"Do you remember Gouverneur Morris, General?" asked Ben.

"Of course."

"He spoke passionately against slavery, Tom. The issue reached its most heated in the debate over how many persons each member of Congress should represent. The senators represented all the citizens of their states. But in the House, the smaller the number of citizens represented by a member of Congress, the closer the House of Representatives would be to the people."

"Another question of national identity," observed Tom.

"Virginia and South Carolina protested," said Ben. "They said their congressmen would be at a numerical disadvantage, as most of their residents were slaves. And then Morris rose and suggested that representation be limited to 'free' inhabitants in each state. He called slavery a nefarious institution and cursed the states where it was allowed to flourish."

"I thought that issue alone might sink the deliberations," said the General.

"George Mason was also furious," said Ben. "It was one of the most explosive speeches. He called slavery 'this infernal traffic' and predicted it would destroy America."

"I wonder if it has," said Tom. "The three-fifths rule was shameful in its way."

"If Alex were here, he would say, 'shameful, perhaps, but necessary,'" said the General.

"The greater sin in my view was when General Thomas Pinckney, at the last minute, moved to forestall the ban on importing slaves until 1808. We had originally proposed 1800."

"I had a letter from James Madison about that," said Tom. "James was outraged."

"Yes," said Ben. "Roger Sherman, of Massachusetts, insisted that we not use the term 'slaves,' as it suggested that they were property. But Rufus King, also from Massachusetts, spoke for many exhausted delegates when he observed that such was the price to be paid to form this union."

"A victory for the pragmatists," said Tom.

Emily, their docent, had been standing at the back of the hall, listening to their conversation.

"I can't imagine you actors need any more coaching to learn your parts," she said. "That must be quite a reenactment they're planning down in DC. Allow me to show you the back exit."

They followed her out to the gardens and walked for a bit.

"Delighted we came," said the General. "I understand now why no one else could play our parts."

They grabbed an Uber to City Tavern, and joined their friends there. They spoke of history, and aviation, of republican democracy and insurgent armies. Then they called Saul for a ride back to the airport, up and away in the clouds, with their General at the helm.

SCENE 22

Ben's Trial

As they arrived for his trial, Ben was surprised to see the crush of people outside the E. Barrett Prettyman Courthouse on Constitution Avenue.

"Do you think there's been a fire?" he asked his lawyer.

"No fire," said Jonathan Turley. "That's just the blob."

"The blob?"

"That's what I call the bubble of elitists, media folk, and celebrity hunters who flock to events such as your trial. Smile, wave, or frown, but whatever you do, never engage. No eye contact."

On the third floor, they encountered another blob, so deputies escorted them through the judges' chambers. When Ben finally saw the courtroom, he smiled. Its architecture borrowed something from a Philadelphia church—a middle aisle, pews on either side, an altar flanked by symbols of authority, even a choir box. But he sensed this courtroom was hardly a site of spiritual uplift.

"This will not be a wedding," said Ben.

Jonathan looked at him quizzically.

"No, but neither will it be a funeral. We have a very strong case, Dr. Franklin."

At that moment, a deputy announced, "All rise. Chief Judge Charles Lindbergh presiding."

Jonathan had told Ben that Lindbergh, a distant relative of the famed aviator and a fierce critic of President Trump, would be hostile.

"Steel yourself for us to be overruled frequently and just tell yourself that all of the judge's excesses can be turned into successful appeals," Jonathan had said in their last planning meeting.

But Ben thought the judge looked ordinary, sort of a middling man.

The judge gaveled the proceeding to order, and everyone sat down.

Ben looked around the room. Sergeant Bilk was in the audience, alongside that man called Christina from the Wax Museum who started all the nonsense. He noticed a contingent from DOGE, including Big Balls. He spotted Tom, Alex, Mercy, Will, and the General sitting with Kendra Blackett. She waved.

"The defendant will rise," the judge said.

Ben and Jonathan rose.

"State your name."

"My name is…my name is…"

From the balcony, someone shouted, "Benjamin Franklin."

Laughter ensued.

"Benjamin Franklin was my name in another—well, another chapter of life. Now I am Josiah Folger."

"And, Mr. Folger, how do you plead to the charge of violating the District's hate crime statute?"

Ben whispered something to Jonathan, who spoke.

"Your honor, my client was a famous scientist and would like to be referred to as Dr. Folger."

Lindbergh smirked.

"Fine, I'll play along with the charade. How do you plead, Dr. Folger?

"As God is my witness, not guilty, Your Honor."

At this there was much laughter in the courtroom.

The prosecution began its case, and, according to later reports in *The Washington Post,* Ben fell asleep during the early testimony from the government. But as the *Post*'s equally bored correspondent put it, had he been awake, he would have heard only a recap of the incident with which he was all too familiar.

When Sergeant Bilk called him "a recidivist troublemaker," according to the *Post,* Ben's eyes opened, and he whispered something to his lawyer.

On cross-examination, Jonathan asked Sergeant Bilk why he called the defendant a repeat offender.

"I caught him prowling around the day of the protests at the Archives. He and his buddies were trying to get photos of the protestors' signs."

"Getting photos of protestors? Is that, in your view, illegal?" said Jonathan.

There was much laughter in the audience at that. Judge Lindbergh frowned and ordered the crowd to remain silent or they would be escorted from his courtroom.

The man called Christina testified that Josiah Folger and his friends, "who claimed to be actors, triggered my anxiety and forced me to take a brief absence to recover my Zen."

There was laughter in the courtroom at that too. This time, Judge Lindbergh did not use his gavel.

At lunchtime the courtroom emptied. Jonathan escorted Ben up to the lawyers' offices, where he had been given a small warren. Soon, all kinds of well-wishers—including the General, Will, and Mercy—barged in to congratulate him on staying awake through most of the proceedings. Then, to everyone's delight, Big Balls personally delivered a lunch of barbecue chicken and fries.

"Elon sent them with his best regards," said Edward.

"I had no idea he could cook," said Ben. "Truly a man of many talents."

In the afternoon session, Jonathan called Mercy Otis Warren to the stand. She faltered when the clerk asked her if she would "swear to tell the truth, the whole truth, and nothing but the truth."

"I will affirm to do that, sir," she said. "But I was raised never to swear."

Even Judge Lindbergh laughed at that.

She confirmed details of the events at the Wax Museum.

"How long have you known the defendant?" asked Jonathan.

"I have known Dr. Franklin for more than two hundred fifty years," she began.

Judge Lindbergh admonished her to refer to the witness as Josiah Folger. "And remember that even if you did not swear, you did pledge to tell the truth."

"But I am telling the truth! And I tell you that Ben—I mean Josiah—meant no disrespect. It's just that none of us had ever seen a man who wanted to be a woman. In our world, in our time, it just was not done. We didn't know the meaning of the word 'misgender.' It never occurred to us that people would try to change pronouns. All his life, Josiah was a force for good—an inventor, a diplomat, a civic leader, a person who founded lending libraries and universities to uplift those without. He would never hurt anyone's feelings deliberately."

"Objection," said the prosecutor.

"On what grounds?"

"Counsel did not ask her a question."

"Sustained."

Jonathan looked over at the prosecutor with amazement.

"Mrs. Warren, can you tell the court what you saw and how you assessed Dr. Folger's behavior?"

"Do you want me to repeat what I just said?"

"That would be fine."

And she did, word for word.

"Objection," said the prosecutor.

"Grounds?"

"Coaching. It is obvious this witness was coached. Otherwise, she could not have repeated her answer verbatim."

"Your Honor, is the prosecution suggesting that his witnesses were not prepared?"

"As you know, counsel, the line between coaching and preparing is important. Yes, you want your witnesses to know how to conduct themselves in court, but it is unethical to teach tampering."

"Tampering, your honor? If you need any evidence of the ethical character of this witness, I would refer you to her biography."

"Perhaps, Counselor, you should ask that question."

"Mrs. Warren, could you tell us a little of your biography?"

"I was born in 1728 in Barnstable, Massachusetts, one of thirteen children of James and Mary Allyne Otis. I was the oldest girl. My father, who was a member of the Massachusetts Legislature, allowed me to sit in on my brothers' tutoring sessions at home. After marrying James Warren, who was also a member of the Massachusetts Legislature, we moved to Plymouth, Massachusetts, where we raised our five boys and I became a writer, albeit under pen names. We were friends with Abigail and John Adams, and at first, Mr. Adams helped me with my writing career. But then we had a falling-out over the Constitution. He thought it just fine, and I thought it needed a First Amendment."

"Your Honor," said the prosecutor, "may counselor and I approach the bench?"

Jonathan accompanied him to the well before the judge's throne.

"This is absurd. Defense is making a mockery of justice."

"Agreed," said Judge Lindbergh. "We cannot have witnesses claiming to be nearly three hundred years old."

"And yet, we have Social Security recipients claiming that age," said Jonathan.

"She must be mental," said the prosecutor.

"You don't believe in Heaven?" asked Jonathan.

"You're kidding. Really, you bought the Kool-Aid on this one?"

"Do you have a more plausible explanation? You can call them actors if you want, but in the several months they have been here, no one has ever heard them speak out of character."

"You're telling me that the guy I'm prosecuting is really Ben Franklin? That's sad. I always liked him."

"You know the old saying, 'Keep your friends close and your enemies closer.'"

"Is that from *Poor Richard's Almanac*?"

"I don't know. Do you want me to ask my client?"

"Gentlemen, this is a court of law, not of fantasies. I will not admonish this lady, as she seems very sincere. But please, no more witnesses claiming to have lived in three centuries."

As the lawyers returned to their desks, the judge turned to Mercy.

"The court appreciates your time and your candor," said Judge Lindbergh. "You may go now."

Mercy walked off the stand, smiling at Ben on her way to the gallery.

"Do you have another witness?" asked Judge Lindbergh.

"We do, Your Honor," said Jonathan. "The defense calls Evelyn Michaels."

"Who is that?" Ben whispered to Jonathan.

"You'll see."

After she was sworn in, Jonathan asked her to state her name and occupation. That's when Ben found out, as did everyone else in the courtroom, that Evelyn was a waitress at Old Ebbitt's Grill.

"And do you remember the defendant?"

"Yes, sir," she said. "He and his friends came in for lunch at one of my tables. I remember them because they were dressed in costumes."

"What kind of costumes?"

"You know, those kind from our Revolution."

"So colonial outfits?"

"I guess."

"And what was your interaction with the defendant?"

"Mr. Turley, in my job I take a lot of guff from people. Sometimes, when men get drunk, they make crude references to my body parts—not in quiet conversation with each other but right out loud! But that gentleman treated me as if I were special."

"Can you be more specific?"

"He was curious about my iPad, you know, on account of him being an inventor and all, so I showed him how it worked. As we talked, he called me 'my dear lady.' I loved how it sounded."

"You didn't consider it a sexist comment?"

"Oh, no. Trust me, I know a sexist remark when I hear it. No, this was more like a melody. It kept singing in my head for days."

"No further questions."

"Mr. Prosecutor?"

"No questions, Your Honor."

"Mr. Turley, do you have any further witnesses?"

"We do your honor. The defense calls Elon Musk."

The prosecutor coughed. The judge rolled his eyes. Elon took the stand and swore to tell the truth.

"Mr. Musk, can you, as Mrs. Warren just did, give us a brief biography?"

"Objection," said the prosecutor.

"Grounds?"

"This is a waste of the court's time. Everyone knows who Elon Musk is. He's the guy who decimated the federal government."

"Objection," said Jonathan.

"Grounds?"

"Libel."

"Mr. Prosecutor, save your commentary for the press conference. I'll allow it in."

"I was born in 1971 in Pretoria, South Africa, and immigrated to Canada at the age of eighteen. I graduated from the University of Pennsylvania and then moved to California to pursue business ventures. I created several technology start-ups before founding SpaceX, which developed reusable rockets. I also founded an online payment company that later merged with PayPal, acquired by eBay in 2002. That year, I became a US citizen. I also have a neurotechnology company called Neuralink, which is developing brain implants to help spinal cord patients walk, and the Boring Company, which I developed to help major cities relief traffic congestion with tunnels. I was an early investor in Tesla, which pioneered electric vehicles, and became its CEO in 2008. In 2022, I acquired the social media network Twitter. The next year I rebranded it as X."

"And what have you been doing lately?"

Even the judge smiled at that.

"Last year, President Trump named me director of the Department of Government Efficiency, which we call DOGE after the cryptocurrency. In the first hundred days, my team of high-tech sleuths eliminated tremendous waste and fraud, saving the American taxpayer two hundred billion dollars. I have since returned to my business interests, but I stay in touch with the team."

"And how did you meet the defendant?"

"I met Dr. Franklin—Dr. Folger—when he and his colleagues came to visit the DOGE team. He and I had a long conversation about inventions. We even argued a bit about whether the wheel was more important than the printing press. He impressed me when he suggested that, although separated by several millennia, the two were connected. The printing press, he said, may have influenced more minds, but it would not have been possible without the wheel."

"And what did that tell you about him?"

"That he had an agile mind, one that could draw conclusions on a macro level."

"And what did you think when you heard about his arrest?"

"Perfect."

"Explain."

"In my mind, biology is determinant. Even if a man has cosmetic surgery to change his appearance and takes hormones to diminish his testosterone and wears dresses and makeup, his body will always carry the XY chromosome. When I heard about this gentleman's arrest for innocently misgendering someone, I thought it was a perfect metaphor for the craziness of our times. The most brilliant mind of his century had no way to absorb the concept of a man deliberately adopting the ways of the opposite sex."

"But we have laws against offending people, don't we?"

"Not when it concerns free speech. As Mrs. Warren's testimony suggested, the First Amendment is the bedrock of our governance. You can't copyright an idea, and pronouns are figures of speech, not politics. We use language to communicate, to exercise our free speech rights. If someone calls me a jerk—and trust me, this is a daily experience—there is no law to prevent that. Even if someone threatens to kill me, which is unfortunately another regular occurrence, he can be investigated, but absent any evidence of plans to proceed, he will not be prosecuted."

"I take it you are saying that hate speech is protected?"

"Exactly. If Dr. Folger had hit Christina because of his dressing as a woman, that would be a crime. Assault is a crime. But, in fact, it was Christina who hit him, sending him reeling to the ground and breaking his famous bifocals. The only crime here is that some are still trying to enforce these kinds of laws. But they are really laws designed to rob people like Dr. Folger of their right to speak."

"Your witness," said Jonathan.

"When did you become such an expert on the First Amendment?" the prosecutor asked Elon.

"When I became a US citizen."

"Let me refresh your memory. The First Amendment says, 'Congress shall make no law respecting an establishment of religion, or prohibiting the free exercise thereof; or abridging the freedom of speech, or of the press; or the right of the people peaceably to assemble, and to petition the government for a redress of grievances.' I don't hear anything in that text that would stop a jurisdiction such as the District of Columbia from banning hate speech against transgender people."

"Seriously?" asked Elon. "I don't hear anything that allows it."

"Then, in your view, could we prohibit bullying?"

"No, but you can discourage it."

"Cursing in public?"

"That may be nice, but I doubt it's effing constitutional."

"And what about shouting 'fire' in a crowded theater?"

"I believe there are already laws against that. Doesn't that come under malicious intent to do harm?"

"May, I say, you are a shame to our country. Nothing further, Your Honor."

"Objection," said Jonathan.

"Grounds?"

"Malice toward the witness."

"I'll let it go. Have you any more witnesses, Mr. Turley?"

"Yes, Your Honor. I call Dr. Josiah Folger."

The courtroom quieted in anticipation. The *Post* reporter said Ben looked a little sleepy as he walked to the witness stand. He took the oath and sat down.

"Dr. Folger, at the risk of offending the court's sensibilities to historic figures, I will not ask you to recite your biography. Perhaps I can ask instead what brought you to Washington, DC?"

"I am an actor, Mr. Turley. I came to DC to participate in a reenactment of our signing the Declaration of Independence on July 4, 1776, and the events that led to the American Revolution."

"And how are rehearsals going?"

"So far, quite well. A few Americans have snuck in to watch them, so we are getting some positive social media attention, including from our friend the Original Will Lee."

The galleries broke into applause. Judge Lindbergh gaveled them to silence with a grave look.

"And what have you learned while preparing for the reenactment?"

"A delightful question, Mr. Turley. In the weeks since our arrival, I have learned that the government the founders bequeathed us is very similar to the one Americans live under today. For the founders, the central question was how much power to give the central government and how much to leave to the states. Since I've been in this town, I have learned more about the Civil War and realize that it was a necessary correction to the slavery that had bedeviled us since the beginning. It was a very bloody war, but it was imperative to deliver on the Declaration's promise. But the essential tension—between the states and the central government—that is still there, animating the national debate."

"Let us turn to the events on the day when you and your fellow actors decided to tour Madame Tussauds Wax Museum on F Street. When the person who greeted you at the museum had a nametag that said 'Christina,' what did you think?"

"I thought maybe I needed new bifocals."

A flurry of laughter from the gallery.

"But when this person insisted that was the name that they answered to, what did you think?"

"I didn't know what to think. My only thought was that he seemed a nice person, so I decided to respect his position by calling him 'young man.'"

"Because you thought he was a male?"

"Yes, that was evident from the Adam's apple."

At that moment there was an outburst from behind the banister that separated the audience from the prosecutor's desk.

"You have no right to mock me," shouted Christina. "The First Amendment does not give you the right to mock me!"

Judge Lindbergh pounded his gavel and told Christina to sit down and be quiet or be arrested for disorderly behavior.

"I'd like to answer that, if I may," said Ben. "Counselor?"

"Dr. Folger, do you think the First Amendment gives you the right to mock someone?"

"It was not my intention to mock, Mr. Turley. But I have often quoted Thomas Gordon, a radical of his time, who said, 'Whoever would overthrow the liberty of a nation, must begin by subduing the freeness of speech.' I was exercising mine."

"Dr. Folger, is there anything you'd like to say now to Christina?"

Ben turned toward Christina and addressed him.

"I meant you no harm. You assumed I did because in your worldview, you see calling someone by their name as mockery, grounds for cancelation and, apparently, arrest. In my culture, there is no such thing, as gender was decided by God and codified by nature. I suppose you could say we were both speaking English, but of different dialects. And, if I may, whatever you choose to call yourself, you should show more strength of character, for that is what defines all of us. I am here, after all, pretending to be Dr. Folger, but everyone knows who I am. By my name I have left a footprint, one I am proud of. Do something with your life that will made you proud, that will leave a legacy."

"The defense rests, Your Honor."

Ben was making his way back to the defense table when Judge Lindbergh said, "I am ready to rule."

Jonathan raised his eyebrows.

"No closing arguments, Your Honor?"

"This is not a jury trial, Counselor."

"And you, as the judge, do not want to hear closing arguments?"

"Ah, I can already hear you framing your appeal, Mr. TV Lawyer. All right, then. Mr. Prosecutor, closing argument?"

There was much bustle at the prosecutor's table, two lawyers conferring in whispers. At one point they were joined by Sergeant Bilk, who did not look happy.

"Your Honor," said the lead prosecutor, "may we approach the bench?"

Both he and Jonathan went to the well.

"If the defense pursues an appeal on grounds of the First Amendment," the prosecutor whispered to the judge, "we fear it could jeopardize all the gendered hate speech laws still on the books."

"Why don't we let the judge rule first?" suggested Jonathan. "Or do you have some inside information on how the judge will rule?"

"Watch it, Mr. Turley," the judge said sharply. "If you're suggesting a conspiracy between me and the prosecutor, I can throw you in jail for contempt."

"Your Honor, I suggest no such thing. I only wonder why he seems to think he's won the case."

"Your Honor, prosecution would like to withdraw the charges to avoid a First Amendment problem on appeal that could prove binding on many other worthy cases."

The judge looked flummoxed.

"Return to your seats. I will hear closing arguments, then I will rule."

The prosecutor looked rattled but did an admirable job of making his case. He began by speaking of the trauma and pain visited on the transgendered, seeking to find acceptance in a hostile society. He made nametags sound like a rite of passage, dictation to anyone who came in contact with them. He ended by quoting Tom's Declaration of Independence, where he said Americans had the right to pursue happiness not by the government's definition, but by their own.

But it was Jonathan's closing arguments that became the talk of the town. He talked about the founding and how the founders bequeathed us the First Amendment for a reason: so we could fight tyranny wherever it bubbled up. He talked of Abraham Lincoln at Gettysburg and Martin Luther King in Selma, using their voices to plead for the rights of African Americans. He even mentioned the long fight for women's right to vote, a one-hundred-year battle to assert their suffrage.

"I believe, Your Honor, that these earlier struggles have left a lasting impression on today's young people, and they lament that they were not alive for those noble causes. So now they embrace violent protests and abort babies and model transgender behavior to signal their virtue, to expand the meaning of natural rights. Dr. Folger is from an older generation unfamiliar with these contemporary causes. He and Christina clashed not over the latter's choices, but over the former's principles. And I would submit, Your Honor, in the name of justice and in the memory of Martin Luther King Jr., that no one should be punished for the content of his character."

The courtroom was utterly silent when he sat down. Judge Lindbergh's face looked mottled.

"Defendant, please rise," he said.

Ben and Jonathan rose.

"Dr. Folger, I find you guilty of a hate crime against Christina. But I also recognize that you come from an older generation without awareness of our current cultural tolerance. Therefore, I waive any penalty and expunge the record of any conviction. You are free to go."

"Free?" said Ben. "I have been free since 1776."

The courtroom burst into applause. Mercy and the others rushed over to Ben to congratulate him.

"Mercy, if you hadn't insisted on a Bill of Rights, I might have been marched off to prison."

"As today's Americans say," she said, "what are old friends for?"

"I'm disappointed," said Jonathan. "How I would have liked to argue the appeal before the Supreme Court on First Amendment grounds."

"I imagine the argument has already reached their ears," said Ben. "Where is Elon? I want to compliment him on his cooking."

SCENE 23

Alex and Scott at the Fed

Now that Scott Bessent was serving as both treasury secretary and unofficial czar of the Federal Reserve, he invited Alexander Hamilton to have lunch at the Fed. Of course, first he offered him a tour of what Trump loyalists were calling "Powell's Palace on the Potomac," the $2.7 billion, or maybe it was $3.2 billon, renovation, the one that Jerome Powell had built as his legacy.

"Ugly, isn't it?" said Scott. "Larry Kudlow said that if you wanted to re-create the Taj Mahal, quite a beautiful place of décor and reverence, in today's dollars it cost about the same."

"I am glad Tom is not here," said Alex. "He was a big fan of neoclassical architecture. This would not appeal to his elegant standards."

"President Trump feels the same way. He issued an order requiring all public buildings—courthouses and agency headquarters—to use classical architectural designs. He believes design can 'uplift and beautify public spaces and inspire the human spirit.' This Fed does neither."

"I sometimes think businessmen like Trump are the real optimists," said Alex.

"That is very astute. Few people understand that."

"Precisely why I wanted a National Bank, to spur the markets and our manufacturing base. Tom thought the ideal was a nation of farmers maintaining their liberties through landownership. He and the attorney general lobbied against the bill. The General asked me to defend it."

"*Report on the Subject of Manufactures.* I know it well. They teach it in business schools, you know. It is considered the most clear-eyed economic manifesto for a thriving marketplace."

"I'm delighted to hear it was widely remembered. My central thesis was that unlike slavery, which underpinned the plantation oligarchy in the South, and unlike profits, which drove the mercantile oligarchy in the North, the US as a manufacturing giant called on all of us—rural, urban, intellect, laborer—to use our God-given creativity. As I wrote, 'There is, in the genius of the people of this country, a peculiar aptitude for mechanic improvements.' Still true, I think."

"I suspect Elon would agree with that. President Trump too."

"President Trump and I talked about it at the White House dinner. Like our administration, his does focus on restoring the country's manufacturing base, and on tariffs. What he added to the mix—and I told him I thought it was brilliant—is to use tariffs as a negotiating tool."

"Why brilliant?"

Alex paused.

"In my view," said Alex, "he is leading a second American Revolution, this time against the globalists and Marxists who want to erase national borders and coopt federal governments.

He is intent on reclaiming America's sovereignty and restoring the republic we created two hundred fifty years ago."

"Let's continue the conversation over lunch. I've reserved a table. Although I have to warn you, Mr. Powell may be there. He seems unwilling to leave the building."

"Very few leave power as honorably as George Washington did."

"Or as you did."

"Very few today seem to understand that a duel is a measure of a man's honor," said Alex.

"Virtue is returning, but I'm not sure the duel ever will."

They rode up in an elevator.

"This seems far quieter than other elevators I have ridden on, as if the hydraulics have been buffered with padded cushions."

"Yes, Chairman Powell decided to insulate the walls and then wrap them in velvet."

"More Taj Mahal?" Alex asked, raising his eyebrows.

"On the taxpayer dime."

"How I wish Woodrow Wilson had never passed the income tax."

"We're working on it. Here we go."

The members' dining room was hushed, like an old British men's club. It was moments like this—when he was treated as an elite—that always made Alex marvel at the trajectory of his life, and now his afterlife. Eliza had been more religious than he, but when he encountered blessings from above, he always felt humbled. Surely not only history but even God was smiling on him.

The menu was impressive.

"Have you a favorite dish?" Alex asked.

"The filet mignon is excellent. But so are the fish tacos. Depends on your mood."

"What are fish tacos?"

"Think bland Hawaiian fish meets spicy Mexican bread."

"With a recommendation like that," said Alex, smiling, "I will try it."

Scott ordered a Caesar salad topped with grilled salmon.

"Let's start with the similarities between our two presidents," suggested Scott.

"Phenomenon of nature, with so much energy," said Alex. "And their height! If you look at their images side by side, both are so similar, yet two centuries apart."

"I also notice that both put value on presentation. President Trump always dresses elegantly—unless he's working at McDonald's that day—and I gather that George Washington did too."

"Yes, he never went out in public, never went before his troops, never addressed Congress, unless his uniform was clean and brushed, his horse saddle polished, his posture erect."

"A reporter once asked President Reagan, on his exit from the White House, what it was like to have been the only actor elected to the presidency. He cocked his head, smiled, and said, 'Everyone who has ever served in this noble office has been an actor.' On Wall Street, too, projecting calm and confidence is key. To Reagan it was the ability to persuade through acting."

"I had not thought of that, but it is true," said Alex. "To lead is to convey meaning by demonstrating character, and I suppose charm. They both did that."

"In President Trump's case, there's one more key. He's running the country like a business. Powell refused to lower the interest rates, so Trump mocked him, calling him "Too-Late Powell." He went after another Fed member, Lisa Cook, for allegations of mortgage fraud. And then he instructed me not to issue long-term government bonds until rates came down."

"Watching Trump, sometimes I wish the General had been a little more, well..."

"Badass? Just the other day President Trump instructed me to slap sanctions on Brazilian Supreme Court Justice Alexandre de Moraes for targeting free speech against US and Brazilian citizens and companies. His assets are frozen, and he can't do business with US entities. So now the US Treasury is standing up for the principles that you and the other founders bequeathed us."

"That is what I was thinking. President Washington was courtly. Maybe President Trump is more of a business tycoon, using all tools at his disposal to achieve his goals."

"Do you know the story of Franklin Delano Roosevelt? He was elected four times, navigating the Depression and World War II. He led from a wheelchair, a victim of polio. After his death, Congress passed a constitutional amendment limiting presidents to two terms."

"That was the standard the General set."

"And that Congress, after FDR, codified," said Scott. "Now some fervent Trump supporters—led by activist Steve Bannon, who went to jail rather than testify before a Congress that was conspiring to topple Trump—are pushing to rewrite things to give him a third term."

Just then Jerome Powell walked up, smirking as he greeted Scott.

"Have you joined the rogues pushing for a third term?"

"Not at all, Mr. Powell. I was just explaining to Alexander Hamilton the fervor for Trump among some of his supporters. Alex, this is Jerome Powell."

"Pleased to meet you," said Alex, as he stood and reached to shake Powell's hand.

"I make it a habit never to shake hands with actors pretending to be their characters."

"So you have no interest in talking to the nation's first treasury secretary?" asked Scott.

"Mad, the lot of you, all gone mad," Powell muttered as he retreated.

Just then their food arrived, and the two of them dove in. Alex was enthralled by his tacos.

"After my interview with Joe Rogan was canceled, I missed my chance to try food in Austin. And now you have brought this delicious Tex-Mex food up here to the capital city. Delightful."

"What did Rogan want to talk to you about?"

"He wanted to discuss my duel with Aaron Burr. He said history has not paid the event enough attention. He kept saying, 'We lost a Founding Father to an effing duel!'"

"What would you have told him?"

"I thought Aaron Burr unprincipled both as a public and private man. And I said so."

"Do you wish you hadn't said those things?"

"No. I believed them true. This seems to have fallen from the history books, but after Burr lost the presidency to Jefferson, he lost his mind."

"I have a vague memory—something about a plot?"

"He concocted a secessionist scheme to wrest power away from Jefferson's Republicans. And this was after he had served as Jefferson's first-term vice president! He planned to capture the western lands and the Louisiana Territory and lead a rival nation. The plot was hatched a few months before our duel, and, after my death, I am told, President Jefferson had him arrested for treason, but he was acquitted and escaped. He never gave up the dream of conquest, soliciting funds in Europe to renew his plans. Both Britain and France kicked him out."

"Why was he acquitted?"

"Because we wrote in the Constitution that treason required two eyewitnesses."

"That passage has been making the rounds lately at the White House. Why did you do that?"

"The feeling in the room was that treason was a serious crime, not to be trivialized by politics."

"And did you have a strategy for the duel?"

Alex nodded.

"I had the first shot and deliberately missed, convinced it would shame him into being similarly restrained. It did not. He had no shame."

"Regrets?"

"None. I'm told I had a huge funeral. Wall Street turned out. My wife wept. I was missed and long remembered. Why they wrote a musical about me, I imagine."

"And Burr?"

"They say he became the Benedict Arnold of his day—widely seen as the villain he was."

"So reputation in death over longevity in life?"

"Perhaps so."

"I love it that you told me this story instead of Rogan. I can't wait to tell the president."

"Does the duel have a modern equivalent?"

Scott looked pensive.

"Hedge fund trading? Maybe not as noble, but such volatile investing with enormous capital holds similar nerve-wracking qualities."

"Remind me not to try it."

"What else has history forgotten? What else should we know about Washington's character?"

"During the French and Indian War, he gained a firsthand look at British military procedures—and their arrogance. He told me he knew Virginia better than they did—he had been a land surveyor—but they never took his advice about the best routes to take to confront the enemy. After the war, he wanted to continue in His Majesty's service—clearly, he had an aptitude for the military—but they demoted him. He was furious. He went home, ran successfully for a seat in the Virginia House of Burgesses, and married Martha Dandridge Custis."

"And the demotion—it angered him?"

"It is fair to say his treatment by the British produced a simmering anger in him, tension just below the surface. It is also true he was insecure about his lack of a formal education. His older brothers were sent to college in England. But after their mother died, Augustine Washington married again. George was the first son of the new marriage, and when he was eleven, his father died. They did not have money for college. So he became a land surveyor and a farmer."

Scott sat back, looking thoughtful.

"Trump simmers too. Oh, he explodes on occasion. But at your own risk do you underestimate how deeply the lawfare against him affected his soul. There is a sense of aggrieved wrongdoing, an insult to character, which I imagine is much like your duel or Washington's demotion."

Now it was Alex's turn to ponder the conversation.

"Is that what drove these two presidents two centuries apart—a mission to avenge wrongs?"

"Perhaps," said Scott. "But I believe what really drives Trump is you."

"Me?"

"The founders, the figures of history who birthed our nation. Your principles, your values, even your debates—he stands on your shoulders as he surveys the modern landscape."

"I am glad I lived when I did," said Alex. "But maybe you feel that way too."

"I've never enjoyed any job as much as I'm enjoying this one. To sit in the office where Salmon P. Chase sat, the treasury secretary who single-handedly financed the Union's war effort, to be present on the couch in the Oval Office when Trump entertains foreign visitors, to formulate tariff policy globally that will secure this nation's financial future, it is a thrilling experience."

"And what of this institution, this Federal Reserve?"

"That is a more complicated question. The Fed was created in 1913 by bankers, for bankers, but also for Americans, to ensure sound currency."

"Was our currency in danger?"

"In 1893, the US suffered a recession larger than it had ever experienced before, primarily because of the overexpansion of the railroad industry after the Civil War. Factories closed, towns emptied, and the US Treasury went broke. President Grover Cleveland, a Democrat, borrowed money from J. P. Morgan and the Rothschilds, but the crisis pushed him out of office. In 1896, President McKinley, a Republican, was elected. He called on the major capitalists of the day—sometimes they are disparaged as robber barons, but they were patriots—and asked them to loan the federal government money, which they did. Soon, the US was running a surplus."

"Is that why President Trump reveres McKinley?"

"Perhaps, though he also admires his stance on tariffs. In any event, on McKinley's assassination in 1901, Vice President Theodore Roosevelt was sworn in. A Republican but also a populist, Roosevelt had a grand time spending down the surplus, and another economic downturn, the Panic of 1907, ensued. The Fed was an effort to institutionalize stability, where economists could keep an eye on the trends and adjust interest rates as needed to avoid huge dips."

"And has it worked?"

Scott paused.

"You could make a case that for the most part the Fed smoothed out the rough edges, though some think the Fed caused the Great Depression in the 1930s. But like everything else in Washington, it has mushroomed beyond its intended scope. There are three thousand people working for the Federal Reserve Board itself, and another twenty thousand working in the whole system—twelve regional federal reserve boards, the Federal Open Market Committee, and advisers spread across the country. I've heard some people wonder why we need all those PhDs in economics."

"And President Trump wants to disrupt that?"

Scott smiled.

"You may have noticed we have already begun resetting the global trading system, flipping the US dollar's reserve status from a burden into a bargaining chip, turning our towering debt from an embarrassment into leverage, reorienting the entire global economy in Washington's favor. Have you ever heard the line President Reagan used about this?"

Alex shook his head.

"President Reagan once said that he was looking to hire a one-handed economist, because otherwise all he would hear on asking for advice would be 'on the one hand, and on the other.'"

Alex smiled.

"The pontificating class," he observed. "I wonder if they were inevitable. What will happen to this massive complex now, and to the bureaucracy?"

Scott smiled.

"There's been a lot of debate about that lately. Some in Congress want to eliminate the Fed altogether and vest duty for monitoring the economy in the treasury secretary. Others think we should just sell the three buildings to pay down the national debt. President Trump just wants a Fed that thinks as he does. But he also likes the idea of turning this campus into a Museum of the Deep State, where tourists could come and be reminded of Lord Acton."

"British?"

"Yes, a British historian. 'Power tends to corrupt. Absolute power corrupts absolutely.'"

"Maybe we should have that sentiment emblazoned on our currency."

"Which reminds me—I hear you are unhappy with your placement on the ten-dollar bill."

"My goodness, this town permits of no secrets."

"It was always thus, I assume."

Alex nodded.

"The nation was lucky to have you when we did."

"Thank you, Mr. Secretary."

"And thank you, our first Mr. Secretary. Oh, and good luck with the reenactment."

SCENE 24
Epilogue

At play's end, Mercy stood center stage at the National Archives, surrounded by heavenly and earthly cast, as thunderous applause washed over them. Flowers flew onto the stage, and one man in the audience yelled, "Take that, King George!" Plus, an unprecedented four curtain calls.

Reviews were sparkling. President Trump called the performance "bigger and more beautiful than I could have imagined." Lin-Manuel Miranda said he might buy the rights. *The Washington Post* conceded the play had been an epic success, though *The New York Times* smirked that it was hardly up to Broadway standards. Even *Variety*, that daily bible of Hollywood's most deranged Trump haters, said it was the only good thing POTUS 47 had ever produced, which prompted the Nobel Committee to reconsider its decision to give Trump the Peace Prize.

Now it was time to leave.

As a venue to say their goodbyes and recap their journey, President Trump had offered them the use of the Truman Balcony at the White House, where they could sit, reminisce, and look out at the landscapes they had now lived not once but twice. The only person joining their conversation on the balcony from outside the heavenly circle was Thomas Sowell.

"I find myself thinking of my older brother James," said Ben. "Perhaps in retrospect, I failed to give him credit for all that I became. I was an apprentice at his Boston newspaper, *The New-England Courant.* I published my first literary efforts there—under the pen name of Silence Dogood, a widow with a gift for satire."

"But why do you think of him now?" asked the Director.

"James sometimes drank, and when he did, he often beat me. I fled Boston for Philadelphia, like a slave escaping bondage, to chart my own path as a printer. I vowed never to communicate with him again. Now I wish I had been more in touch with him, because I suspect he would think that on this visit, we did not explain well enough the long history of rebellion."

"I thought we did that pretty well in the play," said Mercy, "with Sam Adams talking in my parlor, and all the other Tea Party participants having their moment on the stage."

"I thought the OBBR was splendid," said the Director. "It introduced a new generation to the constitutional principles that can sustain a nation for centuries to come."

"Perhaps," said Ben, "but how many of today's Americans know that in 1684, one hundred years before our movement, Britain revoked the first Massachusetts charter?"

"I did not know that," said Will. "Why should today's Americans?"

"Elisha Cooke Jr., speaker of the Massachusetts House, called it the beginning of the rebellion because it targeted our most precious asset—democratic town meetings that allowed every citizen a voice. My brother James grew up hearing their stories. He didn't live long enough to read the Declaration of Independence, but I believe he would have wanted us to make that link."

"My favorite moment of the OBBR was when the actor portraying John Hancock leaned back and fell over," said Alex. "The audience roared as if it intentional."

"I always feared the production would trivialize us," said Tom. "But there were other moments so poignant they brought tears. That soldier who deserted, only to face the General's wrath—Mercy, that was so beautifully written."

"Thank you."

"My favorite scene was when Alex and Mercy read their letters to each other during the ratification fight," said Ben. "I had no idea you two were in contact."

Mercy smiled at Alex.

"Actually, Dr. Franklin, those were fabricated from our imaginations," said Mercy. "We had to find a way to describe the raging debate over ratification."

"For what it is worth," said Alex, "I thought they captured our differences brilliantly. And, frankly, the exercise left me more appreciative of the debate. Important things to argue about."

"We've had many letters about that scene," said the Director. "One young history student wrote that she was so inspired by the exchange she was going to switch her PhD dissertation from the slaveholding founders to the debate over what the nation should become."

"Dear Lord, let this be the beginning of a trend," said Tom.

"Maybe this is the time to tell you, Mr. Jefferson, that your memorial has been restored to its glory. No more rewriting at the Tidal Basin. Now we just have to work on Monticello."

Tom smiled.

"I, too, have been thinking of the generation before us," said Alex. "From the beginning, the British tried to strangle our credit, suppress our natural instinct to create. Two generations before our Declaration, landowners and artisans in Boston opened a Land Bank—Sam Adams Sr. was its creator—and issued fifty thousand pounds in paper, not British silver. Parliament declared them traitors and wiped them out. It angered the father, and I suspect that's what made his son a rebel."

"The son avenging the father's pain," said Will.

"Then, in 1764, Parliament passed the Currency Act, demanding that we exchange our script for Bank of England notes with devastating impact on American commerce."

"I remember that," said Mercy. "In one year, conditions were so reversed that an era of prosperity ended, filling the cobblestone streets of the colonies with the unemployed."

"That social memory is why I had such a hard time convincing everyone"—here Alex smiled at Tom—"that unlike the British version, the US National Bank would provide the seeds for expanding industry and commerce that was in the public interest, not those of speculators."

"There was nothing in the Constitution, Alex, about a National Bank," said Tom.

"There was. The Necessary and Proper Clause gave the government broad implied powers."

"The governor of Maine is trying to use the Nullification Clause to defy Trump's efforts to keep men out of women's sports," said Will. "One of my followers called it ironic that far-left Democrats—for whom race is a wedge issue—are now channeling the pro-slavery Confederacy."

"I do not understand either why men want to dress as women or why any governor would want to encourage it," said Ben.

"Christina would say I am mocking these people. Sometimes I wonder if perhaps they are mocking us."

"I leave convinced we are appreciated," said the General. "I found people interested in hearing the details of the work we did the first time we were here. We have much to smile about."

"Is that a denture joke?" said Will, to laughter. "My journey has been both enlightening and discouraging. So many died, on both sides, to free the slaves. Yet so many of their descendants now belittle that sacrifice and dismiss the political fights waged to enact three Reconstruction amendments that cemented their rights in the Constitution, instead seeking reparations for a wrong already righted. They seem ignorant of their own history, victims to the past. Meanwhile, I now have more than one million followers, so perhaps there is a lane for reason."

"I, too, have been thinking of the Civil War, for different reasons," said Tom. "I have been struck by how often Lincoln, in navigating the searing issues of that war, appropriated our biographies."

"Example?" asked Will.

"During his famous debates with Stephen Douglas, he said most signers to the Constitution opposed slavery, that we meant to put that cruel institution on a course of eventual extinction."

"There may be something to that," said Ben. "We were none of us saints, but maybe our cause was saintly and of use to this improbable president."

"Lincoln was not alone in using you as lodestars," said Director Sowell. "When the Confederacy issued its postage stamps, the South's President Jefferson Davis was on the five-cent stamp, but Tom was on the ten-cent stamp and, General, you were on the twenty-cent stamp."

"How very amazing," said the General. "An indication that we really were a nation of shared values. Even as it was fighting the North, the South was still saluting us."

"We were united around the issue of British tyranny and yearning to be free," said Ben. "I remember how impressed I was when you, General, of Virginia, rode off to Boston to save the citizens of that New England state. Slavery, that was our Achilles' heel."

"It was certainly mine," said Tom. "If this visit has done nothing else, it has awakened my consciousness to the barbarity of that institution and to the long shadows it cast on this nation. Yet, we were creatures of our time. Only lately has it become a sin to be a product of your era."

"I fear the issue of slavery will never be closed," said Will. "It seems more of an open wound."

"It must heal," said the General. "And I believe it will. I, too, have been thinking about war. I counted twelve major wars after the Revolution. And that doesn't count hundreds of incursions and other excuses to meddle in other lands. I even found one called nation-building."

"I wonder if presidents went to war often to improve their public appeal," said Alex. "I believe they now call it the 'rally around the flag' phenomenon. If citizens feel threatened by military incursions of other countries, they often see the president as their savior, at least in the moment."

The General was thoughtful for a moment.

"Perhaps that is why President Trump believes in peace through strength. He understands the weaponry is more and more deadly and uses it for leverage in diplomacy instead of war."

"Will," said Director Sowell, "any final thoughts?"

"I have so enjoyed this sojourn back to Earth, this reacquaintance with the country we once knew, even the debates we have had over the country's values, then and now," said Will. "If the rest of you feel the same way, why don't we request a reunion, say, for our five hundredth birthday?"

"Count me in," said Alex. "I leave energized by a country of perpetual reinvention."

"Now that I have earthly teeth, I would be happy to return whenever called," said the General. "It is nice to be remembered kindly."

"I agree with Alex that creativity will always form a large part of this country's character. I worry about AI taking over all human cognitive functions, but we will know on our return visit."

"I extended myself beyond the comfort of the familiar, speaking to mixed audiences, conferring in the White House with the president of the United States, even narrating One Big Beautiful Reenactment," said Mercy. "I look forward to our return."

There was a silence then, and everyone looked in Tom's direction.

"This journey," he said, "has forced me to look in the mirror at the contradictions in my character. Tommy Blackett seems to respect me now, but others still look at me with disdain."

"A victory that you've changed at least one mind corrupted by modern schools," said the Director.

"Perhaps. It seems to me that unless President Trump can topple them, the government officials who run this place will remain eager to erase us founders and our founding, smearing us with the lie that our intentions were all racist. Yet I would return, if only to wage anew the battle with a new generation. But I wonder, would we even be welcome here in another two hundred fifty years?"

There was a silence as they pondered the end of their journey

"I would hope that you would be invited," said Director Sowell. "I would also hope that some of my students showed such command of our nation's history as you have during your visit. Some of your encounters here—Ben's trial for a hate crime, Tom's reunion with his books at the Library of Congress, Will becoming an influencer—might be deposited in the Earthly Library."

"Not to forget Mercy's conversation at the DAR, where a pregnant lady in the audience asked if she could name her child Mercy," said Tom. "Or Alex learning to play golf with Eric Trump."

"Or the General at the Pentagon, kneeling down to pay his respects to the captain of the plane that was hijacked to terrorize America on 9/11," said Alex.

"I think I speak for everyone, perhaps even John and Sam, when I thank you for summoning us, Mr. Director," said the General. "I will miss our conversations about politics and economics."

"No worries," said Director Sowell. "I suppose this is the time to tell you I'm coming with you."

There was silence first, then claps on the back and laughter.

"You will love it," said Mercy, "surrounded by the ones you love, in a place of honor."

The founders circled the Director. Then they all vanished into thin air, evaporating into the skies.

A few moments later, President Trump and First Lady Melania Trump walked to the balcony to say their final goodbyes, surprised to find the founders all gone. Director Sowell was slumped over in a chair, asleep. The president held out his hand to the First Lady, and they danced. Then they looked up to the sky.

"The stars are bright tonight," whispered Melania.

"Yes," said Trump. "Maybe it's a sign, that the stars are still shining brightly on this nation."

"Perhaps we should wake the Director," said Melania.

They found him without a pulse. Trump called the physician, and soon the Director was transported to hospital, where he was pronounced dead.

After his death, Priscilla planned a huge memorial service in the Archives. She spoke last.

"I think it is fair to say that he was proudest of bringing patriotism back to America, of instilling in today's Americans pride about the founders who blessed us with this country. And he would want to thank them for reminding us and all the generations between us of the gift of liberty we share together. Rest in peace, our beloved Dr. Sowell, and enjoy the company."